ELIZABETH VON ARNIM

Elizabeth von Arnim was born on 31 August 1866 in Australia. She was cousin to the writer Katherine Mansfield. In 1890 she married her first husband, Count Henning August von Arnim-Schlagenthin, a Prussian aristocrat, with whom she had five children. *Elizabeth and her German Garden*, published anonymously in 1898, was a barely fictionalised account of Elizabeth's life and the creation of her garden at the family home of Nassenheide in Pomerania, where Hugh Walpole and E. M. Forster were tutors to her children. Its instant success was followed by many more novels, including *Vera* (1914) and *The Enchanted April* (1922), and another almost-autobiography, *All the Dogs of My Life* (1936). She separated from Count von Arnim in 1908, and after his death two years later she built a house in Switzerland, marrying John Francis Stanley Russell in 1916. This marriage also ended in separation in 1919 when Elizabeth moved to America, where she died on 9 February 1941, aged seventy-four.

ALSO BY ELIZABETH VON ARNIM

ELIZABETH VON ARNIM

Fräulein Schmidt and Mr Anstruther

VINTAGE

1 3 5 7 9 10 8 6 4 2

Vintage
20 Vauxhall Bridge Road,
London SW1V 2SA

Vintage Classics is part of the Penguin Random House group of companies
whose addresses can be found at global.penguinrandomhouse.com.

 Penguin
Random House
UK

First published in Great Britain by Smith, Elder & Co in 1907

www.vintage-books.co.uk

A CIP catalogue record for this book is
available from the British Library

ISBN 9781784872342

Typeset in 11.5/13.75 pt Bembo
by Jouve (UK), Milton Keynes
Printed and bound by Clays Ltd, St Ives plc

Penguin Random House is committed to a sustainable future
for our business, our readers and our planet. This book is made
from Forest Stewardship Council® certified paper.

I

DEAR ROGER,—This is only to tell you that I love you, supposing you should have forgotten it by the time you get to London. The letter will follow you by the train after the one you left by, and you will have it with your breakfast the day after tomorrow. Then you will be eating the marmalade Jena could not produce, and you'll say, 'What a very indiscreet young woman to write first.' But look at the 'Dear Roger,' and you'll see I'm not so indiscreet after all. What could be more sober? And you've no idea of all the nice things I could have put instead of that, only I wouldn't. It is a most extraordinary thing that this time yesterday we were on the polite-conversation footing, you, in your beautiful new German, carefully calling me *gnädiges Fräulein* at every second breath, and I making appropriate answers to the Mr Anstruther who in one bewildering hour turned for me into Dear Roger. Did you always like me so much?— I mean, love me so much? My spirit is rather unbendable as yet to the softnesses of these strange words, stiff for want of use, so forgive a tendency to go round them. Don't you think it is very wonderful that you should have been here a whole year, living with us, seeing me every day, practising your German on me—oh, wasn't I patient?—and never have shown the least sign that I could see of thinking of me or of caring for me at all except as a dim sort of young lady who assisted her stepmother in the work of properly mending and feeding you? And then an hour ago, just one hour by that absurd cuckoo-clock here in this

I

room where we said good-bye, you suddenly turned into something marvellous, splendid, soul-thrilling—well, into Dear Roger. It is so funny that I've been laughing, and so sweet that I've been crying. I'm so happy that I can't help writing, though I do think it rather gushing—loathsome word—to write first. But then you strictly charged me not to tell a soul yet, and how can I keep altogether quiet? You, then, my poor Roger, must be the one to listen. Do you know what Jena looks like tonight? It is the most dazzling place in the world, radiant with promise, shining and dancing with all sorts of little lovely lights that I know are only the lamps being lit in people's rooms down the street, but that look to me extraordinarily like stars of hope come out, in defiance of nature and fog, to give me a glorious welcome. You see, I'm new, and they know it. I'm not the Rose-Marie they've twinkled down on from the day I was born till to-night. She was a dull person: a mere ordinary, dull person, climbing doggedly up the rows of hours each day set before her, doggedly doing certain things she was told were her daily duties, equally doggedly circumventing certain others, and actually supposing she was happy. Happy? She was not. She was most wretched. She was blind and deaf. She was asleep. She was only half a woman. What is the good or the beauty of anything, alive or dead, in the world, that has not fulfilled its destiny? And I never saw that before. I never saw a great many things before. I am amazed at the suddenness of my awaking. Love passed through this house today, this house that other people think is just the same dull place it was yesterday, and behold—well, I won't grow magnificent, and it is what you do if you begin a sentence with 'Behold.' But really there's a splendour—oh well. And as for this room where you—where I—where we—well, I won't grow sentimental either, though now I know, I who

2

always scoffed at it, how fatally easy a thing it is to be. That is, supposing one has had great provocation; and haven't I? Oh, haven't I?

I had got as far as that when your beloved Professor Martens came in, very much agitated because he had missed you at the station, where he had been to give you a send-off. And what do you think he said? He said, why did I sit in this dreary hole without a lamp, and why didn't I draw the curtains, and shut out the fog and drizzle. Fog and drizzle? It really seemed too funny. Why, the whole sky is shining. And as for the dreary hole—gracious heavens, is it possible that just being old made him not able to feel how the air of the room was still quivering with all you said to me, with all the sweet, wonderful, precious things you said to me? The place was full of you. And there was your darling coffee-cup still where you had put it down, and the very rug we stood on still all ruffled up.

'I think it's a glorious hole,' I couldn't help saying.

'*De gustibus*,' said he, indulgently; and he stretched himself in the easy-chair—the one you used to sit in—and said he should miss young Anstruther.

'Shall you?' said I.

'Fräulein Rose-Marie,' said he, solemnly, 'he was a most intelligent young man. Quite the most intelligent young man I have ever had here.'

'Really?' said I, smiling all over my silly face.

And so of course you were, or how would you ever have found out that I—well, that I'm not wholly unlovable?

Yours quite, quite truly,

R.-M.

II

DEAR ROGER,—You left on Tuesday night—that's yesterday—and you'll get to London on Thursday morning— that's tomorrow—and first you'll want to wash yourself, and have breakfast—please notice my extreme reasonableness— and it will be about eleven before you are able to begin to write to me. I shan't get the letter till Saturday, and today is only Wednesday, so how can I stop myself from writing to you again, I should like to know? I simply can't. Besides, I want to tell you all the heaps of important things I would have told you yesterday, if there had been time when you asked me in that amazing sudden way if I'd marry you.

Do you know I'm poor? Of course you do. You couldn't have lived with us a year and not seen by the very sort of puddings we have that we are poor. Do you think that anybody who can help it would have *dicker Reis* three times a week? And then if we were not, my stepmother would never bother to take in English young men who want to study German; she would do quite different sorts of things, and we should have different sorts of puddings—proud ones, with *Schlagsahne* on their tops—and two servants instead of one, and I would never have met you. Well, you know then that we are poor; but I don't believe you know *how* poor. When girls here marry, their parents give them, as a matter-of-course, house-linen enough to last them all their lives, furniture enough to furnish all their house, clothes enough for several generations, and so much a year besides. Then, greatly impoverished, they spend the evenings of their days

4

doing without things and congratulating themselves on having married off their daughter. The man need give only himself. You've heard that my own mother, who died ten years ago, was English? Yes, I remember I told you that, when you were so much surprised at what you called, in politest German, my colossally good English. From her I know that people in England do not buy their son-in-law's carpets and saucepans, but confine their helpfulness to suggesting Maple. It is the husband, they think, who should, like the storks of the Fatherland, prepare and beautify the nest for the wife. If the girl has money, so much the better; but if she has not, said my mother, it doesn't put an absolute stop to her marrying.

Here, it does; and I belong here. My mother had some money, or my father would never have let himself fall in love with her—I believe you can nip these things in the bud if you see the bud in time—and you know my father is not a mercenary man; he only, like the rest of us, could not get away altogether from his bringing-up and the points of view he had been made to stare from ever since he stared at all. It was a hundred a year (pounds, thank Heaven, not marks), and it is all we have except what he gets for his books, when he does get anything, which is never, and what my stepmother has, which is an annuity of a hundred and fifty pounds. So the hundred a year will be the whole sum of my riches, for I have no aunts. What I want you to consider is the awfulness of marrying a woman absolutely without saucepans. Not a single towel will she be able to add to your linen-room, not a single pot to your kitchen. All Jena when it hears of it will say, 'Poor, infatuated young man,' and if I had sisters all England would refuse in future to send its sons to my stepmother. Why, if you were making a decently suitable marriage do you suppose your

Braut would have to leave off writing to you at this point, in the very middle of luminous prophecy, and hurry into the kitchen and immerse herself in the preparation of potato soup? Yet that is exactly what your *Braut*, who has caught sight of the clock, is about to do. So good-bye.

Your poor, but infinitely honest

R.-M.

See how wise and practical I am today. I believe my letter last night was rather aflame. Now comes morning with its pails of cold water, and drenches me back into discretion. Thank God, say I, for mornings.

III

DEAR ROGER,—I can't leave you alone, you see. I must write. But though I must write you need not read. Last night I was seized with misgivings—awful things for a hitherto placid Fräulein to be seized with—and I wrestled with them all night, and they won. So now, in the calm frostiness of the early morning atmosphere, I wish to inquire very seriously, very soberly, whether you have not made a mistake. In one sense, of course, you have. It is absurd, from a worldly point of view, for you to marry me. But I mean more than that: I mean, have you not mistaken your own feelings, being hurled into the engagement by impulsiveness, by, if you choose, some spell I may unconsciously have put upon you? If you have even quite a faint misgiving about what you really feel for me, tell me—oh, tell me straight and plainly, and we will both rub out that one weak hour with a sponge well soaked in common sense. It would not hurt so much, I think, now as it might later on. Up to last night, since you left, I've been walking on air. It is a most pleasant form of exercise, as perhaps you know. You not only walk on air, but you walk in what seems to be an arrested sunset, a bath of liquid gold, breathing it, touching it, wrapped in it. It really is most pleasant. Well, I did that till last night; then came my stepmother, and catching at my flying feet pulled them down till they got to the painted deal floors of Rauchgasse 5, Jena, and once having got there, stuck there. Observe, I speak in images. My stepmother, so respectable, so solidly Christian, would not dream of

7

catching hold of anybody's feet and spoiling their little bit of happiness. Quite unconsciously she blew on that glow of sunset in which I was flying, and it went out with the promptness and completeness of a tallow candle, and down came Rose-Marie with a thud. Yes, I did come down with a thud. You will never be able to pretend, however much you try, that I'm one of your fairy little women that can be lifted about, and dandled, and sugared with dainty diminutives, will you? Facts are things that are best faced. I stand five feet ten without my heels, and when I fall I do it with a thud. Said my stepmother, then, after supper, when Johanna had cleared the last plate away, and we were sitting alone—my father is not back yet from Weimar—she on one side of the table, I on the other, the lamp in the middle, your chair gaping empty, she, poor herself, knitting wool into warmth for the yet poorer at Christmas, I mending the towels you helped to wear out, while my spirit soared and made a joyful noise somewhere far away, up among angels and archangels and other happy beings—said my stepmother, 'Why do you look so pleased?'

Slightly startled, I explained that I looked pleased because I was pleased.

'But nothing has happened,' said my stepmother, examining me over her spectacles. 'You have been nowhere today, and not seen any one, and the dinner was not at all good.'

'For all that, I'm pleased. I don't need to go somewhere or see some one to be pleased. I can be it quite by myself.'

'Yes, you are blest with a contented nature, that is true,' said my stepmother, with a sigh, knitting faster. You remember her sighs, don't you? They are always to me very unaccountable. They come in such odd places. Why should she sigh because I have a contented nature? Ought she not rather to rejoice? But the extremely religious people

8

I have known have all sighed an immense deal. Well, I won't probe into that now, though I rather long to.

'I suppose it's because it has been a fine day,' I said, foolishly going on explaining to a person already satisfied.

My stepmother looked up sharply. 'But it has not been fine at all, Rose-Marie,' she said. 'The sun has not appeared once all day.'

'What?' said I, for a moment genuinely surprised. I couldn't help being happy, and I don't believe really happy people are ever in the least aware that the sun is not shining. 'Oh well,' I hurried on, 'perhaps not an Italian blue sky, but still mild, and very sweet, and November always smells of violets, and that's another thing to be pleased about.'

'Violets?' echoed my stepmother, who dislikes all talk about things one can neither eat nor warm one's self with nor read about in the Bible. 'Do you not miss Mr Anstruther,' she asked, getting off such flabbinesses as quickly as she could, 'with whom you were so constantly talking?'

Of course I jumped. But I said 'Yes,' quite naturally, I think.

It was then that she pulled me down by the feet to earth.

'He has a great future before him,' she said. 'A young man so clever, so good looking, and so well connected may rise to anything. Martens tells me he has the most brilliant prospects. He will be a great ornament to the English diplomatic service. Martens says his father's hopes are all centred on this only son. And as he has very little money and much will be required, Roger'—she said it indeed—'is to marry as soon as possible, some one who will help him in every way, some one as wealthy as she is well born.'

I murmured something suitable; I think a commendation of the plan as prudent.

'No one could help liking Roger,' she went on—Roger,

do you like being Rogered?—'and my only fear is, and Martens fears it too, that he will entangle himself with some undesirable girl. Then he is ruined. There would be no hope for him.'

'But why——' I began; then suffocated a moment behind a towel. 'But why,' I said again, gasping, 'should he?'

'Well, let us hope he will not. I fear, though, he is soft. Still, he has steered safely through a year often dangerous to young men. It is true his father could not have sent him to a safer place than my house. You so sensible——' oh, Roger!—'Besides being arrived at an age when serious and practical thoughts replace the foolish sentimentalness of earlier years,'—oh, Roger, I'm twenty-five, and not a single one of my foolish sentimentalnesses has been replaced by anything at all. Do you think there is hope for me? Do you think it is very bad to feel exactly the same, just exactly as calf-like now as I did at fifteen?—'so that under my roof,' went on my stepmother, 'he has been perfectly safe. It would have been truly deplorable if his year in Germany had saddled him with a German wife from a circle beneath his own, a girl who had caught his passing fancy by youth and prettiness, and who would have spent the rest of her life dragging him down, an ever-present punishment with a faded face.'

She is eloquent, isn't she? Eloquent with the directness that instinctively finds out one's weak spots and aims straight at them. 'Luckily,' she concluded, 'there are no pretty faces in Jena just now.'

Then I held a towel up before my own, before my ignominious face, excluded by a most excellent critic from the category pretty, and felt as though I would hide it for ever in stacks of mending, in tubs of soup, in everything domestic and drudging and appropriate. But some of the words you rained down on me on Tuesday night between all those kisses came throbbing through my head, throbbing with great throbs through my whole body—Roger, did I hear wrong, or were they not 'Lovely—lovely—lovely'? And always kisses between, and always again that 'Lovely—lovely—lovely'? Where am I getting to? Perhaps I had better stop.

R.-M.

IV

DEAREST OF LIVING CREATURES,—The joy your dear, dear letters gave me! You should have seen me seize the postman. His very fingers seemed rosy-tipped as he gave me the precious things. Two of them—two love-letters all at once. I could hardly bear to open them, and put an end to the wonderful moment. The first one, from Frankfurt, was so sweet—oh, so unutterably sweet—that I did sit gloating over the unbroken envelope of the other for at least five minutes, luxuriating, purring. I found out exactly where your hand must have been, by the simple process of getting a pen and pretending to write the address where you had written it, and then spent another five minutes most profitably kissing the place. Perhaps I ought not to tell you this, but there shall be no so-called maidenly simperings between you and me, no pretences, no affectations. If it was silly to kiss that blessed envelope, and silly to tell you that I did, why then I was silly, and there's an end of it.

Do you know that my mother's maiden name was Watson? Well, it was. I feel bound to tell you this, for it seems to add to my ineligibleness, and my duty plainly is to take you all round that and expatiate on it from every point of view. What has the grandson of Lord Grasmere—you never told me of Lord G. before, by the way—to do with the granddaughter of Watson? I don't even rightly know what Watson was. He was always for me an obscure and rather awful figure, shrouded in mystery. Of course Papa could tell me about him, but as he never has, and my mother rarely mentioned him, I fancy he was not anything I should be proud of. Do not, then, require of me that I shall tear the veil from Watson.

And of course your mother was handsome. How dare you doubt it? Look in the glass and be grateful to her. You know, though you may only have come within the spell of what you so sweetly call my darling brown eyes during the last few weeks, I fell a victim to your darling blue ones in the first five minutes. And how great was my joy when I discovered that your soul so exactly matched your outside. Your mother had blue eyes, too, and was very tall, and had an extraordinarily thoughtful face. Look, I tell you, in the glass, and you'll see she had, for I refuse to believe that your father, a man who talks port wine and tomatoes the whole of the first meal he has with his only son after a year's separation, is the parent you are like. Heavens, how I shake when I think of what will happen when you tell him about me. 'Sir,' he'll say in a voice of thunder—or don't angry English parents call their sons 'sir' any more? Anyhow, they still do in books—'Sir, you are far too young to marry. Young men of twenty-five do not do such things. The lady, I conclude, will provide the income?'

Roger, rushing to the point: She hasn't a pfenning.

Incensed Parent: Pfenning, sir? What, am I to understand she's a German?

Roger, dreadfully frightened: Please.

I. P., forcing himself to be calm: Who is this young person?

Roger: Fräulein Schmidt, of Jena.

I. P., now of a horrible calmness: And who, pray, is Fräulein Schmidt of Jena?

Roger, pale but brave: The daughter of old Schmidt, in whose house I boarded. Her mother was English. She was a Watson.

I. P.: Sir, oblige me by going to the——

Roger goes.

Seriously, I think something of the sort will happen. I don't see how it can help giving your father a dreadful shock; and suppose he gets ill, and his blood is on my head? I can't see how it is to be avoided. There is nothing to recommend me to him. He'll know I'm poor. He'll doubt if I'm respectable. He won't even think me pretty. You might tell him that I can cook, darn, manage as well as the thriftiest of *Hausfraus*, and I believe it would leave him cold. You might dwell on my riper age as an advantage: say I have lived down the first fevers of youth—I never had them; say, if he objects to it, that Eve was as old as Adam when they started life in their happy garden, and yet they got on very well; say that I'm beautiful as an angel, or so plain that I am of necessity sensible, and he'll only answer 'Fool.' Do you see anything to be done? I don't; but I'm too happy to bother.

Later.

I had to go and help get supper ready. Johanna had let the fire out, and it took rather ages. Why do you say you feel like screaming when you think of me wrestling with Johanna? I tell you I'm so happy that nothing any Johanna can do or leave undone in the least affects me. I go about the house on tiptoe; I am superstitious, and have an idea that all sorts of little envious Furies are lying about in dusty corners asleep, put to sleep by you, and that if I don't move very delicately I shall wake them—

O Freude, habe Acht,
Sprich leise, dass nicht der Schmerz erwacht....

That's not Goethe. By the way, *poor* Goethe. What an unforeseen result of a year in the City of the Muses, half

14

an hour's journey from the Ilm Athens itself, that you should pronounce his poetry coarse, obvious, and commonplace. What would Papa say if he knew? Probably that young Anstruther is not the intelligent young man he took him for. But then Papa is soaked in Goethe, and the longer he soaks the more he adores him. In this faith, in this Goethe-worship, I have been brought up, and cannot, I'm afraid, get rid of it all at once. It is even possible that I never shall, in spite of London and you. Will you love me less if I don't? Always I have thought Goethe uninspired. The Muse never seized and shook him till divinenesses dropped off his pen without his knowing how or whence, divinenesses like those you find sometimes in the pages of lesser men, lesser all-round men, stamped with the unmistakable stamp of heavenly birth. Goethe knew, very well, very exactly, where each of his sentences had come from. But I don't see that his poetry is either of the three things you say. I'm *afraid* it is not the last two, for the world would grow very interesting if thinking and writing as he did were so obvious that we all did it. As to its being coarse, I'm incurably incapable of seeing coarseness in things. To me

> All is clean for ever and ever.

Everything is natural and everything is clean, except for the person who is afraid it isn't. Perhaps, dear Roger, you won't, as Papa says, quite apprehend my meaning; if you cannot, please console yourself with the reflection that probably I haven't got one.

What you say about the money you'll have dazzles me. Why, it's a fortune. We shall be richer than our *Bürgermeister.* You never told me you were so rich. Five hundred pounds a year is ten thousand marks; nearly double what we have always lived on, and we've really been quite comfortable, now, haven't we? But think of our glory when my hundred pounds is added, and we have an income of twelve thousand marks. The *Bürgermeister* will be utterly eclipsed. And I'm such a good manager. You'll see how we'll live. You'll grow quite fat. I shall give you lovely food; and Papa says that lovely food is the one thing that ever really makes a man give himself the trouble to rise up and call his wife blessed.

It is so late. Good night.

R.-M.

Don't take my Goethe-love from me. I know simply masses of him, and can't let him go. My mind is decked out with him as a garden is decked with flowers. Now, isn't that pretty? Or is it only silly? Anyhow, it's dreadfully late. Good night.

V

No letter from you today. I am afraid you are being worried, and because of me. Here am I, quiet and cheerful, nobody bothering me, and your dear image in my heart to warm every minute of life; there are you, being forced to think things out, to make plans for the future, decide on courses of action, besides having to pass exams. and circumvent a parent whom I gather you regard as refractory. How lucky I am in my dear father! If I could have chosen, I would have chosen him. Never has he been any trouble. Never does he bore me. Never am I forced to criticisms. He knows that I have no brains, and has forgiven me. I know he hasn't much common sense, and have forgiven him. We spend our time spoiling and petting and loving each other—do you remember how you sometimes laughed?

But I wish you were not worried. It is all because I'm so ineligible. If I could come to you with a pot of money in each hand, turned by an appreciative ruler into Baroness von Schmidt, with a Papa in my train weighed down by Orders, and the road behind me black with carts containing clothes, your father would be merciful unto us and bless us. As things are, you are already being punished, you have already begun to pay the penalty for that one little hour's happiness; and it won't be quite paid ever, not so long as we both shall live. Do you, who think so much, ever think of the almost indecent haste with which punishments hurry in the wake of joys? They really seem to tumble over one another in their eagerness each to get there first. You took me to your

17

heart, told me you loved me, asked me to be your wife. Was it so wrong? So wrong to let one's self go to happiness for those few moments that one should immediately be punished? My father will not let me believe anything. He says—when my stepmother is not listening; when she is he doesn't—that belief is not faith, and you can't believe if you do not know. But he cannot stop my silently believing that the Power in whose clutches we are is an amazing disciplinarian, a relentless grudger of joys. And what pitiful small joys they are, after all. Pitiful little attempts of souls doomed to eternal solitude to put out feelers in the dark, to get close to each other, to touch each other, to try to make each other warm. Now I am growing lugubrious; I who thought never to be lugubrious again. And at ten o'clock on a fine November morning, of all times in the world.

Papa comes back from Weimar today. There has been a prolonged meeting there of local lights about the damage done by some Goth to the Shakespeare statue in the park; and though Papa is not a light, still he did burn with indignation over that, and has been making impassioned speeches, and suggesting punishments for the Goth when they shall have caught him. I think I shall go over by the two o'clock train and meet him and bring him home, and look in at Goethe's sponge on the way. You know how the little black thing lies in his bedroom there, next to a basin not much bigger than a breakfast-cup. With this he washed and was satisfied. And whenever I feel depressed, out of countenance with myself and life, I go and look at it and come home cheered and strengthened. I wonder if you'll be able to make out why? Bless you my dearest.

R.-M.

VI

THAT sponge had no effect yesterday. I stared and stared at it, and it only remained a sponge, far too small for the really cleanly, instead of what it has up to now been, the starting-point for a train of thrilling, enthusiastic thoughts. I'm an unbalanced creature. Do you divide your time too, I wonder, between knocking your head against the stars and, in some freezing depth of blackness, listening to your heart, how it will hardly beat for fear? Of course you don't. You are much too clever. And then you have been educated, trained, taught to keep your thoughts within bounds, and not let them start off every minute on fresh and aimless wanderings. Yet the star-knocking is so wonderful that I believe I would rather freeze the whole year round for one hour of it than go back again to the changeless calm, the winter-afternoon sunshine, in which I used to sit before I knew you. All this only means that you have not written. See how variously one can state a fact.

I have run away from the sitting-room and the round table and the lamp, because Papa and my stepmother had begun to discuss you again, your prospects, your probable hideous fate if you were not prudent, your glorious career if you were. I felt guilty, wounded, triumphant, vain, all at once. Papa, of course, was chiefly the listener. He agreed; or at most he temporized. I tell you, Roger, I am amazed at the power a woman has over her husband if she is in every way inferior to him. It is not only that, as we say, *der Klügere giebt nach*, it is the daily complete victory of the coarser over the finer, the rough over the gentle, the ignorant over the wise. My stepmother is an uneducated person, shrewd about all the things that do not matter, unaware of the very existence of the things that do, ready to be charitable, helpful, where the calamity is big enough, wholly unsympathetic, even antagonistic, towards all those many small calamities that make up one's years; the sort of woman parsons praise, and who get tombstones put over them at last peppered with frigid adjectives like virtuous and just. Did you ever chance to live with a just person? They are very chilling, and not so rare as one might suppose. And Papa, laxest, most tolerant of men, so lax that nothing seems to him altogether bad, so tolerant that nobody, however hard he tries, can pass, he thinks, beyond the reach of forgiveness and love, so humorous that he has to fight continually to suppress it—for humour lands one in odd morasses of dislike and misconception here—married her a year after my mother died, and did it wholly for my sake. Imagine it. She was to make me happy. Imagine that too. I was not any longer to be a solitary *Backfisch*, with holes in her stockings and riotous hair. There came a painful time when Papa began to suspect that the roughness of my hair might conceivably be a symbol of the dishevelment of my soul. Neighbouring matrons pointed out the possibility to him. He took to peering anxiously at unimportant parts of me, such as my nails, and was startled to see them often black. He caught me once or twice red-eyed in corners, when it had happened that the dear ways and pretty looks of my darling mother had come back for a moment with extra vividness. He decided that I was both dirty and wretched, and argued, I am sure during sleepless nights, that I would probably go on being dirty and wretched for ever. And so he put on his best clothes one day, and set out doggedly in search of a wife.

He found her quite easily, in a house in the next street. She was making doughnuts, for it was the afternoon of New Year's Eve. She had just taken them out of the oven, and they were obviously successful. Papa loves doughnuts. His dinner had been uneatable. The weather was cold. She took off her apron, and piled them on a dish, and carried them, scattering fragrance as they went, into the sitting-room; and the smell of them was grateful; and they were very hot.

Papa came home engaged. 'I am not, as a rule, in favour of second marriages, Rose-Marie,' he began, breaking the news to me with elaborate art.

'Oh, horrid things,' I remarked, my arm round his neck, my face against his, for even then I was as tall as he. You know how he begins abruptly about anything that happens to cross his mind, so I was not surprised.

He rubbed his nose violently. 'I never knew anybody with such hair as yours for tickling a person,' he said, trying to push it back behind my ears. Of course it would not go. 'Would it do that,' he added suspiciously, 'if it were properly brushed?'

'I don't know. Well, *Papachen?*'

'Well, what?'

'About second marriages.'

He had forgotten, and he started. In an instant I knew. I took my arm away quickly, but put it back again just as quickly and pressed my face still closer: it was better we should not see each other's eyes while he told me.

'I am not, as a rule, in favour of them,' he repeated, when he had coughed and tried a second time to induce my hair to go behind my ears; 'but there are cases where they are— imperative.'

'Which ones?'

'Why, if a man is left with little children, for instance.'

'Then he engages a good nurse.'

'Or his children run wild.'

'Then he gets a severe aunt to live with him.'

'Or they grow up.'

'Then they take care of themselves.'

'Or he is an old man left with, say, one daughter.'

'Then she would take care of him.'

'And who would take care of her, Rose-Marie?'

'He would.'

'And if he is an incapable? An old person totally unable to notice lapses from convention, from social customs? If no one is there to tell her how to dress and how to behave? And she is growing up, and yet remains a barbarian, and the day is not far distant when she must go out, and he knows that when she does go out Jena will be astounded.'

'Does the barbarian live in Jena?'

'My dear, she is universal. Wherever there is a widower with an only female child, there she is.'

'But if she had been happy?'

'But she had not been happy. She used to cry.'

'Oh, of course she used to cry sometimes, when she thought more than usual of her sweet—of her sweet—— But for all that she had been happy, and so had he. Why, you know he had. Didn't she look after him, and keep house for him? Didn't she cook for him? Not very beautifully, perhaps, but still she did cook, and there was dinner every day. Didn't she go to market three times a week, and taste all the butter? Didn't she help to do the rooms? And in the evenings weren't they happy together, with nobody to worry them? And then, when he missed his darling wife, didn't the barbarian always know he was doing it, and come and sit on his knee, and kiss him, and make up for it? Didn't she? Now didn't she?'

Papa unwound himself, and walked up and down with a desperate face.

'Girls of sixteen must learn how to dress and to behave. A father cannot show them that,' he said.

'But they do dress and behave.'

'Rose-Marie, unmended stockings are not dressing. And to talk to a learned stranger well advanced in years with the freedom of his equal in age and knowledge, as I saw one doing lately, is not behaving.'

'Oh, papa, she wouldn't do that again, I'm certain.'

'She wouldn't have done it that once if she had had a mother.'

'But the poor wretch hadn't got a mother.'

'Exactly. A mother, therefore, must be provided.'

Here, I remember, there was a long pause. Papa walked, and I watched him in despair. Despair, too, was in his own face. He had had time to forget the doughnuts, and how cold he had been, and how hungry. So shaken was I that I actually suggested the engagement of a finishing governess to finish that which had never been begun, pointing out that she, at least, having finished would go; and he said he could not afford one; and he added the amazing statement that a wife was cheaper.

Well, I suppose she has been cheap: that is, she has made one of Papa's marks go as far as two of other people's; but oh how expensive she has been in other ways! She has ruined us in such things as freedom, and sweetness, and light. You know the sort of talk here at meals. I wish you could have heard it before her time. She has such a strong personality that somehow we have always followed her lead; and Papa, who used to bubble out streams of gaiety when he and I sat untidily on either side of a tureen of horrible bad soup, who talked of all things under heaven, and with undaunted audacity of many things in it, and who somehow put a snap and a sparkle into whatever he said, sits like a schoolboy invited to a meal at his master's, eager to agree, anxious to give satisfaction. The wax cloth on the table is clean and shiny; the spoons are bright; a cruet with clear oil and nice-looking vinegar stands in the midst; the food, though simple, is hot and decent; we are quite comfortable; and any of the other Jena *Hausfraus* coming in during a meal would certainly cry out *Wie gemütlich*. But of what use is it to be whitewashed and trim outside, to have pleasant creepers and tidy shutters, when inside one's soul wanders through empty rooms, mournfully shivers in damp and darkness, is hungry and no one brings it food, is cold and no one lights a fire, is miserable and tired and there's not a chair to sit on?

Why I write all this I can't think; except that I feel as if I were talking to you. You must tell me if I bore you. When I begin a letter to you the great difficulty is to leave off again. Oh, how warm it makes one feel to know that there is one person in the world to whom one is everything. A lover is the most precious, the most marvellous possession. No wonder people like having them. And I used to think that so silly. Heavens, what an absurd person I have been! Why, love is the one thing worth having. Everything else, talents, work, arts, religion, learning, the whole *tremblement*, are so many drugs with which the starved, the loverless, try to dull their pangs, to put themselves to sleep. Good night, and God bless you a thousand times.

R.-M.

VII

DEAREST,—Your letter came this afternoon. How glad I was to get it. And I do think it a good idea to go down into the country to those Americans before your exam. Who knows but they may, by giving you peace at the right moment, be the means of making you pass extra brilliantly? That you should not pass at all is absolutely out of the question. Why have the gods showered gifts on you if not for the proper passing of exams.? For I suppose in this as in everything else there are different ways, ways of excellence and mediocrity. I know which way yours will be. If only the presence of my spirit by your side on Saturday could be of use. But that's the worst of spirits: they never seem to be the least good unless they take their bodies with them. Yet mine burns so hotly when I am thinking of you—and when am I not thinking of you?—that I feel as if you actually must feel the glow of it as it follows you about. How strange and dreadful love is! Till you know it, you are so sure the world is very good and pleasant up in those serene, frost-bitten regions where you stand alone, breathing the thin air of family affection, shone upon gently by the mild and misty sun of general esteem. Then comes love, and pulls you down. For isn't it a descent? Isn't it? Somehow, though it is so great a glory, it's a coming-down as well—down from the pride of absolute independence of body and soul, down from the high-mightiness of indifference, to something fierce, and hot, and consuming. Oh, I daren't tell you how little of serenity I have left. At first, just at first, I didn't feel like this. I think I was stunned. My soul seemed to stand still. Surely it was extraordinary, that tempestuous crossing from the calm of careless friendship to the place where love dashes madly against the rocks? Don't laugh at my images. I'm in deadly earnest tonight. I do feel that love hurts. I do feel as if I'd been thrown on to rocks, left by myself on them to come slowly to my senses and find I am lying alone in a new and burning sun. It's an exquisite sort of pain, but it's very nearly unbearable. You see, you are so far away. And I, I'm learning for the first time in my life what it means, that saying about eating out one's heart.

R.-M.

VIII

REALLY, my dear Roger, nicest of all *Bräutigams*, pleasantest,
best, and certainly most charming, I don't think I'll write
to you again in the evenings. One of those hard clear hours
that lie round breakfast-time will be the most seemly for
consecration to you. Moods are such queer things, each one
so distinct and real, so seemingly eternal, and I am
influenced by them to an extraordinary degree. The
weather, the time of day, the light in the room—yes, actually
the light in the room, sunlight, cloudlight, lamplight—the
scent of certain flowers, the sound of certain voices—the
instant my senses become aware of either of these things I
find myself flung into the middle of a fresh mood. And the
worst part of it is the blind enthusiasm with which I am
sure that as I think and feel at that moment so will I think
and feel for ever. Nothing cures me. No taking of myself
aside, no weight of private admonishment, no bringing of
my spirit within the white glare of pure reason. Oh, women
are fools; and of all fools the most complete is myself. But
that's not what I want to talk about. I want to say that I
had to go to a *Kaffee-Klatsch* yesterday at four, which is why
I put off answering your letter of the 13th till the evening.
My dear Roger, you must take no notice of that letter. Pray
think of me as a young person of sobriety; collected, discreet,
cold to frostiness. Think of me like that, my dear, and in
return I'll undertake to write to you only in my after-
breakfast mood, quite the most respectable I possess. It is
nine now. Papa, in the slippers you can't have forgotten, is

in his corner by the stove, loudly disagreeing with the morning paper; he keeps on shouting *Schafskopf.* Johanna is carrying coals about and dropping them with a great noise. My stepmother is busy telling her how wrong it is to drop dirty coals in clean places. I am writing on a bit of the breakfast-table, surrounded by crumbs and coffee-cups. I will not clear them away till I've finished my letter, because then I am sure you'll get nothing either morbid or love-sick. Who, I'd like to know, could flame into love-talk or sink into the mud of morbidness from a starting-point of anything so sprightly as crumbs and coffee-cups?

It was too sweet of you to compare me to Nausicaa in your letter yesterday. Nobody ever did that before. Various aunts, among whom a few years ago there was a great mortality, so that they are all now aunts in heaven, told me in divers tones that I was much too long for my width, that I was like the handle of a broom, like the steeple of the *Stadtkirche*, like a tree walking; but none of them ever said anything about Nausicaa. I doubt if they had ever heard of her. I'm afraid if they had they wouldn't have seen that I am like her. You know the blindness of aunts. Jena is full of them (not mine, *Gott sei Dank*, but other people's) and they are all stone-blind. I don't mean, of course, that the Jena streets are thick with aunts being led by dogs on strings, but that they have that tragic blindness of the spirit that misses seeing things that are hopeful and generous and lovely; things alight with young enthusiasms, or beautiful with a patience that has had time to grow grey. They also have that odd, unfurnished sort of mind that can never forget and never forgive. Yesterday at the *Kaffee-Klatsch* I met them all again, the Jena aunts I know so well and who are yet for ever strange, for ever of a ghastly freshness. It was the first this season, and now I suppose I shall waste

many a good afternoon *klatsch*ing. How I wish I had not
to go. My stepmother says that if I do not show myself I
shall be put down as eccentric. 'You are not very popular,'
says she, 'as it is. Do not, therefore, make matters worse.'
Then she appeals, should a more than usual stubbornness
cloud my open countenance, to Papa. 'Ferdinand,' she says,
'shall she not, then, do as others of her age?' And of course
Papa says, bless him, that girls must see life occasionally, and
is quite unhappy if I won't. Life? God bless him for a dear,
innocent Papa. And how they talked yesterday. Papa
would have writhed. He never will talk or listen to talk
about women unless they've been dead some time, so
uninteresting, so unworthy of discussion does he consider
all live females except Johanna to be. And if I hadn't had
my love-letter (I took it with me tucked inside my dress,
where my heart could beat against it), I don't think I would
have survived that *Klatsch*. You've no idea how proudly I
set out. Hadn't I just been reading the sweetest things about
myself in your letter? Of course I was proud. And I felt so
important, and so impressive, and simply gloriously good-
tempered. The pavement of Jena, I decided as I walked over
it, was quite unworthy to be touched by my feet; and if the
passers-by only knew it, an extremely valuable person was
in their midst. In fact, my dear Roger, I fancied myself
yesterday. Didn't Odysseus think Nausicaa was Artemis when
first he met her among the washing, so god-like did she
appear? Well, I felt god-like yesterday, made god-like by your
love. I actually fancied people would *see* something wonderful
had happened to me, that I was transfigured, *verklärt*.
Positively, I had a momentary feeling that my coming in,
the coming in of anything so happy, must blind the *Kaffee-
Klatsch*, that anything so burning with love must scorch it.
Well, it didn't. Never did torch plunged into wetness go

out with a drearier fizzle than did my little shining. Nobody noticed anything different. Nobody seemed even to look at me. A few careless hands were stretched out, and the hostess told me to ask the servant to bring more milk.

They were talking about sin. We don't sin much in Jena, so generally they talk about sick people, or their neighbour's income and what he does with it. But yesterday they talked sin. You know, because we are poor and Papa has no official position and I have come to be twenty-five without having found a husband, I am a *quantité négligeable* in our set, a being in whose presence everything can be said, and who is expected to sit in a draught if there is one. Too old to join the young girls in the corner set apart for them, where they whisper and giggle and eat amazing quantities of whipped cream, I hover uneasily on the outskirts of the group of the married, and try to ingratiate myself by keeping on handing them cakes. It generally ends in my being sent out every few minutes by the hostess to the kitchen to fetch more food and things. 'Rose-Marie is so useful,' she will explain to the others when I have been extra quick and cheerful; but I don't suppose Nausicaa's female acquaintances said more. The man Ulysses might take her for a goddess, but the most the women would do would be to commend the way she did the washing. Sometimes I have great trouble not to laugh when I see their heads, often quite venerable, gathered together in an eager bunch, and hear them expressing horror, sympathy, pity, in every sort of appropriate tone, while their eyes, their tell-tale eyes, betrayers of the soul, look pleased. Why they should be pleased when somebody has had an operation or doesn't pay his debts, I can't make out. But they do. And after a course of *Klatsches* throughout the winter, you are left towards April with one firm conviction in a world where everything else is shaky, that there's not a single person who isn't either extraordinarily ill, or, if he's not, who does not misuse his health and strength by not paying his servants' wages.

Yesterday the *Klatsch* was in a fearful flutter. It had got hold of a tale of sin, real or suspected. It was a tale of two people who, after leading exemplary lives for years, had suddenly been clutched by the throat by Nature; and Nature, we know, cares nothing at all for the claims of husbands and wives or any other lawfulnesses, and is a most unmoral and one-idea'd person. They have, says Jena, begun to love each other in defiance of the law. Nature has been too many for them, I suppose. All Jena is a-twitter. Nothing can be proved, but everything is being feared, said the hostess; from her eyes I'm afraid she wanted to say hoped. Isn't it ugly?— *pfui*, as we say. And so stale, if it's true. Why can't people defy Nature and be good? The only thing that is always fresh and beautiful is goodness. It is also the only thing that can make you go on being happy indefinitely.

I know her well. My heart failed me when I heard her being talked about so hideously. She is the nicest woman in Jena. She has been kind to me often. She is very clever. Perhaps if she had been more dull she would have found no temptation to do anything but jog along respectably— sometimes I think that to be without imagination is to be so very safe. He has only come to these parts lately. He used to be in Berlin, and has been appointed to a very good position in Weimar. I have not met him, but Papa says he is brilliant. He has a wife, and she has a husband, and they each have a lot of children; so you see if it's true it really is very *pfui*.

Just as the *Kaffee-Klatsch* was on the wane, and crumbs were being brushed off laps, and bonnet-strings tied, in she

31

walked. There was a moment's dead silence. Then you should have heard the effusion of welcoming speeches. The hostess ran up and hugged her. The others were covered with pleasant smiles. Perhaps they were grateful to her for having provided such thrilling talk. When I had to go and kiss her hand I never in my life felt baser. You should have seen her looking round cheerfully at all the Judases, and saying she was sorry to be late, and asking if they hadn't missed her; and you should have heard the eager chorus of assurances.

Oh, *pfui, pfui.*

R.-M.

How much I love goodness, straightness, singleness of heart—*you.*

Later.

I walked part of the way home with the calumniated one. How charming she is. Dear little lady, it would be difficult not to love her. She talked delightfully about German and English poetry. Do you think one can talk delightfully about German and English poetry and yet be a sinner? Tell me, do you think a woman who is very intellectual, but very, *very* intellectual, could yet be a sinner? Would not her wits save her? Would not her bright wits save her from anything so dull as sin?

IX

DEAREST,—I don't think I like that girl at all. Your letter
from Clinches has just come, and I don't think I like her
at all. What is more, I don't think I ever shall like her. And
what is still more, I don't think I even want to. So your
idea of her being a good friend to me later on in London
must retire to that draughty corner of space where abortive
ideas are left to eternal shivering. I'm sorry if I am
offensively independent. But then I know so well that I
won't be lonely if I'm with you, and I think rooting up,
which you speak of as a difficult and probably painful
process, must be very nice if you are the one to do it, and
I am sure I could never by any possibility reach such depths
of strangeness and doubt about what to do next as would
induce me to stretch out appealing hands to a young
woman with eyes that, as you put it, tilt at the corners. I
wish you hadn't told her about us, about me. It has profaned
things so, dragged them out into the streets, cheapened
them. I don't in the least want to tell my father, or any one
else. Does this sound as though I were angry? Well, I don't
think I am. On the contrary, I rather want to laugh. You
dear silly! So clever and so simple, so wise and crammed
with learning, and such a dear, ineffable goose. How old
am I, I wonder? Only as old as you? Really only as old?
Nonsense: I'm fifteen, twenty years your senior, my dear sir.
I've lived in Jena, you in London. I frequent *Kaffee-Klatsches*,
and you the great world. I talk much with Johanna in the
kitchen, and you with Heaven knows what in the way of

geniuses. Yet no male Nancy Cheriton, were his eyelids never so tilted, would wring a word out of me about a thing so near, so precious, so much soul of my soul as my lover.

How would you explain this? I've tried and can't.

Your rebellious

ROSE-MARIE.

Darling, darling, don't ask me to like Nancy. The thing's unthinkable.

Later.

Now I know why I am wiser than you: life in kitchens and *Klatsches* turns the soul grey very early. Didn't one of your poets sing of somebody who had a sad lucidity of soul? I'm afraid that is what's the matter with me.

X

OH, what nonsense everything seems,—everything of the
nature of differences, of arguments, on a clear morning up
among the hills. I am ashamed of what I wrote about Nancy;
ashamed of my eagerness and heat about a thing that does
not matter. On the hills this morning, as I was walking in
the sunshine, it seemed to me that I met God. And He took
me by the hand, and let me walk with Him. And He showed
me how beautiful the world is, how beautiful the
background He has given us, the spacious, splendid
background on which to paint our large charities and
loves. And I looked across the hilltops, golden, utterly
peaceful, and amazement filled me in the presence of that
great calm at the way I flutter through my days and at the
noise I make. Why should I cry out before I am hurt? flare
up into heat and clamour? The pure light up there made
it easy to see clearly, and I saw that I have been silly and
ungrateful. Forgive me. You know best about Nancy, you
who have seen her; and I, just come down from that holy
hour on the hills, am very willing to love her. I will not
turn my back upon a ready friend. She can have no motive
but a good one. Roger, I am a blunderer, a clumsy creature
with not one of my elemental passions bound down yet
into the decent listlessness of chains. But I shall grow better,
grow more worthy of you. Not a day shall pass without my
having been a little wiser than the day before, a little kinder,
a little more patient. I wish you had been with me this
morning. It was so still and the sky so clear that I sat on

the old last year's grass as warmly as in summer. I felt irradiated with life and love; light shining on to every tiresome incident of life and turning it into beauty, love for the whole wonderful world, and all the people in it, and all the beasts and flowers, and all the happy living things. Indeed, blessings have been given me in full measure, pressed down and running over. In the whole of that little town at my feet, so quiet, so bathed in lovely light, there was not, there could not be, another being so happy as myself. Surely I am far too happy to grudge accepting a kindness? I tell you I marvel at the energy of my protest yesterday. Perhaps it was—oh, Roger, after those hours on the hills I will be honest, I will pull off the veil from feelings that the female mind generally refuses to uncover—perhaps the real reason, the real, pitiful, mean reason was that I felt sure somehow from your description of her that Nancy's *blouses* must be very perfect things, things beyond words very perfect. And I was jealous of her blouses. There now. Good-bye.

XI

I AM glad you did not laugh at that silly letter of mine
about scorching in the sun on rocks. Indeed, I gather, my
dear Roger, that you liked it. Make the most of it, then, for
there will be no more of the sort. A decent woman never
gets on to rocks, and if she scorches she doesn't say so. And
I believe that it is held to be generally desirable that she
should not, even under really trying circumstances, part with
her dignity. I rather think the principle was originally laid
down by the husband of an attractive wife, but it is a good
one, and so long as I am busy clinging to my dignity
obviously I shall have no leisure for clinging to you, and
then you will not be suffocated with the superabundance
of my follies.

About those two sinners who are appalling us: how can
I agree with you? To do so would cut away the ground
from under my own feet. The woman plays such a losing
game. She gives so much, and gets so little. So long as the
man loves her I do see that he is worth the good opinion
of neighbours and relations, which is one of the chilliest
things in the world; but he never seems able to go on loving
her once she has begun to wither. That is very odd. She
does not mind his withering. And has she not a soul? And
does not that grow always lovelier? But what, then, becomes
of her? For wither she certainly will, and years rush past at
such a terrific pace that almost before she has begun to be
happy it is over. He goes back to his wife, a person who
has been either patient or bitter, according to the quantity

37

of her vitality and the quality of her personal interests, and concludes, while he watches her sewing on his buttons in the corner she has probably been sitting in through all his vagrant years, that marriage has its uses, and that it is good to know there will be some one bound to take care of you up to the last, and who will shed decent tears when you are buried. She goes back—but where, and to what? They have gone long ago, her husband, her children, her friends. And she is old, and alone. You too, like everybody else, seem unable to remember how transient things are. Time goes, emotions wear out. You say these people are in the hands of Fate, and can no more get out of them and do differently than a fly in a web can walk away when it sees the hungry spider coming nearer. I don't believe in webs and spiders; at least, I don't today. Today I believe only in my unconquerable soul—

> I am the master of my fate,
> I am the captain of my soul.

And you say that a person in the grip of a great feeling should not care a straw for circumstance, should defy it, trample it under foot. Heaven knows that I too am for love and laughter, for the snatching of flying opportunities, for all that makes the light and the glory of life; but what afterwards? The Afterwards haunts me like a weeping ghost. It is true, there is still the wide world, the warm sun, seed-time and harvest, Shakespeare, the Book of Job, singing birds, flowers; but the soul that has transgressed the laws of man seems for ever afterwards unable to use the gifts of God. If supreme joy could be rounded off by death, death at the exact right moment, how easy things would be. Only death has a strange way of shunning those persons who want him most. To long to die seems to make you as nearly immortal as it is possible to become. Now, just think what would have happened if Tristan had not been killed, had lived on quite healthily. King Mark, than whom I know no man in literature more polite, would have handed Isolde over to him as he declared himself ready to have done had he been aware of the unfortunately complicated state of things, and he would have done it with every expression of decent regret at the inconvenience he had caused. Isolde would have married Tristan. There would have been no philosophy, no divine hours in the garden, no acute, exquisite anguish of love and sorrow. But there would presently have been the Middle Ages equivalent for a perambulator, a contented Tristan coming to meet it, a faded Isolde who did not care for poetry admonishing, perhaps with sharpness, a mediaeval nursemaid, and quite quickly afterwards a Tristan grown too comfortable to move, and an Isolde with wrinkles. Would we not have lost a great deal if they had lived? It is certain that they themselves would have lost a great deal; for I don't see that contentment beaten out thin enough to cover a long life—and beat as thin as you will, it never does cover quite across the years—is to be compared with one supreme contentment heaped in one heap on the highest, keenest point of living we reach. Now, I am apparently arguing on your side, but I'm not really, because you, you know, think of love as a perpetual *crescendo*, and I, though I do hear the *crescendo* and follow it with a joyful clapping of hands up to the very top of its splendour, can never forget the drop on the other side, the inevitable *diminuendo* to the dead level—and then? Why, the rest is not even silence, but a querulous murmur, a querulous, confused whining, confused complaining, not very loud, not very definite, but always there till the last chord is reached a long time afterwards—that satisfactory common chord of death. My point is, that if you want to let yourself go to great emotions you ought to have the luck to die at an interesting moment. The alternative makes such a dreary picture; and it is the picture I always see when I hear of love at defiance with the law. The law wins; always, inevitably. Husbands are best; always, inevitably. Really, the most unsatisfactory husband is a person who should be clung to steadily from beginning to end, for did not one marry him of one's own free will? How ugly then, because one had been hasty, foolish, unacquainted with one's usually quite worthless mind, to punish him. The brilliant professor, the fascinating little lady, what are they but grossly selfish people, cruelly punishing the husband and wife who had the misfortune to marry them? Oh, it's a mercy most of us are homely, slow of wit, heavy of foot; for so at least we stay at home and find our peace in fearful innocence and household laws. (Please note my familiarity with the British poets.) But isn't that a picture of frugal happiness, of the happiness that comes from a daily simple obedience to the Stern Daughter of the Voice of God, beside which stormy, tremendous, brief things come off very badly? I don't believe you do in your heart side with the two sinners. Bother them. They have made me feel like a Lutheran pastor on a Sunday afternoon. But you know I love you.

R.-M.

XII

WHEN do you go back to Jermyn Street? Surely today, for is not the examination tomorrow? Your description of the Cheriton *ménage* at Clinches is like fairyland. No wonder you feel so happy there. My mother used to tell me about life in England, but apparently the Watson family did not dwell in houses like Clinches. Anyhow, I had an impression of little houses with little staircases, and oilcloth, and a servant in a cap with streamers, and round white balls of suet with currants in them very often for dinner. But Clinches, beautiful and dignified in the mists and subtleties of a November afternoon, its massed greyness melting into that other greyness, its setting of mysterious blurred wood and pale light of water, its spaciousness, its pleasant people, its daughter with the dusky hair and odd grey eyes—is a vision of fairyland. I cannot conceive what life is like in such places; nor, I am sure, could any other inhabitant of Jena. What, for instance, can it be like to live in a thing so big that you do not hear the sounds nor smell the smells of the kitchen? Ought not people who live in such places to have unusually beautiful ways of looking at life? of thinking? of speaking? One imagines it all very noble, very gracious, altogether worthy. That complete separation from the kitchen is what wrings the biggest sigh of envy out of me. Is it my English blood that makes me rebel against kitchens? Or is it only my unfortunate sensitiveness to smell? I wish I had no nose. It has always been a nuisance. It is as extravagantly delighted by exquisite scents as it is

41

extravagantly horrified by nasty ones. Why, a beautiful smell, if it is delicate, subtle, intermittent, can ruin a morning for me. It fills me with a quite unworthy rapture. Things that ought to be hard in me melt. Things that ought to be fixed are scattered Heaven knows where. I go soft, ecstatic, basely idle. I forget that my business is to get dinner, and not to stand still and just sniff. In March I dare not pass the house Schiller used to live in on my way to market, because the people who live there now have planted violets along the railings. It is the shortest way, and it takes ten more minutes out of a busy morning to go round by the Post Office; but really for a grown woman to stand lost in what is mere voluptuous pleasure, leaning against somebody else's railing while the family dinner lies still unbought in the market-place, is conduct that I cannot justify. As for a beanfield—my dear Roger, did you ever come across a beanfield in flower? It is the divinest experience the nose can give us. Two years ago an Englishman came and spent a spring and summer in the little house in the apple orchard up on the road over the Galgenberg—the little house with the blue shutters—and he was a great gardener. And he dug a big patch, and planted a beanfield, and it was the first beanfield Jena had ever seen; for those beans called broad that you eat in England and are properly thankful for are only grown in Germany for the use of pigs, and there are no pigs in Jena. Sow-beans they are called here, mindful of their destiny. The Englishman, who possessed no visible sow, was a source of astonishment to us. The things came up, and were undoubtedly sow-beans. A great square patch of them grew up just over the fence on which Jena leaned and pondered. The man himself was seen in his shirt-sleeves weeding them on rainy afternoons. Jena could only suspect a pig concealed in the parlour, and was indulgent; and it

42

was indulgent because no one, in its opinion, can be both English and sane. 'God made us all,' was its invariable helpless conclusion as it went, shaking its head, home down the hill. When in June the beanfield flowered I blessed that Englishman. No one hung over his fence more persistently than I. It was the first time I had smelt the like. It became an obsession. I wanted to be there at every sort of time and under every sort of weather-condition. At noon, when the sun shone straight down on it, drawing up its perfume in hot breaths, I was there; in the morning, so early that it was still in the blue shadow of the Galgenberg and every grey leaf and white petal was drenched with dew, I was there; on wet afternoons, when the scent was crushed out of it by the beating of heavy rain, and the road for half a mile, the slippery clay road with its puddles and amazing mud, was turned into a bath of fragrance fit for the tenderest, most fastidious goddess to bare her darling little limbs in, I was there; and once, after lying awake in my hot room so near the roof for hours thinking of it out there on the hillside in the freshness under the stars, I got up and dressed, and crept with infinite caution past my stepmother's door, and stole the latchkey, and slunk, my heart in my mouth, through the stale streets, along all the railings and dusty front gardens, out into the open country, up on to the hill, to where it stood in straight and motionless rows, sending out waves of fragrance into that wonderful clean air you find in all the places where men leave off and God begins. Did you ever know a woman before who risked her reputation for a beanfield? Well, it is what I did. And I'll tell you, I who am so incurably honest that I can never for long pretend, why I write all this about it. It is that I am sick with anxiety—oh, sick, cold, shivering with it— about your exam. I didn't want you to know. I've tried to

43

write of beanfields instead. I didn't want you to be bothered. The clamourings for news of the person not on the spot are always a worry, and I did not want to worry. But the letter I got from you this morning never mentions the exam., the thing on which, as you told me, everything depends for us. You talk about Clinches, about the people there, about the shooting, the long days in woods, the keen-wittedness of Nancy who goes with you, who understands before you have spoken, who sympathizes so kindly about me, who fits, you say, so strangely into the misty winter landscape in her paleness, her thinness, her spiritualness. There was one whole page—oh, I grudged it—about her loosely done dark hair, how softly dusky it is, how it makes you think of twilight, and her eyes beneath it of the first faint shining of stars. I wonder if these things really fill your thoughts, or whether you are only using them to drive away useless worry about Saturday. I know you are a poet, and a poet's pleasure in eyes and hair is not a very personal thing, so I do not mind that. But tomorrow is Saturday. Shall you send me a telegram, I wonder? A week ago I would not have wondered; I should have been so sure you would let me have one little word at once about how you felt it had gone off—one little word for the person so far away, so helpless, so dependent on your kindness for the very power to go on living. Oh, what stuff this is. Worse even than the beanfield. But I must be sentimental sometimes, now mustn't I? or I would not be a woman. But really, my darling, I am very anxious.

R.-M.

XIII

I HAVE waited all day, and there has been no telegram. Well, on Monday I shall get a letter about it, and how much more satisfactory that is. Today after all is nearly over, and there is only Sunday to be got through first, and I shall be helped to endure that by the looking forward. Isn't it a mercy that we never get cured of being expectant? It makes life so bearable. However regularly we are disappointed and nothing whatever happens, after the first blow has fallen, after the first catch of the breath, the first gulp of misery, we turn our eyes with all their old eagerness to a point a little further along the road. I suppose in time the regular repetition of shocks does wear out hope, and then I imagine one's youth collapses like a house of cards. Real old age begins then, inward as well as outward; and one's soul, that kept so bravely young for years after one's face got its first wrinkles, suddenly shrivels up. Its light goes out. It is suddenly and irrecoverably old, blank, dark, indifferent.

Sunday Night.

I didn't finish my letter last night because, observing the strain I had got into, I thought it better for your comfort that I should go to bed. So I did. And while I went there I asked myself why I should burden you with the dull weight of my elementary reflections. You who are so clever and who think so much and so clearly, must laugh at their elementariness. They are green and immature, the acid juice of an imperfect fruit that has always hung in the shadow.

45

And yet I don't think you must laugh, Roger. It would, after all, be as cruel as the laughter of a child watching a blind man ridiculously stumbling among the difficulties of the way.

The one Sunday post brought nothing from you. The day has been very long. I cannot tell you how glad I am night has come, and only sleep separates me now from Monday morning's letter. These Sundays now that you are gone are intolerable. Before you came they rather amused me,—the furious raging of Saturday, with its extra cleaning and feverish preparations till far into the night; Johanna more than usually slipshod all day, red of elbow, wispy of hair, shuffling about in her felt slippers, her skirt girded up very high, a moist mop and an overflowing pail dribbling soapy tracks behind her in her progress; my stepmother baking, and not lightly to be approached; Papa fled from early morning till supper-time; and then the dead calm of Sunday, day of food and sleep. Cake for breakfast—such a bad beginning. Church in the University chapel, with my stepmother in her best hat with the black feathers and the pink rose—it sounds frivolous, but you must have noticed the awe-inspiring effect of it coming so unexpectedly on the top of her long respectable face and oiled-down hair. A fluffy person in that hat would have all the students offering to take her for a walk or share their umbrella with her. My stepmother stalks along panoplied in her excellences, and the feather waves and nods gaily at the passing student as he slinks away down by-streets. Once last spring a silly bee thought the rose must be something alive and honeyful, and went and smelt it. I think it must have been a very young bee; anyhow, nobody else up to now has misjudged my stepmother like that. She sits near the door in church, and has never yet heard the last half of the sermon because she has to go out in time to put the goose or other Sunday succulence safely into the oven. I wish she would let me do that, for I don't care for sermons. When you were here and condescended to come with us, at least we could criticize them comfortably on our way home; but alone with my stepmother I may do nothing but praise. It is the most tiring, tiresome of all attitudes, the one of undiscriminating admiration. To hear you pull the person who had preached to pieces, and laugh at the things he had said that would not bear examination, used to be like having a window thrown open in a stuffy room on a clear winter's morning. Shall you ever forget the elaborateness of the Sunday dinner? For that, chiefly, is Saturday sacrificed, a whole day that might be filled with lovely leisure. I do hope you never thought that I too looked upon it as a nice way of celebrating Sunday. How amazing it is, the way women waste life. Men waste enough of it, Heaven knows, but never anything like so much as women. Papa and I both hate that Sunday dinner, both dread the upheavals of Saturday made necessary by it, and you, I know, disliked them just as much, and so has every other young man we have had here; yet my stepmother inflicts these things on us with an iron determination that nothing will ever alter. And why? Only because she was brought up in the belief that it was proper, and because, if she omitted to do the proper, female Jena would be aghast. Well, I think it's a bad thing to be what is known as brought up, don't you? Why should we poor helpless little children, all soft and resistless, be squeezed and jammed into the rusty iron bands of parental points of view? Why should we have to have points of view at all? Why not, for those few divine years when we are still so near God, leave us just to guess and wonder? We are not given a chance. On our pulpy little minds our parents carve their opinions, and the mass slowly hardens, and all those deep, narrow, up and down strokes harden with it, and the first thing the best of us have to do on growing up is to waste precious time rubbing and beating at the things to try to get them out. Surely the child of the most admirable, wise parent is richer with his own faulty but original point of view than he would be fitted out with the choicest selection of maxims and conclusions that he did not have to think out for himself? I could never be a schoolmistress. I should be afraid to teach the children. They know more than I do. They know how to be happy, how to live from day to day in godlike indifference to what may come next. And is not how to be happy the secret we spend our lives trying to guess? Why then should I, by forcing them to look through my stale eyes, show them as through a dreadful magnifying-glass the terrific possibilities, the cruel explosiveness of what they had been lightly tossing to each other across the daisies and thinking were only toys!

Today at dinner, when Papa had got to the stage immediately following the first course at which, his hunger satisfied, he begins to fidget and grow more and more unhappy, and my stepmother was conversing blandly but firmly with the tried and ancient friend she invites to bear witness that we too have a goose on Sundays, and I had begun to droop, I hope poetically, like a thirsty flower, let us say, or a broken lily, over my plate, I thought—oh, how longingly I thought—of the happy past meals, made happy because you were here sitting opposite me and I could watch you. How short they seemed in those days. You didn't know I was watching you, did you? But I was. And I learned to do it so artfully, so cautiously. When you turned your head and talked to Papa I could do it openly; when you talked to me I could look straight in your dear eyes while I answered; but when I wasn't answering I still looked at you, by devious routes carefully concealed, routes that grew so familiar by practice that at last I never missed a single expression, while you, I suppose, imagined you had nothing before you but a young woman with a vacant face. What talks and laughs we will have about that odd, foolish year we spent here together in our blindness when next we meet! We've had no time to say anything at all yet. There are thousands of things I want to ask you about, thousands of little things we said and did that seem so strange now in the light of our acknowledged love. My heart stands still at the thought of when next we meet. These letters have been so intimate, and we were not intimate. I shall be deadly shy when in your presence I remember what I have written and what you have written. We are still such strangers, bodily, personally; strangers with the overwhelming memory of that last hour together to make us turn hot and tremble.

Now I am going to bed,—to dream of you, I suppose, considering that all day long I am thinking of you; and perhaps I shall have a little luck, and dream that I hear you speaking. You know, Roger, I love you for all sorts of queer and apparently inadequate reasons—I won't tell you what they are, for they are quite absurd; things that have to do with eyebrows, and the shape of hands, so you see quite foolish things—but most of all I love you for your voice. A beautiful speaking voice is one of the best of the gifts of the gods. It is so rare; and it is so irresistible. Papa says heaps of nice poetic things, but then the darling pipes. The most eloquent lecturer we have here does all his eloquence, which is really very great read afterwards in print, in a voice of beer, loose, throaty, reminiscent of barrels. Not one of the preachers who come to the University chapel has a voice that does not spoil the merit there may be in what he says. Sometimes I think that if a man with the right voice were to get up in that pulpit and just say, 'Children, Christ died for you,'—oh, then I think that all I have and am, body, mind, soul, would be struck into one great passion of gratefulness and love, and that I would fall conquered on my face before the Cross on the altar, and cry and cry. . . .

XIV

Jena, Nov. 25. Monday Night.
THE last post has been. No letter. If you had posted it in London on Saturday after the examination I ought to have had it by now. I am tortured by the fear that something has happened to you. Such dreadful things do happen. Those great, blundering, blind fists of Fate, laying about in mechanical cruelty, crushing the most precious lives as indifferently as we crush an ant in an afternoon walk, how they terrify me. All day I have been seeing foolish, horrible pictures—your train to London smashing up, your cab coming to grief—the thousand things that might so easily happen really doing it at last. I sent my two letters to Jermyn Street, supposing you would have left Clinches, but now somehow I don't think you did leave it, but went up from there for the exam. Do you know it is three days since I heard from you? That wouldn't matter so much—for I am determined never to bother you to write, I am determined I will never be an exacting woman—if it were not for the all-important examination. You said that if you passed it well and got a good place in the Foreign Office you would feel justified in telling your father about us. That means that we would be openly engaged. Not that I care for that, or want it except as the next step to our meeting again. It is clear that we cannot meet again till our engagement is known. Even if you could get away and come over for a few days I would not see you. I will not be kissed behind doors. These things are too wonderful to be handled after the manner of kitchen-maids. I am willing to be as silent as the

grave for as long as you choose, but so long as I am silent we shall not meet. I tell you I am incurably honest. I cannot bear to lie. And even these letters, this perpetual writing when no one is likely to look, this perpetual watching for the postman so that no one will be likely to see, does not make me love myself any better. It is true, I need not have watched quite so carefully lately, need I? Oh, Roger, why don't you write? What has happened? Think of my wretched plight if you are ill. Just left to wonder at the silence, to gnaw away at my miserable heart. Or, if some one took pity on me and sent me word,—your servant, or the doctor, or the kind Nancy—what could I do even then but still sit here and wait? How could I, a person of whom nobody has heard, go to you? It seems to me that the whole world has a right to be with you, to know about you, except myself. I cannot wait for the next post. The waiting for these posts makes me feel physically sick. If the man is a little late, what torments I suffer lest he should not be coming at all. Then I hear him trudging up the stairs. I fly to the door, absolutely vainly trying to choke down hope. 'There will be no letter, no letter, no letter,' I keep on crying to my thumping heart so that the disappointment shall not be quite so bitter; and it takes no notice, but thumps back wildly, 'Oh, there will, there will.' And what the man gives me is a circular for Papa.

It is quite absurd, madly absurd, the anguish I feel when that happens. My one wish, my only wish, as I creep back again down the passage to my work, is that I could go to sleep, and sleep and sleep and forget that I have ever hoped for anything; sleep for years, and wake up quiet and old, with all these passionate, tearing feelings gone from me for ever.

XV

Jena, Nov. 28.

LAST night I got your letter written on Sunday at Clinches, a place from which letters do not seem to depart easily. My knowledge of England's geography is limited, so how could I guess that it was so easy to go up to London from there for the exam. and back again the same day? As you had no time, you say, to go to Jermyn Street, I suppose the two letters I sent there will be forwarded to you. If they are not it does not matter. They were only a string of little trivial things that would look really quite too little and trivial to be worth reading in the magnificence of Clinches. I am glad you are well; glad you are happy; glad you feel you did not do badly on Saturday. It is a good thing to be well and happy and satisfied, and a pleasant thing to have found a friend who takes so much interest in you, and to whom you can tell your most sacred thoughts: doubly pleasant, of course, when the friend chances to be a woman, and she is pretty, and young, and rich, and everything else that is suitable and desirable. The world is an amusing place. My stepmother talked of you this morning at breakfast. She was, it seems, in a prophetic mood. She shook her head after the manner of the more gloomy of the prophets, and hoped you would steer clear of entanglements.

'And why should he not, *meine Liebste?*' inquired Papa.

'Not for nothing has he got that mouth, Ferdinand,' answered she.

ROSE-MARIE SCHMIDT.

53

XVI

My darling, forgive me. If I could only get it back! I who
hate unreasonableness, who hate bitterness, who hate
exacting women, petty women, jealous women, to write a
thing so angry. How horrible this letter-writing is. If I had
said all that to you in a sudden flare of wrath, I would have
been sorry so immediately, and at once have made
everything fair and sweet again with a kiss. And I never
would have got beyond the first words, never have
reached my stepmother's silly and rude remarks, never have
dreamed of repeating the unkind, unjust things. Now, Roger,
listen to me: my faith in you is perfect, my love for you is
perfect, but I am so undisciplined, so new to love, that you
must be patient, you must be ready to forgive easily for a
little while, till I have had time to grow wise. Just think,
when you feel irritated, of the circumstances of my life.
Everything has come so easily, so naturally to you. But I
have been always poor, always second-rate—oh, it's true—
shut out from the best things and people, lonely because
the society I could have was too little worth having, and
the society I would have liked didn't want me. How could
it? It never came our way, never even knew we were there.
I have had a shabby, restricted, incomplete life; I mean the
last ten years of it, since my father married again. Before
that, if the shabbiness was there I did not see it; there
seemed to be sunshine every day, and room to breathe, and
laughter enough; but then I was a child, and saw sunshine
everywhere. Is there not much excuse for some one who

has found a treasure, some one till then very needy, if his anxiety lest he should be robbed makes him—irritable? You see, I put it mildly. I know very well that irritable isn't the right word. I know very well what are the right words, and how horrid they are, and how much ashamed I am of their bitter truth. Pity me. A person so unbalanced, so stripped of all self-control that she writes things she knows must hurt to the being she loves so utterly, does deserve pity from better, serener natures. I do not understand you yet. I do not understand the ways yet of people who live as you do. I am socially inferior, and therefore sensitive and suspicious. I am groping about, and am so blind that only sometimes can I dimly feel how dark it really is. I have built up a set of ideals about love and lovers, absurd crude things, clumsy fabrics suited to the conditions of Rauchgasse, and the first time you do not exactly fit them I am desperately certain that the world is coming to an end. But how hopeless it is, this trying to explain, this trying to undo. How shall I live till you write that you do still love me?

Your wretched

ROSE-MARIE.

XVII

I COUNTED up my money this morning to see if there would be enough to take me to England, supposing some day I should wake up and find myself no longer able to bear the silence. I know I should be mad if I went, but sometimes one is mad. There was not nearly enough. The cheapest route would cost more than comes in my way during a year. I have a ring of my mother's with a diamond in it, my only treasure, that I might sell. I never wear it; my red hands are not pretty enough for rings, so it is only sentiment that makes it precious. And if it would take me to you and give me just one half-hour's talk with you and sweep away the icy fog that seems to be settling down on my soul and shutting out everything that is wholesome and sweet, I am sure my darling mother, whose one thought was always to make me happy, would say, 'Child, go and sell it, and buy peace.'

XVIII

LAST night I dreamed I did go to England, and I found you in a room with a crowd of people, and you nodded not unkindly, and went on talking to the others, and I waited in my corner till they should have gone, waited for the moment when we would run into each other's arms; and with the last group you too went out talking and laughing, and did not come back again. It was not that you wanted to avoid me; you had simply forgotten that I was there. And I crept out into the street, and it was raining, and through the rain I made my way back across Europe to my home, to the one place where they would not shut me out, and when I opened the door all the empty future years were waiting for me there, grey, vacant, listless.

XIX

THESE scraps of letters are not worth the postman's trouble, are not worth the stamps; but if I did not talk to you a little every day I do not think I could live. Yesterday you got my angry letter. If you were not at Clinches I could have had an answer tomorrow; as it is, I must wait till Wednesday. Roger, I am really a cheerful person. You mustn't suppose that it is my habit to be so dreary. I don't know what has come over me. Every day I send you another shred of gloom, and deepen the wrong impression you must be getting of me. I know very well that nobody likes to listen to sighs, and that no man can possibly go on for long loving a dreary woman. Yet I cannot stop. A dreary man is bad enough, but he would be endured because we endure every variety of man with so amazing a patience; but a dreary woman is unforgivable, hideous. Now, am I not luminously reasonable? But only in theory. My practice lies right down on the ground, wet through by that icy fog that is freezing me into something I do not recognize. You do remember I was cheerful once? During the whole of your year with us I defy you to recollect a single day, a single hour of gloom. Well, that is really how I always am, and I can only suppose that I am going to be ill. There is no other way of accounting for the cold terror of life that sits crouching on my heart.

XX

DEAREST,—You will be pleased to hear that I feel gayer tonight, so that I cannot, after all, be sickening for anything horrid. It is an ungrateful practice, letting one's self go to vague fears of the future when there is nothing wrong with the present. All these days during which I have been steeped in gloom and have been taking pains to put some of it into envelopes and send it to you were good days in themselves. Life went on here quite placidly. The weather was sweet with that touching, forlorn sweetness of beautiful worn-out things, of late autumn when winter is waiting round the corner, of leaves dropping slowly down through clear light, of the smell of oozy earth sending up faint whiffs of corruption. From my window I saw the hills every day at sunset, how wonderfully they dressed themselves in pink; and in the afternoons, in the free hour when dinner was done and coffee not yet thought of, I went down into the Paradies valley and sat on the coarse grey grass by the river, and watched the water slipping by beneath the osiers, the one hurried thing in an infinite tranquillity. I ought to have had a volume of Goethe under my arm and been happy. I ought to have read nice bits out of 'Faust,' or about those extraordinary people in the Elective Affinities, and rejoiced in Goethe, and in the fine days, and in my good fortune in being alive, and in having you to love. Well, it is over now, I hope,—I mean the gloom. These things must take their course, I suppose, and while they are doing it one must grope about as best one can by the flickering lantern-light of one's own affrighted spirit. My stepmother looked at me at least once on each of these miserable days, and said: 'Rose-Marie, you look very odd. I hope you are not going to have anything expensive. Measles are in Jena, and also the whooping-cough.'

'Which of them is the cheapest?' I inquired.

'Both are beyond our means,' said my stepmother, severely.

And today at dinner she was quite relieved because I ate some *dicker Reis,* after having turned from it with abhorrence for at least a week. Goodbye, dearest.

Your almost cured
ROSE-MARIE.

XXI

YOUR letter has come. You must do what you know is best. I agree to everything. You must do what your father has set his heart on, since quite clearly your heart is set on the same thing. All the careful words in the world cannot hide that from me. And they shall not. Do you think I dare not look death in the face? I am just the girl you kissed once behind a door, giving way before a passing gust of temptation. You cannot, shall not marry me as the price of that slight episode. You say you will if I insist. Insist? My dear Roger, with both hands I give you back any part of your freedom I may have had in my keeping. Reason, expediency, all the prudences are on your side. You depend entirely on your father; you cannot marry against his wishes; he has told you to marry Miss Cheriton; she is the daughter of his oldest friend; she is extremely rich; every good gift is hers; and I cannot compete. Compete? Do you suppose I would put out a finger to compete? I give it up. I bow myself out.

But let us be honest. Apart from anything to do with your father's commands, you have fallen into her toils as completely as you did into mine. My stepmother was right about your softness. Any woman who chose and had enough opportunity could make you think you loved her, make you kiss her. Luckily this one is absolutely suitable. You say, in the course of the longest letter you have written me—it must have been a tiresome letter to have to write—that father or no father you will not be hurried, you will not marry for a long time, that the wound is too fresh, etc., etc. What is this talk of wounds? Nobody knows about me. I shall not be in your way. You need observe no period of mourning for a corpse people don't know is there. True, Miss Cheriton herself knows. Well, she will not tell; and if she does not mind, why should you? I am so sorry I have written you so many letters full of so many follies. Will you burn them? I would rather not have them back. But I enclose yours, as you may prefer to burn them yourself. I am so very sorry about everything. At least it has been short, and not dragged on growing thinner and thinner till it died of starvation. Once I wrote and begged you to tell me if you thought you had made a mistake about me, because I felt I could bear to know better then than later. And you wrote back and swore all sorts of things by heaven and earth, all sorts of convictions and unshakable things. Well, now you have another set of convictions, that's all. I am not going to beat the big drum of sentiment and make a wailful noise. Nothing is so dead as a dead infatuation. The more a person was infatuated the more he resents an attempt to galvanize the dull dead thing into life. I am wise, you see, to the end. And reasonable, too, I hope. And brave. And brave, I tell you. Do you think I will be a coward, and cry out? I make you a present of everything; of the love and happy thoughts, of the pleasant dreams and plans, of the little prayers sent up, and the blessings called down—there were a great many every day—of the kisses, and all the dear sweetness. Take it all. I want nothing from you in return. Remember it as a pleasant interlude, or fling it into a corner of your mind where used-up things grow dim with cobwebs. But do you suppose that, having given you all this, I am going to give you my soul as well? To moan my life away, my beautiful life? You are not worth it. You are not worth anything, hardly. You are quite invertebrate. My life shall be splendid in spite of you. You shall not cheat me of one single chance of heaven. Now, goodbye. Please burn this last one too. I suppose no one who heard it would quite believe this story, would quite believe it possible for a man to go such lengths of—shall we call it unkindness? to a girl in a single month; but you and I know it is true.

ROSE-MARIE SCHMIDT.

XXII

Jena, March 5.

DEAR MR ANSTRUTHER,—It was extremely kind of you to remember my birthday and to find time in the middle of all your work to send me your good wishes. I hope you are getting on well, and that you like what you are doing. Professor Martens seems to tell you all the Jena news. Yes, I was ill; but we had such a long winter that it was rather lucky to be out of it, tucked away comfortably in bed. There is still snow in the ditches and on the shady side of things. I escaped the bad weather as thoroughly as those persons do who go with infinite trouble during these months to Egypt.

Yours sincerely,
ROSE-MARIE SCHMIDT.

My father and stepmother beg to be remembered to you.

XXIII

Jena, March 18.

Dear Mr Anstruther,—It is very kind indeed of you to want to know how I am and what was the matter with me. It wasn't anything very pleasant, but quite inoffensive aesthetically. I don't care to think about it much. I caught cold, and it got on to my lungs and stayed on them. Now it is over, and I may walk up and down the sunny side of the street for half an hour on fine days.

We all hope you are well, and that you like your work.

Yours sincerely,

Rose-Marie Schmidt.

XXIV

Jena, March 25.

DEAR MR ANSTRUTHER,—You ask me to tell you more about my illness, but I am afraid I must refuse. I see no use in thinking of painful past things. They ought always to be forgotten as quickly as possible; if they are not, they have a trick of turning the present sour, and I cling to the present, to the one thing one really has, and like to make it as cheerful as possible—like to get, by industrious squeezing, every drop of honey out of it. Just now I cannot tell you how thankful I am simply to be alive with nothing in my body hurting. To be alive with a great many things in one's body hurting is a poor sort of amusement. It is not at all a game worth playing. People talk of sick persons clinging to life however sick they are, say they invariably do it, that they prefer it on any terms to dying; well, I was a sick person who did not cling at all. I did not want it. I was most willing to be done with it. But Death, though he used often to come up and look at me, and once at least sat beside me for quite a long while, went away again, and after a time left off bothering about me altogether; and here I am, walking out in the sun every day, and listening with immense pleasure to the chaffinches.

Yours sincerely,

ROSE-MARIE SCHMIDT.

XXV

Jena, March 31.

DEAR MR ANSTRUTHER,—Yes, of course I will be friends. And if I can be of any use in the way of admonishment, which seems to be my strong point, pray, as people say in books, command me. Naturally we are all much interested in you, and shall watch your career, I hope, with pleasure. I am sorry the Foreign Office bores you so much. Do you really have to spend your days gumming up envelopes? Not for that did you win all those scholarships and things at Eton and Oxford, and study Goethe and the minor German prophets so diligently here. You say it will go on for a year. Well, if that is your fate and you cannot escape it, gum away gaily, since gum you must. Later on, when you are an ambassador and everybody is talking to you at once, you will look back on the envelope time as a blessed period when at least you were left alone. But I hope you have a nice wet sponge to do it with, and are not so lost to what is expedient as to be like a little girl I sat next to yesterday at a coffee party, who had smudged most of the cream that ought to have gone inside her outside her, and when I suggested a handkerchief said she didn't hold with handkerchiefs and never had one. 'But what does one do, then,' I asked, looking at her disgraceful little mouth, 'in a case like this? You can't borrow somebody else's—it wouldn't be being select.' 'Oh,' she said airily, 'don't you know? You take your tongue.' And in a twinkling the thing was done. But please do not you do that with the envelopes. My father and stepmother send you many kind messages.

Yours sincerely,

ROSE-MARIE SCHMIDT.

XXVI

Jena, April 9.

DEAR MR ANSTRUTHER,—No, I do not in the least mind
your writing to me. Do, whenever you feel you want to
talk to a friend. It is pleasant to be told that my letters
remind you of so many nice things. I expect your year in
Jena seems much more agreeable, now that you have had
time to forget the uncomfortable parts of it, than it really
was. But I don't think you would have been able to endure
it if you had not been working so hard. I am sorry you do
not like your father. You say so straight out, so I see no
reason for roundaboutness. I expect he will be calmer when
you are married. Why do you not gratify him, and have a
short engagement? Yes, I do understand what you feel about
the mercifulness of being often left alone, though I have
never been worried in quite the same way as you seem to
be; when I am driven it is to places like the kitchen, and
your complaint is that you are driven to what most
people would call enjoying yourself. Really, I think my
sort of driving is best. There is so much satisfaction
about work, about any work. But just to amuse one's self,
and to be, besides, in a perpetual hurry over it because
there is so much of it and the day can't be made to stretch,
must be a sorry business. I wonder why you do it. You say
your father insists on your going everywhere with the
Cheritons, and the Cheritons will not miss a thing; but,
after all, isn't it rather weak to let yourself be led round by
the nose if your nose doesn't like it? It is as though instead
of a dog wagging its tail the tail should wag the dog. And

68

all Nature surely would stand aghast before such an improper spectacle.

The wind is icy, and the snow patches are actually still here, but in the nearest garden I can get to I saw violets yesterday in flower, and crocuses and scillas, and one yellow pansy staring up at the sun astonished and reproachful because it had bits of frozen snow stuck to its little cheeks. Dear me, it is a wonderful feeling, this resurrection every year. Does one ever grow too old, I wonder, to thrill over it? I know the blackbirds are whistling in the orchards if I could only get to them, and my father says the larks have been out in the bare places for these last four weeks. On days like this, when one's immortality is racing along one's blood, how impossible it is to think of death as the end of everything. And as for being grudging and disagreeable, the thing's not to be done. Peevishness and an April morning? Why, even my stepmother opened her window today and stood for a long time in the sun, watching how

> proud-pied April, dressed in all his trim,
> Hath put a spirit of youth in everything.

The first part of the month with us is generally bustling and busy, a great clatter and hustling while the shrieking winter is got away out of sight over the hills, a sweeping of the world clear for the marsh-marigolds and daffodils, a diligent making of room for the divine calms of May. I always loved this first wild frolic of cold winds and catkins and hurriedly crimsoning pollards, of bleakness and promise, of roughness and sweetness—a blow on one cheek and a kiss on the other—before the spring has learned good manners, before it has left off being anything but a boisterous, naughty, charming *Backfisch*; but this year, after having been ill so long, it is more than love, it is passion. Only people who have been buried in beds for weeks, getting used to listening for Death's step on the stairs, know what it is to go out into the stinging freshness of the young year and meet the first scilla, and hear a chaffinch calling out, and feel the sun burn red patches of life on their silly, sick white faces.

My parents send you kind remembrances. They were extremely interested to hear, through Professor Martens, of your engagement to Miss Cheriton. They both think it a most excellent thing.

Yours sincerely,

ROSE-MARIE SCHMIDT.

XXVII

DEAR MR ANSTRUTHER,—You tell me I do not answer
your letters, but really I think I do quite often enough. I
want to make the most of these weeks of idle getting strong
again, and it is a sad waste of time writing. My stepmother
has had such a dose of me sick and incapable, of doctor's bills
and physic and beef-tea and night-lights, that she is
prolonging the convalescent period quite beyond its just limits
and will have me do nothing lest I should do too much. So
I spend strange, glorious days, days strange and glorious to
me, with nothing to do for anybody but myself and a clear
conscience to do it with. The single sanction of my
stepmother's approval has been enough to clear my conscience,
from which you will see how illogically consciences can be
cleared; for have I not always been sure she has no idea
whatever of what is really good? Yet just her approval, a thing
I know to be faulty and for ever in the wrong place, is
sufficient to prop up my conscience and make it feel secure.
How then, while I am busy reading Jane Austen and Fanny
Burney and Maria Edgeworth—books foreordained from all
time for the delight of persons getting well—shall I find time
to write to you? And you must forgive me for a certain
surprise that you should have time to write so much to me.
What have I done to deserve these long letters? How many
Foreign Office envelopes do you leave ungummed to write
them? *Es ist zu viel Ehre.* It is very good of you. No, I will
not make phrases like that, for I know you do not do it for
any reason whatever but because you happen to want to.

You are going through one of those tiresome soul-sicknesses that periodically overtake the too comfortable, and you must, apparently, tell somebody about it. Well, it is a form of *Weltschmerz*, and only afflicts the well-fed. Pray do not suppose that I am insinuating that food is of undue interest to you; but it is true that if you did not have several meals a day and all of them too nice, if there were doubts about their regular recurrence, if, briefly, you were a washerwoman or a ploughboy, you would not have things the matter with your soul. Washerwomen and ploughboys do not have sick souls. Probably you will say they have no souls to be sick; but they have, you know. I imagine their souls thin and threadbare, stunted by cold and hunger, poor and pitiful, but certainly there. And I don't know that it is not a nicer sort of soul to have inside one's plodding body than an unwieldy, overgrown thing, chiefly water and air and lightly changeable stuff, so unsubstantial that it flops—forgive the word, but it does flop—on to other souls in search of sympathy, and support, and comfort, and all the rest of the things washerwomen waste no time looking for, because they know they wouldn't find them.

You are a poet, and I do not take a youthful poet seriously; but if you were not I would laugh derisively at your comparing the entrance of my letters into your room at the Foreign Office to the bringing in of a bunch of cottage flowers still fresh with dew. I don't know that my pride does not rather demand a comparison to a bunch of hothouse flowers—a bouquet it would become then, wouldn't it?—or my romantic sense to a bunch of field flowers, wild, graceful, easily wearied things, that would not care at all for Foreign Offices. But I expect cottage is really the word. My letters conjure up homely visions, and I am sure the bunch you see is a tight posy of

Sweet-Williams, with their homely cottage smell.

It was charming of Matthew Arnold to let Sweet-Williams have such a nice line, but I don't think they quite deserve it. They have a dear little name and a dear little smell, but the things themselves might have been manufactured in a Berlin furniture shop where upholstery in plush prevails, instead of made in that sweetest corner of heaven from whence all good flowers come.

Yours sincerely,
ROSE-MARIE SCHMIDT.

XXVIII

DEAR MR ANSTRUTHER,—You seem to be incurably doleful. You talk about how nice it must be to have a sister, a mother, some woman very closely related to whom you could talk. You astonish me; for have you not Miss Cheriton? Still, on reflection, I think I do see that what you feel you want is more a solid bread-and-butter sort of relationship; no sentiment, genial good advice, a helping hand if not a guiding one—really a good thick slice of bread-and-butter as a set-off to a diet of constant cake. I can read between your lines with sufficient clearness; and as I always had a certain talent for stodginess, I will waste no words but offer myself as the bread-and-butter. Somehow I think it might work out my soul's release from self-reproach and doubts if I can help you, as far as one creature can help another, over some of the more tiresome places of life. Exhortation, admonishment, encouragement, you shall have them all, if you like, by letter. In these my days of dignified leisure I have had room to think, and so have learned to look at things differently from the way I used to. Life is so short that there is hardly time for anything except to be, as St Paul says—wasn't it St Paul?—kind to one another. You are, I think, a most weak person. Anything more easily delighted in the first place or more quickly tired in the second I never in my life saw. Does nothing satisfy you for more than a day or two? And the enthusiasm of you at the beginnings of things. And the depression, the despair of you once you have got used to them. I know you are clever, full of brains,

74

intellectually all that can be desired, but what's the good of that when the rest of you is so weak? You are of a diseased fastidiousness. There's not a person you have praised to me whom you have not later on disliked. When you were here I used to wonder as I listened, but I did believe you. Now I know that the world cannot possibly contain so many offensive people, and that it is always so with you—violent heat, freezing cold. I cannot see you drown without holding out a hand. For you are young; you are, in the parts outside your strange, ill-disciplined emotions, most full of promise; and circumstances have knitted me into an unalterable friend. Perhaps I can help you to a greater steadfastness, a greater compactness of soul. But do not tell me too much. Do not put me in an inextricably difficult position. It would not, of course, be really inextricable, for I would extricate myself by the simple process of relapsing into silence. I say this because your letters have a growing tendency to pour out everything you happen to be feeling. That in itself is not a bad thing, but you must rightly choose your listener. Not every one should be allowed to listen. Certain things cannot be shouted out from the housetops. You forget that we hardly know each other, and that the well-mannered do not thrust their deeper feelings on a person who shrinks from them. I hope you understand that I am willing to hear you talk about most things, and that you will need no further warning to keep off the few swampy places. And just think of all the things you can write to me about, all the masses of breathlessly interesting things in this breathlessly interesting world, without talking about people at all. Look round you this fine spring weather and tell me, for instance, what April is doing up your way, and whether, as you go to your work through the park, you too have not seen heavy Saturn laughing and leaping—how that sonnet has got into my head—and do not every day thank God for having bothered to make you at all.

Yours sincerely,

ROSE-MARIE SCHMIDT.

XXIX

Jena, April 30.

DEAR MR ANSTRUTHER,—You know the little strip of balcony outside our sitting-room window, with its view over the trees of the Paradies valley to the beautiful hills across the river? Well, this morning is so fine, the sun is shining so warmly, that I had my coffee and roll there, and now, wrapped up in rugs, am still there writing to you. I can't tell you how wonderful it is. The birds are drunk with joy. There are blackbirds, and thrushes, and chaffinches, and yellow-hammers, all shouting at once; and every now and then, when the clamour has a gap in it, I hear the whistle of the great tit, the dear small bird who is the very first to sing, bringing its pipe of hope to those early days in February when the world is at its blackest. Have you noticed how different one's morning coffee tastes out of doors from what it does in a room? And the roll and butter—oh, the roll and butter I So must rolls and butter have tasted in the youth of the world, when gods and mortals were gloriously mixed up together, and you went for walks on exquisite things like parsley and violets. If Thoreau—I know you don't like him, but that's only because you have read and believed Stevenson about him—could have seen the eager interest with which I ate my roll just now, he would, I am afraid, have been disgusted; for he severely says that it is not what you eat, but the spirit in which you eat it—you are not, that is, to like it too much—that turns you into a glutton. It is, he says, neither the quality nor the quantity, but the devotion to sensual savours that makes your eating horrid. A puritan, he says, may go to his brown bread crust with as gross an appetite as ever an alderman to his turtle. Thus did I go, as grossly as the grossest alderman, this morning to my crust, and rejoiced in the sensual savour of it and was very glad. How nice it is, how pleasant, not to be with people you admire. Admiration, veneration, the best form of love—they are all more comfortably indulged in from a distance. There is too much whalebone about them at close quarters with their object, too much whalebone and not nearly enough slippers. I am glad Thoreau is dead. I love him far too much ever to want to see him; and how thankful I am he cannot see me.

It is my stepmother's birthday, and trusted friends have been streaming up our three flights of stairs since quite early to bring her hyacinths in pots and unhappy roses spiked on wires and make her congratulatory speeches. I hear them talking through the open window, and what they say, wafted out to me here in the sun, sounds like the pleasant droning of bees when one is only half awake. First, there is the distant electric bell and the tempestuous whirl of Johanna down the passage. Then my stepmother emerges from the kitchen and meets the arriving friend with vociferous welcoming. Then the friend is led into the room here, talking in gasps as we all do on getting to the top of this house, and flinging cascades of good wishes for her *liebe Emilie* on to the *liebe Emilie*'s head. Then the hyacinths or the roses are presented:—'I have brought thee a small thing,' says the friend, presenting; and my stepmother, who has been aware of their presence the whole time, but, with careful decency, has avoided looking at them, starts, protests, and launches forth on to heaving billows of enthusiasm. She does not care for flowers, either in pots or on wires or in any other condition, so her gratitude is really most creditably done. Then they settle down in the corners of the sofa and talk about the things they really want to talk about—neighbours, food, servants, pastors, illnesses, Providence; beginning, since I was ill, with a perfunctory inquiry from the visitor as to the health of *die gute* Rose-Marie.

'*Danke, danke,*' says my stepmother. You know in Germany whenever anybody asks after anybody you have to begin your answer with *danke*. Sometimes the results are odd; for instance: 'How is your poor husband today?' 'Oh, *danke*, he is dead.'

So my stepmother, too, says *danke*, and then I hear a murmur of further information, and catch the world *zart*. Then they talk, still in murmurs not supposed to be able to get through the open window and into my ears, about the quantity of beef-tea I have consumed, the length of the chemist's bill, the unfortunate circumstance that I am so overgrown—'Weedy,' says my stepmother.

'Would you call her weedy?' says the friend, with a show of polite hesitation.

'Weedy,' repeats my stepmother emphatically; and the friend remarks quite seriously that when a person is so very long there is always some part of her bound to be in a draught and catching cold. 'It is such a pity,' concludes the friend, 'that she did not marry.' (Notice the tense. Half a dozen birthdays back it used to be 'does not.')

'Gentlemen,' says my stepmother, 'do not care for her.'

'*Armes Mädchen,*' murmurs the friend.

'*Herr Gott, ja,*' says my stepmother; 'but what is to be done? I have invited gentlemen in past days. I have invited them to coffees, to beer evenings, to music on Sunday afternoons, to the reading aloud of Schiller's dramas, each with his part and Rose-Marie with the heroine's; and though they came they also went away again. Nothing was changed, except the size of my beer bill. No, no, gentlemen do not care for her. In society she does not please.'

'*Armes Mädchen*,' says the friend again; and the *armes Mädchen* out in the sun laughs profanely into her furs.

The fact is it is quite extraordinary the effect my illness has had on me. I thought it was bad, and I see it was good. Beyond words ghastly at the time, terrible, hopeless, the aches of my body as nothing compared with the amazing anguish of my soul, the world turned into one vast pit of pain, impossible to think of the future, impossible to think of the past, impossible to bear the present—after all that behold me awake again, and so wide awake, with eyes grown so quick to see the wonder and importance of the little things of life, the beauty of them, the joy of them, that I can laugh aloud with glee at the delicious notion of calling me an *armes Mädchen*. Three months ago with what miserable groanings, what infinite self-pityings, I would have agreed. Now, clear of vision, I see how many precious gifts I have— life, and freedom from pain, and time to be used and enjoyed—gifts no one can take from me except God. Do you know any George Herbert? He was one of the many English poets my mother's love of poetry made me read. Do you remember

I once more smell the dew, the rain,
And relish versing.
O, my only Light!
It cannot be
That I am he
On whom thy tempests fell all night?

Well, that is how I feel: full of wonder and an unspeakable relief. It is so strange how bad things—things we call bad—

bring forth good things, from the manure that brings forth roses lovely in proportion to its manuriness to the worst experiences that can overtake the soul. And as far as I have been able to see (which is not very far, for I know I am not a clever woman) it is also true that good things bring forth bad ones. I cannot tell you how much life surprises me. I never get used to it. I never tire of pondering and watching and wondering. The way in which eternal truths lurk along one's path, lie among the potatoes in cellars (did you ever observe the conduct of potatoes in cellars? their desperate determination to reach up to the light? their absolute concentration on that one distant glimmer?), peep out at one from every apparently dull corner, sit among the stones, hang upon the bushes, come into one's room in the morning with the hot water, come out at night in heaven with the stars, never leave us, touch us, press upon us, if we choose to open our eyes and look, and our ears and listen—how extraordinary it is. Can one be bored in a world so wonderful? And then the keen interest there is to be got out of people, the keen joy to be got out of common affections, the delight of having a fresh day every morning before you, a fresh, long day, bare and empty, to be filled as you pass along it with nothing but clean and noble hours. You must forgive this exuberance. The sun has got into my veins and has turned everything golden.

Yours sincerely,
ROSE-MARIE SCHMIDT.

XXX

DEAR MR ANSTRUTHER,—How can I help it if things look golden to me? You almost reproach me for it. You seem to think it selfish, and talk of the beauty of sympathy with persons less fortunately constituted. That's a grey sort of beauty; the beauty of mists, and rains, and tears. I wish you could have been in the meadows across the river this morning and seen the dandelions. There was not much greyness about them. From the bridge to the tennis-courts—you know that is a long way, at least twenty minutes' walk—they are one sheet of gold. If you had been there before breakfast, with your feet on that divine carpet, and your head in the flickering slight shadows of the first willow leaves, and your eyes on the shining masses of slow white clouds, and your ears filled with the fresh sound of the river, and your nose filled with the smell of young wet things, you wouldn't have wanted to think much about such grey negations as sympathizing with the gloomy. Bother the gloomy. They are an ungrateful set. If they can they will turn the whole world sour, and sap up all the happiness of the children of light without giving out any shining in return. I am all for sun, and heat, and colour, and scent—for all things radiant and positive. If, crushing down my own nature, I set out deliberately to console those you call the less fortunately constituted, do you know what would happen? They would wring me quite dry of cheerfulness, and not be one whit more cheerful for all the wringing themselves. They can't. They were not made that way. People are born in one of three classes: children of light, children of twilight, children of night. And how can they help into which class they are born? But I do think the twilight children can by diligence, by, if you like, prayer and fasting, come out of the dusk into a greater brightness. Only they must come out by themselves. There must be no pulling. I don't at all agree with your notion of the efficacy of being pulled. Don't you, then, know—of course you do, but you have not yet realized—that you are to seek *first* the Kingdom of God and His righteousness, and all these things shall be added unto you? And don't you know—oh, have you forgotten?—that the Kingdom of God is within you? So what is the use of looking to anything outside of you and separated from you for help? There is no help, except what you dig out of your own self; and if I could make you see that I would have shown you all the secrets of life.

How wisely I talk. It is the wisdom of the ever-recurring grass, the good green grass, the grass starred with living beauty, that has got into me; the wisdom of a May morning filled with present joy, of the joy of the moment, without any weakening waste of looking beyond. So don't mock. I can't help it.

Do you, then, want to be pitied? I will pity you if you like, in so many carefully chosen words; but they will not be words from the heart but only, as the charming little child in the flat below us, the child with the flaunting yellow hair and audacious eyes, said of some speech that didn't ring true to her quick ears, 'from the tip of the nose.' I cannot really pity you, you know. You are too healthy, too young, too fortunate for that. You ought to be quite jubilant with cheerfullest gratitude; and, since you are not, you very perfectly illustrate the truth of *le trop* being *l'ennemi du bien*, or, if you prefer your clumsier mother tongue, of the half being better than the whole. How is it that I, bereft of everything you think worth having, am so offensively cheerful? Your friends would call it a sordid existence, if they considered it with anything more lengthy than just a sniff. No excitements, no clothes, acquaintances so shabby that they seem almost moth eaten, the days filled with the same dull round, a home in a little town where we all get into one groove and having got into it stay in it, to which only faint echoes come of what is going on in the world outside, a place where one is amused and entertained by second-rate things, second-rate concerts, second-rate plays, and feels one's self grow cultured by attendance at second-rate debating-society meetings. Would you not think I must starve in such a place? But I don't. My soul doesn't dream of starving; in fact, I am quite anxious about it, it has lately grown so fat. There is so little outside it—for the concerts, plays, debates, social gatherings, are dust and ashes near which I do not go—that it eagerly turns to what is inside it, and finds itself full of magic forces of heat and light, forces hot and burning enough to set every common bush afire with God. That is Elizabeth Barrett Browning; I mean about the common bushes. A slightly mutilated Elizabeth Barrett Browning, but still a quotation; and if you do not happen to know it I won't have you go about thinking it pure Schmidt. Ought I, if I quote, to warn you of the fact by the pointing fingers of inverted commas? I don't care to, somehow. They make such a show of importance. I prefer to suppose you cultured. Oh, I can see you shiver at that impertinence, for I know down in your heart, though you always take pains to explain how ignorant you are, you consider yourself an extremely cultured young man. And so you are; cultured, I should say, out of all reason; so much cultured that there's hardly anything left that you are able to like. Indeed, it is surprising that you should care to write to a rough, unscraped sort of person like myself. Do not my crudities set your teeth on edge as acutely as the juice of a very green apple? You who love half tones, subtleties, suggestions, who, lifting the merest fringe of things, approach them nearer only by infinite implications, what have you to do with the downrightness of an east wind or a green apple? Why, I wonder that just the recollection of my red hands, knobbly and spread with work, does not make you wince into aloofness. And my clothes? What about my clothes? Do you not like exquisite women? Perfectly got-up women? Fresh and dainty, constantly renewed women? It is two years since I had a new hat; and as for the dress that sees me through my days, I really cannot count the time since it started in my company a Sunday and fête-day garment. If you were once, only once, to see me in the middle of your friends over there, you would be cured for ever of wanting to write to me. I belong to your Jena days; days of hard living and working and thinking; days when, by dint of being forced to do without certain bodily comforts, the accommodating spirit made up for it by its own increased comfort and warmth. Probably your spirit will never again attain to quite so bright a shining as it did that year. How can it, unless it is amazingly strong—and I know it well not to be that—shine through the suffocating masses of upholstery your present life piles about it? Poor spirit. At least see to it that its flicker doesn't quite go out. To urge you to strip your life of all this embroidery and let it get the draught of air it needs would be, I know, mere waste of ink.

My people send you every good wish.

Yours sincerely,

ROSE-MARIE SCHMIDT.

XXXI

DEAR MR ANSTRUTHER,—Of course I am full of contradictions. Did you expect me to be full of anything else? And I have no doubt whatever that in every letter I say exactly the opposite from what I said in the last one. But you must not mind this and make it an occasion for reproof. I do not pretend to think quite the same even two days running; if I did I would be stagnant, and the very essence of life is to be fluid, to pass perpetually on. So please do not hold me responsible for convictions that I have changed by the time they get to you, and above all things don't bring them up against me and ask me to prove them. I don't want to prove them. I don't want to prove anything. My attitude towards life is one of open-mouthed wonder and delight, and the open-mouthed cannot talk. You write, too, plaintively, that some of the things I say hurt you. I am sorry. Sorry, I mean, that you should be so soft. Can you not, then, bear anything? But I will smooth my tongue if you prefer it smooth, and send you envelopes filled only with sugar; talk to you about the parks, the London season, the Foreign Office—all things of which I know nothing—and, patting you at short intervals on the back, tell you you are admirable. You say there is a bitter flavour about some of my remarks. I have not felt bitter. Perhaps a little shrewish; a little like, not a mild exhorting elder sister, but an irritated aunt. You see, I am interested enough in you to be fidgety when I hear you groan. What, I ask myself uneasily, can be the matter with this apparently healthy, well-cared-for young man? And then, forced to the conclusion by unmistakable symptoms that there is nothing the matter except a surfeit of good things, I have perhaps pounced upon you with something of the zeal of an aunt moved to anger, and given you a spiritual slapping. You sighed for a sister—you are always sighing for something—and asked me to be one; well, I have apparently gone beyond the sister in decision and authority, and developed something of the acerbity of an aunt.

So you are down at Clinches. How beautiful it must be there this month. I think of it as a harmony in grey and amethyst, remembering your description of it the first time you went there; a harmony in a minor key, that captured you wholly by its tender subtleties. When I think of you inheriting such a place later on through your wife I do from my heart feel that your engagement is an excellent thing. She must indeed be happy in the knowledge that she can give you so much that is absolutely worth having. It is beautiful, beautiful to give; one of the very most beautiful things in life. I quarrel with my poverty only because I can give so little, so seldom, and then never more than ridiculous small trumperies. To make up for them I try to give as much of myself as possible, gifts of sympathy, helpfulness, kindness. Don't laugh, but I am practising on my stepmother. It is easy to pour out love on Papa; so easy, so effortless, that I do not feel as if it could be worth much; but I have made up my mind, not without something of a grim determination that seems to have little enough to do with love, to give my stepmother as much of me, my affections, my services, as she can do with. Perhaps she won't be able to do with much. Anyhow, all she wants she shall have. You know I have often wished I had been a man, able to pull on my boots and go out into the wide world without let or hindrance; but for one thing I am glad to be a woman, and that one thing is that the woman gives. It is so far less wonderful to take. The man is always taking, the woman always giving; and giving so wonderfully, in the face sometimes of dreadful disaster, of shipwreck, of death—which explains perhaps her longer persistence in clinging to the skirts of a worn-out passion; for is not the tenderer feeling on the side of the one who gave and blessed? Always, always on that side? Mixing into what was sensual some of the dear divineness of the mother-love? I think I could never grow wholly indifferent to a person to whom I had given much. He or she would not, could not, be the same to me as other people. Time would pass, and the growing number of the days blunt the first sharp edge of feeling; but the memory of what I had given would bind us together in a friendship for ever unlike any other.

I have not thanked you for the book you sent me. It was very kind indeed of you to wish me to share the pleasure you have had in reading it. But see how unfortunately contrary I am: I don't care about it. And just the passages you marked are the ones I care about least. I do not hold with markings in books. Whenever I have come across mine after a lapse of years I have marvelled at the distance travelled since I marked, and shut up the book and murmured, 'Little fool.' I can't imagine why you thought I should like this book. It has given me rather a surprised shock that you should know me so little, and that I should know you so little as to think you knew me better. Really all the explanations and pointings in the world will not show a person the exact position of his neighbour's soul. It is astonishing enough that the book was printed, but how infinitely more astonishing that people like you should admire it. What is the matter with me that I cannot admire it? Why am I missing things that ought to give me pleasure? You do not, then, see that it is dull? I do. I see it and feel it in every bone, and it makes them ache. It is dull and bad because it is so dreary, so hopelessly dreary. Life is not like that. Life is only like that to cowards who are temporarily indisposed. I do not care to look at it through a sick creature's jaundiced eyes and shudder with him at what he sees. If he cannot see better why not keep quiet, and let us braver folk march along with our heads in the air, held so high that we cannot bother to look at every slimy creepiness that crawls across our path? And did you not notice how he keeps on telling his friends in his letters not to mind when he is dead? Unnecessary advice, one would suppose; I can more easily imagine the friends gasping with an infinite relief. Persons who are everlastingly claiming pity, sympathy, condolences, are very wearing. Surely all talk about one's death is selfish and bad? That is why, though there is so much that is lovely in them, the faint breath of corruption hanging about Christina Rossetti's poetry makes me turn my head the other way. What a constant cry it is that she wants to die, that she hopes to die, that she's going to die, shall die, can die, must die, and that nobody is to weep for her, but that there are to be elaborate and moving arrangements of lilies and roses and winding-sheets. And at least in one place she gives directions as to the proper use of green grass and wet dewdrops upon her grave—implying that dewdrops are sometimes dry. I think the only decent attitude towards one's death is to be silent. Talk about it puts other people in such an awkward position. What is one to say to persons who sigh and tell us that they will no doubt soon be in heaven? One's instinct is politely to murmur, 'Oh no,' and then they are angry. 'Surely not' also has its pitfalls. Cheery words, of the order in speech that a slap on the shoulder is in the sphere of physical expression, only seem to deepen the determined gloom. And if it is some one you love who thinks he will soon be dead and tells you so, the cruelty is very great. When death really comes, is not what the ordinary decent dier wants quiet, that he may leave himself utterly in the hands of God? There should be no massing of temporarily broken-hearted onlookers about his bed, no leave-takings and eager gatherings-up of last words, no revellings of relatives in the voluptuousness of woe, no futile exhortations, using up the last poor breaths, not to weep to persons who would consider it highly improper to leave off doing it, and no administration of tardy blessings. Any blessings the dier has to invoke should have been invoked and done with long ago. In this last hour, at least, can one not be left alone? Do you remember Pater's strange feeling about death? Perhaps you do not, for you told me once you did not care about him. Well, it runs through his books, through all their serenity and sunlight, through exquisite descriptions of summer, of beautiful places, of heat and life and youth and all things lovely, like a musty black riband, very poor, very mean, very rotten, that yet must bind these gracious flowers of light at last together, bruising them into one piteous mass of corruption. It is all very morbid: the fair outward surface of daily life, the gay, flower-starred crust of earth, and just underneath horrible tainted things, things forlorn and pitiful, things which we who still walk on the wholesome grass must soon join, changing our life in the roomy sunshine into something infinitely dependent and helpless, something that can only dimly live if those strong friends of ours in the bright world will spare us a thought, a remembrance, a few minutes from their plenty for sitting beside us, room in their hearts for yet a little love and sorrow. 'Dead cheek by dead cheek, and the rain soaking down upon one from above. . . .' Does not that sound hopeless? After reading these things, sweet with the tainted sweetness of decay, of ruin, of the past, the gone, it is like having fresh spring water dashed over one on a languid afternoon to remember Walt Whitman's brave attitude towards 'delicate death,' 'the sacred knowledge of death,' 'lovely, soothing death,' 'cool, enfolding death,' 'strong deliveress,' 'vast and well-veiled death,' 'the body gratefully nestling close to death,' 'sane and sacred death.' That is the spirit that makes one brave and fearless, that makes one live beautifully and well, that sends one marching straight ahead with limbs that do not tremble and head held high. Is it not natural to love such writers best? Writers who fill one with glad courage and make one proud of the path one has chosen to walk in?

And yet you do not like Walt Whitman. I remember quite well my chill of disappointment when you told me so. At first, hearing it, I thought I must be wrong to like him; but, thank Heaven, I soon got my balance again, and presently was solaced by the reflection that it was at least as likely you were wrong not to. You told me it was not poetry. That upset me for a few days, and then I found I didn't care. I couldn't argue with you on the spot and prove anything, because the only *esprit* I have is that tiresome *esprit d'escalier*, so brilliant when it is too late, so constant in its habit of leaving its possessor in the dreadful condition—or is it a place?—called the lurch; but, poetry or not, I knew I must always love him. You, I suppose, have cultivated your taste in regard to things of secondary importance to such a pitch of sensitiveness that unless the outer shell is flawless you cannot, for sheer intellectual discomfort, look at the wonders that often lie within. I, who have not been educated, am so filled with elementary joy when some one shows me the light in this world of many shadows that I do not stop to consider what were the words he used while my eyes followed his pointing finger. You see, I try to console myself for having an unpruned intelligence. I know I am unpruned, and that at the most you pruned people, all trim and trained from the first, do but bear with me indulgently. But I must think with the apparatus I possess, and I think at this moment that perhaps what you really most want is a prolonged dose of Walt Whitman, a close study of him for several hours every day, shut up with no other book, quite alone with him in an empty country place. Listen to this—you shall listen:

> O we can wait no longer,
> We too take ship, O soul;
> Joyous we too launch out on trackless seas,
> Fearless for unknown shores on waves of ecstasy to sail,
> Amid the wafting winds (thou pressing me to thee, I thee
> to me, O soul).
> Carolling free, singing our song of God,
> Chanting our chant of pleasant exploration,
> O my brave soul!
> O farther, farther sail!
> O daring joy, but safe! are they not all the seas of God?
> O farther, farther sail!

Well, how do you feel now? Can any one, can you, can even you read that without such a tingling in all your limbs, such a fresh rush of life and energy through your whole body that you simply must jump up and, shaking off the dreary nonsense that has been fooling you, turn your back on diseased self-questionings and run straight out to work at your salvation in the sun?

Yours sincerely,
ROSE-MARIE SCHMIDT.

XXXII

DEAR MR ANSTRUTHER,—I am sorry you think me unsympathetic. Hard, I think, was the word; but unsympathetic sounds prettier. Is it unsympathetic not to like fruitless, profitless, barren things? Not to like fogs and blights and other deadening, decaying things? From my heart I pity all the people who are so made that they cannot get on with their living for fear of their dying; but I do not admire them. Is that being unsympathetic? Apparently you think so. How odd. There is a little man here who hardly ever can talk to anybody without beginning about his death. He is perfectly healthy, and I suppose forty or fifty, so that there is every reasonable hope of his going on being a little man for years and years more; but he will have it that as he has never married or, as he puts it, done anything else useful, he might just as well be dead, and then at the word Dead his eyes get just the look of absolute scaredness in them that a hare's eyes do when a dog is after it. 'If only one knew what came next,' he said last time he was here, looking at me with those frightened eyes.

'Nice things I should think,' said I, trying to be encouraging.

'But to those who have deserved punishment?'

'If they have deserved it they will probably get it,' said I, cheerfully.

He shuddered.

'You don't look very wicked,' I went on amiably. He

93

leads a life of sheerest bread-and-milk, so simple, so innocent, so full of little hearthrug virtues.

'But I am,' he declared angrily.

'I shouldn't think half so bad as a great many people,' said I, bent, being the hostess, on a perfect urbanity.

'Worse,' said he, more angrily.

'Oh, come now,' said I, very politely as I thought.

Then he really got into a rage, and asked me what I could possibly know about it, and I said I didn't know anything; and still he stormed and grew more and more terrified, frightening himself by his own words; and at last, dropping his voice, he confessed that he had one particularly deadly fear, a fear that haunted him and gave him no rest, that the wicked would not burn eternally but would freeze.

'Oh,' said I, shrinking; for it was a bitter day, and the north-east wind was thundering among the hills.

'Great cold,' he said, 'seems to be incomparably more terrible than great heat.'

'Oh, incomparably,' I agreed, edging nearer to the stove. 'Only listen to that wind.'

'So will it howl about us through eternity,' said he.

'Oh,' I shivered.

'Piercing one's unprotected—everything about us will be unprotected then—one's unprotected marrow, and turning it to ice within us.'

'But we won't have any marrows,' said I.

'No marrows? Fräulein Rose-Marie, we shall have everything that will hurt.'

'*Oh weh*,' cried I, stopping up my ears.

'The thought frightens you?' said he.

'Terrifies me,' said I.

'How much more fearful, then, will be the reality.'

'Well, I'd like to—I'd like to give you some good advice,' said I, hesitating.

'Certainly; if one of your sex may with any efficacy advise one of ours.'

'Oh—efficacy,' murmured I, with proper deprecation. 'But I'd like to suggest—I daren't advise, I'll just suggest—'

'Fear nothing. I am all ears and willingness to be guided,' said he, smiling with an indescribable graciousness.

'Well—don't go there.'

'Not go there?'

'And while you are here—still here, and alive, and in nice warm woolly clothes, do you know what you want?'

'What I want?'

'Very badly do you want a wife. Why not go and get one?'

His eyes at that grew more frightened than at the thought of eternal ice. He seized his hat and scrambled to the door. He went through it hissing scorching things about *moderne Mädchen*, and from the safety of the passage I heard him call me *unverschämt*.

He hasn't been here since. I would like to go and shake him; shake him till his brains settle into their proper place, and say while I shake, 'Oh, little man, little man, come out of the fog! Why do you choose to die a thousand deaths rather than only one?'

Is that being unsympathetic? I think it is being quite kind.

Yours sincerely,
ROSE-MARIE SCHMIDT.

What I really meant to write to you about today was to tell you that I read your learned and technical and I am sure admirable denouncements of Walt Whitman with the respectful attention due to so much earnestness; and when

I had done, and wondered awhile pleasantly at the amount of time for letter-writing the Foreign Office allows its young men, I stretched myself, and got my hat, and went down to the river; and I sat at the water's edge in the middle of a great many buttercups; and there was a little wind; and the little wind knocked the heads of the buttercups together; and it seemed to amuse them, or else something else did, for I do assure you I thought I heard them laugh.

XXXIII

DEAR MR ANSTRUTHER,—You asked me about your successor in our house, and inquire why I have never mentioned him. Why should I mention him? Must I mention everything? I suppose I forgot him. His name is Collins, and some days he wears a pink shirt, and other days a blue shirt, and in his right cuff there is a pink silk handkerchief on the pink days, and a blue silk handkerchief on the blue days; and he has stuck up the pictures he likes to have about him on the walls of his room, and where your Luini used to be there is a young lady in a voluminous hat and short skirts, and where your Bellini Madonna sat and looked at you with austere, beautiful eyes, there is the winner, complete with jockey, of last year's Derby.

'I made a pot of money over that,' said Mr Collins to me the day he pinned it up and came to ask me for the pin.

'Did you?' said I.

But I think I am tired just now of Luinis and Bellinis and of the sort of spirit in a young man that clothes the walls of his room with them, each in some elaborately simple frame, and am not at all sure that the frank fleshliness of a Collins does not please me best. You see, one longs so much sometimes to get down to the soil, down to plain instincts, to rude nature, to, if you like, elemental savagery.

But I'll go on with Mr Collins; you shall have a dose of him while I am about it. He has bought a canoe, and has won the cup for swimming, wresting it from the reluctant hands of the discomfited Jena young men. He paddles up to the weir, gets out, picks up his canoe, carries it round to the other side, gets in, and vanishes in the windings of the water and the folds of the hills, leaving the girls in the tennis-courts—you remember the courts are opposite the weir—uncertain whether to titter or to blush, for he wears, I suppose, the fewest clothes that it is possible to wear and still be called dressed, and no stockings at all.

'*Nein, dieser Engländer!*' gasp the girls, turning down decent eyes.

'*Höllisch practisch,*' declare the young men, got up in as near an imitation of the flannels you used to wear that they can reach, even their hats bound about with a ribbon startlingly like your Oxford half blue; and before the summer is over I dare say they will all be playing tennis in the Collins canoe costume, stockingless, sleeveless, supposing it to be the latest *cri* in get-ups for each and every form of sport.

Professor Martens didn't care about teaching Mr Collins, and insisted on handing him over to Papa. Papa doesn't care about teaching him, either, and says he is a *dummer Bengel* who pronounces Goethe as though it rhymed with dirty, and who the first time our great poet was mentioned vacantly asked, with every indication of a wandering mind, if he wasn't the joker who wrote the play for Irving with all the devils in it. Papa was so angry that he began a letter to Collins *père*, telling him to remove his son to a city where there are fewer muses; but Collins *père* is a person who makes nails in Manchester with immense skill and application, and is terrifyingly rich, and my stepmother's attitude towards the terrifyingly rich is one of large forgiveness; so she tore up Papa's letter just where it had got to the words *erbärmlicher Esel*, said he was a very decent boy, that he should stay as long as he wanted to, but that, since he seemed to be troublesome about learning, Papa must write and demand a higher scale of payment. Papa wouldn't; my stepmother did; and behold Joey—his Christian name is Joey—more lucrative to us by, I believe, just double than any one we have had yet.

'I say,' said Joey to me this morning, 'come over to England some day, and I'll romp you down to Epsom.'

'Divine,' said I, turning up my eyes.

'We'd have a rippin' time.'

'Rather.'

'I'd romp you down in the old man's motor.'

'Not really?'

'We'd be there before you could flutter an eyelash.'

'Are you serious?'

'Ain't I, though. It's a thirty-horse——'

'Can't you get them in London?'

'Get 'em in London? Get what in London?'

'Must one go every time all the way to Epsom?'

Joey ceased from speech and began to stare.

'Are we not talking about salts?' I inquired hastily, feeling that one of us was off the track.

'Salts?' echoed Joey, his mouth hanging open.

'You mentioned Epsom, surely?'

'Salts?'

'You did say Epsom, didn't you?'

'Salts?'

'Salts,' said I, becoming very distinct in the presence of what looked like deliberate wilfulness.

'What's it got to do with salts?' asked Joey, his underlip of a measureless vacancy.

'Hasn't it got everything?'

'Look here, what are you drivin' at? Is it goin' to be a game?'

'Certainly not. It's Sunday. Did you never hear of Epsom salts?'

'Oh—ah—I see—Eno, and all that. Castor oil. Rhubarb and magnesia. Well, I'll forgive you as you're only German. Pretty weird, what bits of information you get hold of. Never the right bits, somehow. I'll tell you what, Miss Schmidt——'

'Oh, do.'

'Do what?'

'Tell me what.'

'Well, ain't I goin' to? You all seem to know everything in this house that's not worth knowin', and not a blessed thing that is.'

'Do you include Goethe?'

'Confound Gerty,' said Joey.

Such are my conversations with Joey. Is there anything more you want to know?

Yours sincerely,
ROSE-MARIE SCHMIDT.

XXXIV

Jena, July 3.

Dear Mr Anstruther,—I am sorry not to have been able to answer your letters for so many weeks, and sorry that you should have been, as you say, uneasy, but my telegram in reply to yours will have explained what has been happening to us. My stepmother died a fortnight ago. Almost immediately after I wrote last to you she began to be very ill. My feelings towards her have undergone a complete upheaval. I cannot speak of her. She is revenging herself, as only the dead in their utter unresentfulness can revenge themselves, for every hard and scoffing thought I had of her in life. I think I told you once about her annuity. Now it is gone Papa and I must see to it that we live on my mother's money alone. It is a hundred pounds a year, so the living will have to be prudent; not so prudent, I hope, but that we shall have everything to enjoy that is worth enjoying, but quite prudent enough to force us to take thought. So we are leaving the flat, grown far too expensive for us, as soon as we can find some other home. We have almost decided on one already. Mr Collins went to England when the illness grew evidently hopeless, and we shall not take him back again, for my father does not care, at least at present, to have strangers with us, and I myself do not feel as though I could cook for and look after a young man in the way my stepmother did. Not having one will make us poor, but I think we shall be able to manage quite well, for we do not want much.

Thank you for your kind letters since the telegram. The ones before that, coming into this serious house filled with the nearness of Death, and of Death in his sternest mood, his hands cruel with scourges, seemed to me so inexpressibly—well, I will not say it; it is not fair to blame you, who could not know in whose shadow we were sitting, for being preoccupied with the trivialities of living. But letters sent to friends a long way off do sometimes fall into their midst with a rather ghastly clang of discord. It is what yours did. I read them sometimes in the night, watching by my stepmother in the half-dark room during the moments when she had a little peace and was allowed to slip away from torture into sleep. By the side of that racked figure and all it meant and the tremendous sermons it was preaching me, wordless, voiceless sermons, more eloquent than any I shall hear again, how strange, how far-away your echoes from life and the world seemed! Distant tinklings of artificialness; not quite genuine writhings beneath not quite genuine burdens; idle questionings and self-criticisms; plaints, doubts, and complicated half-veiled reproaches of myself that I should be able to be pleased with a world so worm-eaten, that I should still be able to chant my song of life in a major key in a world so manifestly minor and chromatic. These things fell oddly across the gravity of that room. Shadows in a place where everything was clear, cobwebs of unreality where everything was real. They made me sigh, and they made me smile, they were so very black and yet so very little. I used to wonder what that usually excellent housemaid Experience is about, that she has not yet been after you with her broom. You know her speciality is the pulling up of blinds and the letting in of the morning sun. But it is unfair to judge you. Your letters since you knew have been kindness itself. Thank you for them.

Yours sincerely,

ROSE-MARIE SCHMIDT.

It seemed so strange for any one to die in June; so strange to be lifeless in the midst of the wanton profusion of life, to grow cold in that quivering radiance of heat. The people below us have got boxes of calla-lilies on their balcony this year. Their hot, heavy scent used to come in at the open window in the afternoons when the sun was on them, the honey-sweet smell of life, intense, penetrating, filling every corner of the room with splendid, pagan summer. And on the bed tossed my stepmother, muttering ceaselessly to herself of Christ.

XXXV

Jena, July 15.

DEAR MR ANSTRUTHER,—Our new address is Galgenberg, Jena,—rather grim, but what's in a name? The thing itself is perfect. It is a tiny house, white, with green shutters, on the south slope of the hill among apple-trees. The garden is so steep that you can't sit down in it except on the north side of the house, where you can because the house is there to stop you from sliding farther. It is a strip of rough grass out of which I shall make haycocks, with three apple-trees in it. There is also a red currant bush, out of which I shall make jelly. At the bottom, below the fence—rotten in places, but I'm going to mend that—begins a real apple orchard, and through its leaves we can look down on the roof of another house, white like ours, but a little bigger, and with blue shutters instead of green. People take it for the summer, and once an Englishman came and made a beanfield there—but I think I told you about the beanfield. Behind us, right away up the slope, are pine trees that brush restlessly backwards and forwards all day long across the clouds, trying to sweep bits of clear blue in the sky, and at night spread themselves out stiff and motionless against the stars. I saw them last night from my window. We moved in yesterday. The moving in was not very easy, because of what Papa calls the precipitous nature of the district. He sat with his back propped against the wall of the house on the only side on which, as I have explained, you can sit, and worked with a pencil at his book about Goethe in Jena with perfect placidity while Johanna and I and the man who urged the furniture-cart up the hill kept on stepping over his legs as we went in and out furnishing the house. There was not much to furnish, which was lucky, there not being much to furnish with. We have got rid of all superfluities, including the canary, which I presented, its cage beautifully tied up with the blue ribbons I wore at my first party, to the little girl with the flame-coloured hair on the second floor. As much of the other things as any one could be induced to buy we sold, and we burnt what nobody would buy or endure having given them. And so, pared down, we fit in here quite nicely, and after a day or two conceded to the suavities of life, such as the tacking up in appropriate places of muslin curtains and the tying of them with bows, I intend to buy a spade and a watering-pot and see what I can do with the garden.

I wish it were not quite so steep. If I'm not on the upper side of one of the apple-trees, with my back firmly pressed against its trunk, I don't yet see how I am to garden. It must be disturbing, and a great waste of time, to have to hold on to something with one hand while you garden with the other. And suppose the thing gives way, and you roll down on to the broken fence? And if that, too, gave way, there would be nothing but a few probably inadequate apple trunks between me and the roof of the house with the blue shutters. I should think it extremely likely that until I've got the mountain-side equivalent for what are known as one's sea-legs I shall very often be on that roof. I hope it is strong and new. Perhaps there are kind people inside who will not mind. Soon they'll get so much used to it that when they hear the preliminary rush among their apple-trees and the cracking of the branches, followed by the thud over their heads, they won't even look up from their books, but just murmur to each other, 'There's

Fräulein Schmidt on the roof again,' and go on with their studies.

Now I'm talking nonsense, and the sort of nonsense you like least; but I'm in a silly mood today, and you must take me as you find me. At any time when I have grown too unendurable you can stop my writing to you simply by not writing to me. Then I shall know you have at last had enough of me, of my moods, of my odious fits of bombastic eloquence, of my still more odious facetiousness, of my scoldings of you, and of my complacency about myself. It is true, you actually seem to like my scoldings. That is very abject of you. What you apparently resent are the letters with sturdy sentiments in them and a robust relish of life. It almost seems as though you didn't want me to be happy. That is very odd of you. And I sometimes wonder if it is possible for two persons to continue friends who have a different taste in what, for want of a nicer word, I must call jokes. My taste in them is so elementary that an apple-pie bed makes me laugh tears, and when I go to the play I love to see chairs pulled away just as people are going to sit down. You, of course, shudder at these things. They fill you with so great a dreariness that it amounts to pain. I am at least sensible enough to understand the attitude. But pleasantries quite high up, as I consider, in the scale of humour have not been able to make you smile. I have seen you sit unalterably grave while Papa was piping out the nicest little things, and I know you never liked even your adored Professor Martens when he began to bubble. Well, either I laugh too easily or you don't laugh enough. I can only repeat that if I set your teeth on edge, the remedy is in your own hands.

We are going to be vegetarians this summer. Papa, who hasn't tried it yet, is perfectly willing, and if we live chiefly on nuts and lettuces we shall hardly want any money at all. I read Shelley's *Vindication of Natural Diet* aloud to him before we left the flat to prepare his mind, and he not only heartily agreed with every word, but went at once to the Free Library and dug out all the books he could find about muscles and brains and their surprising dependence on the kind of stuff you have eaten, and brought them home for me to study. I do love Papa. He falls in so sweetly with one's little plans, and lets me do what I want without the least waste of time in questionings or the giving of advice. I have read the books with profound interest. Only a person who cooks, who has to handle meat when it is raw, pick out the internals of geese, peel off the skins of rabbits, scrape away the scales of a fish that is still alive—my stepmother insisted on this, the flavour, she said, being so infinitely superior that way—can know with what a relief, what a feeling of personal purification and turning of the back on evil, one flings a cabbage into a pot of fair water or lets one's fingers linger lovingly among lentils. I brought a bag of lentils up the hill with us, and the cabbage, remnant of my last marketing, came up too in a net, and we had our dinner today of them: lentil soup, and cabbage with bread-and-butter—what could be purer? And for Johanna, who has not read Shelley, there was the last of the Rauchgasse sausage for the soothing of her more immature soul.

That was an hour ago, and Papa has just been in to say he is hungry.

'Why, you've only just had dinner, Papachen,' said I, surprised.

'I know—I know,' he said, looking vaguely troubled.

'You can't really be hungry. Perhaps it's indigestion.'

'Perhaps,' agreed Papa; and drifted out again, still looking troubled.

Before we took this house it had stood empty for several years, and the man it belongs to was so glad to find somebody who would live in it and keep it warm that he lets us have it for hardly any rent at all. I expect what the impoverished want—and only the impoverished would live in a thing so small—is a garden flat enough to grow potatoes in, and to have fowls walking about it, and a pig in a nice level sty. You can't have them here. At least, you couldn't have a sty on such a slope. The poor pig would spend his days either anxiously hanging on with all his claws—or is it paws? I forget what pigs have; anyhow, with all his might—to the hillside, or huddled dismally down against the end planks, and never be of that sublime detachment of spirit necessary to him if he would end satisfactorily in really fat bacon. And the fowls, I suppose, would have to lay their eggs flying—they certainly couldn't do it sitting down—and how disturbing that would be to a person engaged, as I often am, in staring up at the sky, for how can you stare up at the sky under an umbrella? I asked the landlord about the potatoes, and he said I must grow them as the last tenant did, a widow who lived and died here, in a strip against the north side of the house where there is a level space about two yards running from one end of the house to the other, representing a path and keeping the hill from tumbling in at our windows. It really is the only place, for I don't see how Johanna and I, gifted and resourceful as we undoubtedly are, can make terraces with no tools but a spade and a watering-pot; but it will do away with our only path, and it does seem necessary to have a path up to one's front door. Can one be respectable without a path up to one's front door? Perhaps one can, and that too may be a superfluity to those who face life squarely. I am convinced that there must be potatoes, but I am not convinced, on reflection, that there need be a path. Have you ever felt the joy of getting rid of things? It is so great that it is almost ferocious. After each divestment, each casting off and away, there is such a gasp of relief, such a bounding upwards, the satisfied soul, proud for once of its body, saying to it smilingly, 'This, too, then, you have discovered you can do without and yet be happy.' And I, just while writing these words to you, have discovered that I can and will do without paths.

Papa has been in again. 'Is it not coffee-time?' he asked.

I looked at him amazed. 'Darling, coffee-time is never at half-past two,' I said reproachfully.

'Half-past two is it only? *Der Teufel*,' said Papa.

'Isn't your book getting on well?' I inquired.

'Yes, yes,—the book progresses. That is, it would progress if my attention did not continually wander.'

'Wander? Where to?'

'Rose-Marie, there is a constant gnawing going on within me that will not permit me to believe that I have dined.'

'Well, but, Papachen, you have. I saw you doing it.'

'What you saw me doing was not dining,' said Papa.

'Not dining?'

Papa waved his arms round oddly and suddenly.

'Grass, grass,' he cried with a singular impatience.

'Grass?' I echoed, still more amazed.

'Books of an enduring nature, works of any monumentalness, cannot, never were, and shall not be raised on a foundation of grass,' said Papa, his face quite red.

'I can't think what you mean,' said I. 'Where is there any grass?'

'Here,' said Papa, quickly clasping his hands over that portion of him that we boldly talk about and call *Magen*, and you allude to sideways, by a variety of devious expressions. 'I have been fed today,' he said, looking at me quite severely, 'on a diet appropriate only to the mountain goat, and probably only appropriate to him because he can procure nothing better.'

'Why, you had a lentil soup—proved scientifically to contain all that is needed——'

'I congratulate the lentil soup. I envy it. I wish I too contained all that is needed. But here'—he clasped his hands again—'there is nothing.'

'Yes, there is. There is cabbage.'

'Pooh,' said Papa. 'Green stuff. Herbage.'

'Herbage?'

'And scanty herbage, too—appropriate, I suppose, to the mountainous region in which we now find ourselves.'

'Papa, don't you want to be a vegetarian?'

'I want my coffee,' said Papa.

'What, now?'

'And why not now, Rose-Marie? Is there anything more rational than to eat when one is hungry? Let there, pray, be much—very much—bread-and-butter with it.'

'But, Papa, we weren't going to have coffee any more. Didn't you agree that we would give up stimulants?'

Papa looked at me defiantly. 'I did,' he said.

'Well, coffee is one.'

'It is our only one.'

'You said you would give it up.'

'I said gradually. To do so today would not be doing so gradually. Nothing is good that is not done gradually.'

'But one must begin.'

'One must begin gradually.'

'You were delighted with Shelley.'

'It was after dinner.'

'You were quite convinced.'

'I was not hungry.'

'You know he is all for pure water.'

'He is all for many things that seem admirable to those who have lately dined.'

'You know he says that if the populace of Paris at the time of the Revolution had drunk at the pure source of the Seine——'

'There is no pure source of the Seine within reach of the populace of Paris. There would only be cats. Dead cats. And cats interspersed, no doubt, with a variety of objects of the nature of portions of crockery and empty tins.'

'But he says pure source.'

'Then he says pure nonsense.'

'He says if they had done that and satisfied their hunger at the ever-furnished table of vegetable nature——'

'Ever-furnished table? Holy Heaven—the good, the excellent young man.'

'—they would never have lent their brutal suffrage to the proscription list of Robespierre.'

'Rose-Marie, today I care not what this young man says.'

'He says—look, I've got the book in my pocket——'

'I will not look.'

'He says, could a set of men whose passions were not perverted by unnatural stimuli—that's coffee, of course— gaze with coolness on an *auto-da-fé?*'

'I engage to gaze with heat on any *auto-da-fé* I may encounter if only you will quickly——'

'He says——'

'Put down the book, Rose-Marie, and see to the getting of coffee.'

'But he says——'

'Let him say it, and see to the coffee.'

'He says, is it to be believed that a being of gentle feelings rising from his meal of roots——'

'*Gott, Gott*,—meal of roots!'

'—would take delight in sports of blood?'

'Enough. I am not in the temper for Shelley.'

'But you quite loved him a day or two ago.'

'Except food, nobody loves anything—anything at all—while his stomach is empty.'

'I don't think that's very pretty, Papachen.'

'But it is a great truth. Remember it if you should marry. Shape your conduct by its light. Three times every day, Rose-Marie—that is, before breakfast, before dinner, and before supper,—no husband loves any wife. She may be as beautiful as the stars, as wise as Pallas-Athene, as cultured as Goethe, as entertaining as a circus, as affectionate as you please—he cares nothing for her. She exists not. Go, my child, and prepare the coffee, and let the bread-and-butter be cut thick.'

Well, since then I have been cutting bread-and-butter and pouring out cups of coffee. I thought Papa would never leave off. If that is the effect of a vegetarian dinner, I don't think it can really be less expensive than meat. Papa ate half a pound of butter, which is sixty pfennings, and for sixty pfennings I could have bought him a *Kalbsschnitzel* so big that it would have lasted, under treatment, two days. I must go for a walk and think it out.

> Yours sincerely,
> ROSE-MARIE SCHMIDT.

XXXVI

DEAR MR ANSTRUTHER,—I assure you that we have all we
want, so do not, please, go on feeling distressed about us.
Why should you feel distressed? I am not certain that I do
not resent it. Put baldly (you will say brutally), you have no
right to be distressed, uneasy, anxious, and all the other
things you say you are, about the private concerns of persons
who are nothing to you. Even a lamb might conceivably
feel nettled by persistent pity when it knows it has
everything in the world it wants. Come now, if it is a
question of pity, we will have it in the right place, and I
will pity you. There is always, you know, a secret satisfaction
in the soul of him who pities. He does hug himself, and
whether he does it consciously or unconsciously depends
on his aptitude for clear self-criticism. Compared with yours
I deliberately consider my life glorious. And when will you
see that there are kinds of gloriousness that cannot be
measured in money or position? It is plain to me—and it
would be so to you if you thought it over—that the less
one has the more one enjoys. We want space, time,
concentration, for getting at the true sweet root of life. And
I think—and you probably do not—that the true sweet root
of life is in any one thing, no matter what thing, on which
your whole undisturbed attention is fixed. Once I read a
little French story, years ago, with my mother, when I was
a child, and I don't know now who wrote it or what it was
called. It was the story of a prisoner who found a plant
growing between the flags of the court he might walk in,

and I think it was a wallflower; and it, unfolding itself slowly and putting out one tender bit of green after the other in that grey and stony place, stretched out little hands of life and hope and interest to the man who had come there a lost soul. It was the one thing he had. It ended by being his passion. With nothing else to distract him, he could study all its wonders. From that single plant he learned more than the hurried passer-on, free of the treasures of the universe, learns in a life. It saved him from despair. It brought him back to the eager interest in the marvellous world that soul feels which is unencumbered by too heavy a weight of trappings. Why, I still have too much; and here are you pitying me because I have not more when I am distracted by all the claims on my attention. I can look at whole beds of wallflowers every spring, and pass on with nothing but a vague admiration for their massed beauty of scent and colour. I get nothing out of them but just that transient glimpse and whiff. There are too many. There is no time for them all. But shut me up for weeks alone with one of them in a pot, and I too would get out of it the measure of the height and the depth and the wonder of life.

And then you exhort me not to live on vegetables. Is it because you live on meat? I don't think I mind your eating meat, so why should you mind my eating vegetables? I have done it for a week now quite steadily, and mean to give it at least a fair trial. If what the books we have got about it say is true, health and sanity lie that way. And how delightful to have a pure kitchen into which ghastly dead things never come. I will not be a partaker of the nature of beasts. I will not become three parts pig, or goose, or foolish sheep. I turn with aversion from the reddened horror called gravy. I consider it a monstrous ugly thing to have particles of pig rioting up and down my veins, turning into brains, colouring my thoughts, becoming a very part of my body. Surely a body is a wonderful thing? So wonderful that it cannot be treated with too much care and respect? So wonderful that it cannot be too carefully guarded from corruption? And have you ever studied the appearance and habits of pigs?

But I do admit that being a vegetarian is bewildering. None of the books say a word about the odd feeling one has of not having had anything to eat. What Papa felt that first day I have felt every day since. I am perpetually hungry; and it is the unpleasant hunger that expresses itself in a dislike for food, in listlessness, inability to work, flabbiness, even faintness. At eight in the morning I begin with bread and plums. My entire being cries out while I am eating them for coffee with milk in it and butter on my bread. But coffee is a stimulant, and the books say that butter contains no nourishment whatever, and since what I most yearn for is to be nourished I will waste no time eating stuff that doesn't do it. Instead, I eat heaps of bread and stacks of plums, not because I want to, but because I'm afraid the gnawing feeling will follow sooner than ever if I don't. Papa sits opposite me, breakfasting pleasantly on eggs, for he explains he is doing things gradually, and is using the eggs to build wise bridges across the gulf between the end of meat and the beginning of what he persists in describing as herbage. At nine I feel as if I had had no breakfast. All the pains I took to get through the bread were of no real use. I struggle against this for as long as possible, because the books say you mustn't have things between meals, and then I go and eat more plums. I am amazed when I remember that once I liked plums. No words can express my abhorrence of them now. But what is to be done? They are the only fruit we can get. Cherries are over. Apples have not begun. We buy the plums from the neighbour down the hill. To add to my horror of them, I have discovered that hardly one is without a wriggly live thing inside it. I wonder how many of them I have eaten. Can they be brought into the category vegetarian? Papa says yes, because they have lived and moved and had their being in an atmosphere of pure plum. They *are* plum, says Papa, consoling me—bits of plum that have acquired the power to walk about. But according to that beef must be vegetarian too— so much grass grown able to walk about. It is very bewildering. One day the neighbour—he is a nice neighbour, interested in our experiment—sent us some raspberries, a basket of them, all glowing, and downy, and delicious with dew, and covered with a beautiful silvery cabbage leaf; but they were afflicted in just the same way, only more so. Papa says, why do I look? I must look now that I have seen the things once; and so the end of the raspberries was that most of them went out into the kitchen, and Johanna, who has no prejudices, stewed them into compot and ate them, including the inhabitants, for her supper.

For dinner, by which time I am curiously shaky, quite indifferent to food, and possessed of an immense longing to lie down on a sofa and do nothing, we have salad and potatoes and fruit—of course plums—and lentils because they are so good for us (it is a pity they are also so nasty), and cheese because one book says (it is an extraordinarily convincing book) that if a man shall eat beef steadily for a whole morning from six to twelve without stopping, he will not at the end have taken in half the nourishing matter that he would have absorbed after two minutes laid out judiciously on cheese. Unfortunately I don't like cheese. After dinner I shut myself up with the works of Mr Eustace

Miles, which tell me in invigorating language of all the money, time, and energy I have saved, of my increase of bodily health, of how active I am getting, how skilful and of what a tough endurance, how my brains have grown clear and nimble, my morals risen high above the average, and how keen my enjoyment of everything has become, including, strange to say, my food. I read lying down, too spiritless to sit up; and Johanna in the kitchen, who has dined on pig and beer, washes up with the clatter of exuberant energy, singing while she does so in a voice that shakes the house that once she *liebte ein Student*.

It is very bewildering. The advice one gets points in such opposite directions. For instance, the neighbour made friends the very first evening with Papa, who walked with injudicious inattention in our garden and slipped down through a gap in the fence into his orchard and his arms, he being engaged in picking up the fallen plums for his wife to make jam of; and he told me, when he came in one day at dinner and found me struggling through what he considered dark ways and I thought were cabbages, that my salvation lay in almonds. I went down to Jena that afternoon and bought three pounds of them. They were dear, and dreadfully heavy to carry up the hill, and when I was panting past the neighbour's gate his wife, a friendly lady who reads right through the advertisements in the paper every morning and spends her evenings with a pencil working out the acrostics, was standing at it cool and comfortable; and she asked me, with the simple inquisitiveness natural to our nation, what I had got in my parcel; and I, glad to stop a moment and get my breath, told her; and she immediately scoffed both at her husband and at the almonds, and said if I ate them I would lay up for myself an old age steeped in a dreadful thing called xanthin poison. I went home and consulted the books. The neighbour's wife was right. Johanna made macaroons of the almonds, and Papa, who loves macaroons, chose to disbelieve the neighbour's wife and ate them.

But the books are not always so unanimous as they were about this. One exhorted us to eat many peas and beans, which we were cheerfully doing—for are they not in summer pleasant things?—when I read in another that we might as well eat poison, so full were they, too, of qualities ending in xanthin poison. Lentils, recommended warmly by most books, are discountenanced by two because they make you fat. Rice has shared the same condemnation. Lettuces we may eat, but without the oil that soothes and the vinegar that interests, and if you add salt to them you will be thirsty, and you must never drink. An undressed lettuce—a quite naked lettuce—is a very dull thing. Really, I would as soon eat grass. We do refuse at present to follow this cruel advice, and have salad every day in defiance of it, but my conscience forces me to put less and less dressing in it each time, hoping that so shall we wean ourselves from the craving for it— 'gradually,' as Papa says. Carrots, too, the books warn us against. I forget what it is they do to you that is serious, but the neighbour told me they make your skin shine, and since he told me that no carrot has crossed our threshold. Apples we may eat, but we are not to suppose that they will nourish us; they are useful only for preventing, by their bulk, the walls of our insides from coming together. The walls of the vegetarian inside are very apt to come together if the owner strikes out all the things he is warned against from his menu, and then it is, when they are about to do that, that fibrous bulk, most convenient in this form, should be applied; and, like the roasted Sunday goose of our fleshlier days in Rauchgasse, the vegetarian goes about stuffed with

118

apples. Meanwhile there are no apples, and I know not whither I must turn in search of bulk. Do you think that in another week I shall be strong enough to write to you?

Yours sincerely,

ROSE-MARIE SCHMIDT.

XXXVII

Galgenberg, July 28.

DEAR MR ANSTRUTHER,—This is a most sweet evening, dripping, quiet, after a rainy day, with a strip of clear yellow sky behind the pine trees on the crest of the hill. I gathered up my skirts and went down through the soaked grass to where against the fence there is a divine straggly bush of pink China roses. I wanted to see how they were getting on after their drenching; and as I stood looking at them in the calm light, the fence at the back of them sodden into dark greens and blacks that showed up every leaf and lovely loose wet flower, a robin came and sat on the fence near me and began to sing. You will say: Well, what next? And there isn't any next; at least, not a next that I am likely to make understandable. It was only that I felt extraordinarily happy. You will say: But why? And if I were to explain, at the end you would still be saying Why? Well, you cannot see my face while I am writing to you, so that I have been able often to keep what I was really thinking safely covered up; but you mustn't suppose that my letters have always exactly represented my state of mind, and that my soul has made no pilgrimages during this half year. I think it has wandered thousands of miles. And often while I wrote scolding you, or was being wise and complacent, or sprightly and offensive, often just then the tired feet of it were bleeding most as they stumbled among the bitter stones. And this evening I felt that the stones were at an end, that my soul has come home to me again, securely into my keeping, glad to be back, and that there will be no more effort needed when I look life serenely in the face. Till now there was always effort. That I talk to you about it is the surest sign that it is over. The robin's singing, the clear light behind the pines, the dripping trees and bushes, the fragrance of the wet roses, the little white house, so modest and hidden, where Papa and I are going to be happy, the perfect quiet after a stormy day, the perfect peace after discordant months—oh, I wanted to say thank you for each of these beautiful things. Do you remember you gave me a book of Ernest Dowson's poems on the birthday I had while you were with us? And do you remember his—

> Now I will take me to a place of peace,
> Forget my heart's desire—
> In solitude and prayer work out my soul's release?

It is what I feel I have done.

But I will not bore you with these sentiments. See, I am always anxious to get back quickly to the surface of things, anxious to skim lightly over the places where tears, happy or miserable, lie, and not to touch with so much as the brush of a wing the secret tendernesses of the soul. Let us, sir, get back to vegetables. They are so safe as subjects for polite letter-writing. And I have had three letters from you this week condemning their use with all the fervour the English language places at your disposal—really it is generous to you in this respect—as a substitute for the mixed diet of the ordinary Philistine. Yes, sir, I regard you as an ordinary Philistine; and if you want to know what that in my opinion is, it is one who walks along in the ruts he found ready instead of, after sitting on a milestone and taking due thought, making his own ruts for himself. You are one of a flock; and you disapprove of sheep like myself that choose to wander off and browse alone. You condemn all my practices. Nothing that I think or do seems good in your eyes. You tell me roundly that I am selfish, and accuse me, not roundly because you are afraid it might be indecorous, but obliquely, in a mask of words that does not for an instant hide your meaning, of wearing Jaeger garments beneath my outer apparel. Soon, I gather you expect, I shall become a spiritualist and a social democrat; and quite soon after that I suppose you are sure I shall cut off my hair and go about in sandals. Well, I'll tell you something that may keep you quiet: I'm tired of vegetarianism. It isn't that I crave for fleshpots, for I shall continue as before to turn my back on them, on 'the boiled and roast, The heated nose in face of ghost,' but I grudge the time it takes and the thought it takes. For the fortnight I have followed its precepts I have lived more entirely for my body than in any one fortnight of my life. It was all body. I could think of nothing else. I was tending it the whole day. Instead of growing, as I had fondly hoped, so free in spirit that I would be able to draw quite close to the *liebe Gott*, I was sunk in a pit of indifference to everything needing effort or enthusiasm. And it. is not simple after all. Shelley's meal of roots sounds easy and elementary, but think of the exertion of going out, strengthened only by other roots, to find more for your next meal. Nuts and fruits, things that require no cooking, really were elaborate nuisances, the nuts having to be cracked and the fruit freed from what Papa called its pedestrian portions. And they were so useless even then to a person who wanted to go out and dig in the garden. All they could do for me was to make me appreciate sofas. I am tired of it, tired of wasting precious time thinking about and planning my wretched diet. Yesterday I had an egg for breakfast—it gave me one of Pater's 'exquisite moments'—and a heavenly bowl of coffee with milk in it, and the effect was to send me out singing into the garden and to start me mending the fence. The neighbour came up to see what the vigorous hammer-strokes and snatches of *Siegfried* could mean, and when he saw it was I immediately called out—

'You have been eating meat!'

'I have not,' I said, swinging my hammer to show what eggs and milk can do.

'In some form or other you have this day joined yourself to the animal kingdom,' he persisted; and when I told him about my breakfast he wiped his hands (he had been picking fruit) and shook mine and congratulated me. 'I have watched with concern,' he said, 'your eyes becoming daily bigger. It is not good when eyes do that. Now they will shrink to their normal size, and you will at last set your disgraceful garden in order. Are you aware that the grass ought to have been made into hay a month ago?'

He is a haggard man, thin of cheek, round of shoulder, short of sight, who teaches little boys Latin and Greek in Weimar. For thirty years has he taught them, eking out his income in the way we all do in these parts, by taking in foreigners wanting to learn German. In July he shakes his foreigners off and comes up here for six weeks' vacant pottering in his orchard. He bought the house as a speculation, and lets the upper part to any one who will take it, living himself, with his wife and son, on the ground floor. He is extremely kind to me, and has given me to understand that he considers me intelligent, so of course I like him. Only those persons who love intelligence in others and have doubts about their own know the deliciousness of being told a thing like that. I adore being praised. I am athirst for it. Dreadfully vain down in my heart, I go about pretending a fine aloofness from such weakness, so that when nobody sees anything in me—and nobody ever does—I may at least make a show of not having expected them to. Thus does a girl in a ball-room with whom no one will dance pretend she does not want to. Thus did the familiar fox conduct himself towards the grapes of tradition. Very well do I know there is nothing to praise; but because I am just clever enough to know that I am not clever, to be told that I am clever—do you follow me?—sets me tingling.

Now, that's enough about me. Let us talk about you. You must not come to Jena. What could have put such an idea into your head? It is a blazing, deserted place just now, looking from the top of the hills like a basin of hot *bouillon* down there in the hollow, wrapped in its steam. The University is shut up. The professors scattered. Martens is in Switzerland, and won't be back till September. Even the Schmidts, those interesting people, have flapped up with screams of satisfaction into a nest on the side of a precipice. I urge you with all my elder-sisterly authority to stay where you are. Plainly, if you were to come, I would not see you. Oh, I will leave off pretending I cannot imagine what you want here: I know you want to see me. Well, you shall not. Why you should want to is altogether beyond my comprehension. I believe you have come to regard me as a sort of medicine, medicine of the tonic order, and wish to bring your sick soul to the very place where it is dispensed. But I, you see, will have nothing to do with sick souls, and I wholly repudiate the idea of being somebody's physic. I will not be your physic. What medicinal properties you can extract from my letters you are welcome to; but, pray, are you mad that you should think of coming here? When you do come you are to come with your wife, and when you have a wife you are not to come at all. How simple.

Really, I feel inclined to laugh when I try to picture you, after the life you have been leading in London, after the days you are living now at Clinches, attempting to arrange yourself on this perch of ours up here. I cannot picture you. We have reduced our existence to the crudest elements, to the raw material; and you, I know, have grown a very exquisite young man. The fact is you have had time to forget what we are really like, my father and I and Johanna, and since my stepmother's time we have advanced far in the casual scrappiness of housekeeping that we love. You would be like some strange and splendid bird in the midst of three extremely shabby sparrows. That is the physical point of view: a thing to be laughed at. From the moral it is for ever impossible.

Yours sincerely,
ROSE-MARIE SCHMIDT.

XXXVIII

Galgenberg, Aug. 7.

DEAR MR ANSTRUTHER,—It is pleasant of you to take the trouble to emulate our neighbour and tell me that you too think me intelligent. You put it, it is true, more elaborately than he does, with a greater embroidery of fine words, but I will try to believe you equally sincere. I make you a profound *Knix*—it's a more expressive word than curtsey—of polite gratitude. But it is less excellent of you to add on the top of these praises that I am adorable. With words like that, inappropriate, and to me eternally unconvincing, this correspondence will come to an abrupt end. I shall not write again if that is how you are going to play the game. I would not write now if I were less indifferent. As it is, I can look on with perfect calm, most serenely unmoved by anything in that direction you may say to me; but if you care to have letters, do not say them again. I shall never choose to allow you to suppose me vile.

Yours sincerely,

ROSE-MARIE SCHMIDT.

XXXIX

DEAR MR ANSTRUTHER,—You need not have sent me so many pages of protestations. Nothing you can say will persuade me that I am adorable, and I did exactly mean the word vile. Do not quarrel with Miss Cheriton; but if you must, do not tell me about it. Why should you always want to tell one of us about the other? Have you no sense of what is fit? I am nothing to you, and I will not hear these things.

Yours sincerely,
ROSE-MARIE SCHMIDT.

XL

Galgenberg, Aug. 18.

DEAR MR ANSTRUTHER,—You must really write a book. Write a very long one, with plenty of room for all your words. What is your bill for postage now? Johanna, I am sure, thinks you are sending me instalments of manuscript, and marvels at the extravagance that shuts it up in envelopes instead of leaving its ends open and tying it up with string. Once more I must beg you not to write about Miss Cheriton. It is useless to remind me that I have posed as your sister, and that to your sister you may confide anything, because I am not your sister. Sometimes I have written of an elder-sisterly attitude towards you, but that, of course, was only talk. I am not irascible enough for the position. I do think, though, you ought to be surrounded by women who are cross. Six cross and determined elder sisters would do wonders for you. And so would a mother with an iron will. And perhaps an aunt living in the house might be a good thing; one of those aunts—I believe sufficiently abundant—who pierce your soul with their eyes and then describe it minutely at meal-times in the presence of the family, expatiating particularly on what those corners of it look like, those corners you thought so secret, in which are huddled your dearest faults.

Yours sincerely,

ROSE-MARIE SCHMIDT.

XLI

DEAR MR ANSTRUTHER,—Very well; I won't quarrel; I will be friends—friends, that is, so long as you allow me to be so in the only right and possible way. Don't murder too many grouse. Think of my disapproving scowl when you are beginning to do it, and then perhaps your day of slaughter will resolve itself into an innocent picnic on the moors, alone with sky and heather and a bored, astonished dog. Are you not glad now that you went to Scotland instead of coming to Jena to find the Schmidts not at home? Surely long days in the heather by yourself will do much towards making you friends with life. I think those moors must be so beautiful. Really, very nearly as good as my Galgenberg. My Galgenberg, by the by, has left off being quite so admirably solitary as it was at first. The neighbour is, as I told you, extremely friendly, so is his wife, though I do not set such store by her friendliness as I do by his, for, frankly, I find men are best; and they have a son who is an *Assessor* in Berlin. You know what an *Assessor* is, don't you?—it is a person who will presently be a *Landrath*. And you know what a *Landrath* is? It's what you are before you turn into a *Regierungsrath*. And a *Regierungsrath* is what you are before you are a *Geheimrath*. And a *Geheimrath*, if he lives long enough and doesn't irritate anybody in authority, becomes ultimately that impressive and glorious being a *Wirklicher Geheimrath*—implying that before he was only in fun—*mit dem Prädikat Excellenz*. And don't say I don't explain nicely, because I do. Well, where was I? Oh yes; at the son. Well, he appeared a fortnight ago, brown and hot and with a knapsack, having walked all the way from Berlin, and is spending his holiday with his people. For a day or two I thought him quite ordinary. He made rather silly jokes, and wore a red tie. Then one evening I heard lovely sounds, lovely, floating, mellow sounds coming up in floods through the orchard into my garden, where I was propped against a tree-trunk, watching a huge yellow moon disentangling itself slowly from the mists of Jena,—oh, but exquisite sounds, sounds that throbbed into your soul and told it all it wanted to hear, showed it the way to all it was looking for, talked to it wonderfully of the possibilities of life. First they drew me on to my feet, then they drew me down the garden, then through the orchard, nearer and nearer, till at last I stood beneath the open window they were coming from, listening with all my ears. Against the wall I leaned, holding my breath, spell-bound, forced to ponder great themes, themes of life and death, the music falling like drops of liquid light in dark and thirsty places. I don't know how long it lasted or how long I stood there after it was finished, but some one came to the window and put his head out into the freshness, and what do you think he said? He said, '*Donnerwetter, wie man im Zimmer schwitzt.*' And it was the son, brown and hot, and with a red tie.

'Ach, Fräulein Schmidt,' said he, suddenly perceiving me. 'Good evening. A fine evening. I did not know I had an audience.'

'Yes,' said I, unable at once to adjust myself to politenesses.

'Do you like music?'

'Yes,' said I, still vibrating.

'It is a good violin. I picked it up——' And he told me a great many things that I did not hear, for how can you hear when your spirit refuses to come back from its journeyings among the stars?

'Will you not enter?' he said at last. 'My mother is fetching up some beer and will be here in a moment. It makes one warm playing.'

But I would not enter. I walked back slowly through the long orchard grass between the apple-trees. The moon gleamed along the branches. The branches were weighed down with apples. The place was full of the smell of fruit, of the smell of fruit fallen into the grass, that had lain there bruised all day in the sun. I think the beauty of the world is crushing. Often it seems almost unbearable, calling out such an acuteness of sensation, such a vivid, leaping sensitiveness of feeling, that indeed it is like pain.

But what I want to talk about is the strange way good things come out of evil. It really almost makes you respect and esteem the bad things, doing it with an intelligent eye fixed on the future. Here is our young friend down the hill, a young man most ordinary in every way but one, so ordinary that I think we must put him under the heading bad, taking bad in the sense of negation, of want of good; here he is, robust of speech, fond of beer, red of tie, chosen as her temple by that delicate lady the Muse of melody. Apparently she is not very particular about her temples. It is true, while he is playing at her dictation she transforms him wholly, and I suppose she does not care what he is like in between. But I do. I care because in between he thinks it pleasant to entertain me with facetiousness, his mother hanging fondly on every word in the amazing way mothers, often otherwise quite intelligent persons, do. Since that first evening he has played every evening, and his taste in music is as perfect as it is bad in everything else. It is severe, exquisite, exclusive. It is the taste that plays Mozart and

Bach and Beethoven, and wastes no moments with the Mendelssohn sugar or the lesser inspiration of Brahms. I tried to strike illumination out of him on these points, wanted to hear his reasons for a greater exclusiveness than I have yet met, went through a string of impressive names, beginning with Schumann and ending with Wagner and Tchaikowsky, but he showed no interest, and no intelligence either, unless a shrug of the shoulder is intelligent. It is true he remarked one day that he found life too short for anything but the best—'That is why,' he added, unable to forbear from wit, 'I only drink Pilsner.'

'What?' I cried, ignoring the Pilsner, 'and do not these great men'—again I ran through a string of them—'do not they also belong to the very best?'

'No,' he said; and would say no more. So, you see, he is obstinate as well as narrow-minded.

Of course such exclusiveness in art *is* narrow-minded, isn't it? Besides, it is very possible he is wrong. You, I know, used to perch Brahms on one of the highest peaks of Parnassus (I never thought there was quite room enough for him on it); and did you not go three times all the way to Munich while you were with us to hear Mottl conduct the *Ring*? Surely it is probable a person of your all-round good taste is a better judge than a person of his very nearly all-round bad taste? Whatever your faults may be, you never made a fault in ties, never clamoured almost ceaselessly for drink, never talked about *schwitzen*, nor entertained young women from next door with the tricks and facetiousness of a mountebank. I wonder if his system were carried into literature, and life were wholly concentrated on the half-dozen absolutely best writers, so that we who spread our attention out thin over areas I am certain are much too wide knew them as we never can know them, became part of them, lived with them and in them, saw through their eyes and thought with their thoughts, whether there would be gain or loss? I don't know. Tell me what you think. If I might only have the six mightiest books to go with me through life I would certainly have to learn Greek because of Homer. But when it comes to the very mightiest, I cannot even get my six; I can only get four. Of course when I loosely say six books I mean the works of six writers. But beyond my four I cannot get; there must be a slight drop for the other two—very slight, hardly a drop, rather a slight downward quiver into a radiance the faintest degree less blazing, but still a degree less. These two would be Milton and Virgil. The other four—but you know the other four without my telling you. I am not sure that the *Assessor* is not right, and that one cannot, in matters of the spirit, be too exclusive. Exclusiveness means concentration, deeper study, minuter knowledge; for we only have a handful of years to do anything in, and they are quite surely not enough to go round when going round means taking in the whole world.

On the other hand, wouldn't my speech become archaic? I'm afraid I would have a tendency that would grow to address Papa in blank verse. My language, even when praying him at breakfast to give me butter, would be incorrigibly noble. I don't think Papa would like it. And what would he say to a daughter who was forced by stress of concentration on six works to go through life without Goethe? Goethe, you observe, was not one of the two less glorious, and he certainly was not one of the four completely glorious. I begin to fear I should miss a great deal by my exclusions. It would be sad to die without ever having been thrilled by *Werther*, exalted by *Faust*, amazed by the *Wahlverwandtschaften*, sent to sleep by *Wilhelm Meister.*

To die innocent of any knowledge of Schiller's *Glocke*, with no memory of strenuous hours spent getting it by heart at school, might be quite pleasant. But I think it would end by being tiring to be screwed up perpetually to the pitch of the greatest men's greatest moments. Such heights are not for insects like myself. I would hang very dismally, with drooping head and wings, on those exalted hooks. And has not the soul too its longings at times for a dressing-gown and slippers? And do you see how you could do without Boswell?

Yours sincerely,
ROSE-MARIE SCHMIDT.

XLII

DEAR MR ANSTRUTHER,—Yes, of course he does. He plays every evening. And every evening I go and listen, either in the orchard beneath the open window or, more ceremoniously, inside the room with or without Papa. I find it a pleasant thing. I am living in a bath of music. And I hope you don't expect me to agree with your criticism of music as a stirrer-up of, on the whole, second-rate emotions. What are second-rate emotions? Are they the ones that you have? And was it to have them stirred that you used to journey so often to Munich and Mottl? Stirred up I certainly am. Not in the way, I admit, in which a poem of Milton's does it, not affected in the least as I am affected by, for instance, the piled-up majesty of the poem on *Time*, but if less nobly still very effectually. There; I have apparently begun to agree with you. Well, I do see, the moment I begin to consider, that what is stirred is less noble. I do see that what I feel when I listen to music is chiefly *Wehmuth*, and I don't think much of *Wehmuth*. You have no word for it. Perhaps in England you do not have just that form of sentiment. It is a forlorn thing, made up mostly of vague ingredients—vague yearnings, vague regrets, vague dissatisfactions. When it comes over you, you remember all the people who are absent, and you are sad; and the people who are dead, and you sigh; and the times you have been naughty, and you groan. I do see that a sentiment that makes you do that is not the highest. It is profitless, sterile. It doesn't send you on joyfully to the next thing, but keeps you lingering in the dust of churchyards, barren places of the past which should never be revisited by the wholesome-minded. Now, this looks as though I were agreeing with you quite, but I still don't. You put it so extremely. It is so horrid to think that even my emotions may be second-rate. I long ago became aware that my manners were so, but I did like to believe there was nothing second-rate about my soul. Well, what is one to do? Never be soft? Never be sad? Or sorry? Or repentant? Always stay up at the level of Milton's *Time* poem, or of his *At a Solemn Musick*, strung high up to an unchanging pitch of frigid splendour and nobleness? It is what I try to aim at. It is what I would best like. Then comes our friend of the red tie, and in the cool of the day, when the world is dim and scented, shakes a little fugue of Bach's out of his fiddle, a sparkling, sly little fugue, frolicsome for all its minor key, a handful of bright threads woven together, twisted in and out, playing, it would seem, at some game of hide-and-seek, of pretending to want to catch each other into a tangle, but always gaily coming out of the knots, each distinct and holding on its shining way till the meeting at the end, the final embrace when the game is over and they tie themselves contentedly together into one comfortable major chord,—our friend plays this, this manifestly happy thing, and my soul listens, and smiles, and sighs, and longs, and ends by being steeped in *Wehmuth*. I choose the little fugue of Bach as an instance, for of all music it is aimed most distinctly at the intellect, it is the furthest removed from *Wehmuth*; and if it has this effect on me I will not make you uncomfortable by a description of what the baser musics do, the musics of passion, of furious exultations and furious despairs. But my vague wish for I do not know what, gentle, and rather sweetly resigned when the accompaniment is Bach, swells suddenly while I listen to them into a terrifying longing that rends and shatters my soul.

What private things I tell you. I wouldn't if I were talking. I would be affected by your actual presence. But writing is so different and so strange; at once so much more and so much less intimate. The body is safe—far away, unassailable; and the spirit lets itself go out to meet a fellow spirit with the frankness it can never show when the body goes too, that grievous hinderer of the communion of saints, that officious blunderer who can spoil the serenest intercourse by a single blush.

Johanna came in just there. She was decked in smiles, and wanted to say good-bye till tomorrow morning. It is her night out, and she really looked rather wonderful to one used to her kitchen condition. Her skin, cleansed from week-day soilure, was surprisingly fair; her hair, waved more beautifully than mine will ever be, was piled up in bright imposing masses; her starched white dress had pink ribbons about it; she wore cotton gloves; and held the handkerchief I lend her on these occasions genteelly by its middle in her hand. Every second Sunday she descends the mountain at sunset, the door-key in her pocket, and dances all night in some convivial *Gasthof* in the town, coming up again at sunrise or later, according to the amount of fun she was having. On the Monday I do nearly everything alone, for she sleeps half the day, and the other half she doesn't like being talked to. She is a good servant, and she would certainly go if we tried to get her in again under the twelve hours. On the alternate Sundays we allow her to have her young man up for the afternoon and evening. He is a trumpeter in the regiment stationed in Jena, and he brings his trumpet to fill up awkward silences. Engaged couples of that kind don't seem able to talk much, so that the trumpet is a great comfort to them. Whenever conversation flags he whips it out and blows a rousing blast, giving her time to think of something to say next. I had to ask him to do it in the garden, for the first time it nearly blew our roof, which isn't very tightly on, off. Now he and she sit together on a bench outside the door, and the genius down the hill with the exclusive ears suffers, I am afraid, rather acutely. Papa and I wander as far away as we can get among the mountains.

It is rather dreadful when they quarrel. Then, of course, Johanna sulks as girls will, and sulks are silent things, so that the trumpet has to fill up a yawning gulf and never leaves off at all. Last Sunday it blew the whole time we were out, and I expected when I got home to find the engagement broken off. We stayed away as long as we could, climbing higher and higher, wandering further and further, supping at last reluctantly on cucumber salad and cold herrings in the little restaurant up on the Schweizerhöhe because the trumpet wouldn't stop and we didn't dare go home till it did. Its blast pursued us even into the recesses of the dingy wooden hall we took our ears into, vainly trying to carry them somewhere out of range. It seemed to be a serious quarrel. We had a depressing meal. We both esteem Johanna with the craven esteem you feel for a person, at any moment capable of giving notice, who does all the unpleasant things you would otherwise have to do yourself. The state of her temper seriously affects our peace. You see, the house is small, and if her trumpeter has been unsatisfactory and she throws the saucepans about or knocks the broom in sweeping against all the wooden things like doors and skirting-boards, it makes an unendurable clatter and puts an end at once to Papa's work and to my equally earnest play. If, her nerves being already on edge, I were to suggest to her even smilingly to be quiet, she would at once give notice—I know she would—and the dreary search begin again for that impossible treasure you in England call a paragon and we in Jena call a pearl. Where am I to find a clean, honest, strong pearl, able to cook and willing to come and live in what is something like an unopened oyster-shell, so shut-up, so cutoff, so solitary would her existence here be, for eight pounds a year? It is easy for you august persons who never see your servants, who have so many that by sheer force of numbers they become unnoticeable, to deride us who have only one for being so greatly at her mercy. I know you will deride. I see your letter already: 'Dear Fräulein Schmidt, Is not your attitude towards the maid Johanna unworthy?' It isn't unworthy, because it is natural. Defiantly I confess that it is also cringing. Well, it is natural to cringe under the circumstances. So would you. I dare say if your personal servant is a good one, and you depend much on him for comfort, you do do it as it is. And there are very few girls in Jena who would come out of it and take a situation on the side of a precipice for eight pounds a year. Really the wages are small, balanced against the disadvantages. And wages are going up. Down in Jena a good servant can get ten pounds a year now without much difficulty. So that it behoves us who cannot pay such prices to humour Johanna.

About nine the trumpet became suddenly dumb. Papa and I, after waiting a few minutes, set out for home, conjecturing as we went in what state we should find Johanna. Did the silence mean a rupture or a making-up? I inclined towards the rupture, for how can a girl, I asked Papa, murmur mild words of making-up to a lover engaged in blowing a trumpet? Papa said he didn't know; and engrossed by fears we walked home without speaking.

No one was to be seen. The house was dark and empty. Everything was quiet except the crickets. The trumpeter had gone, but so, apparently, had Johanna. She had forgotten to lock the door, so that all we—or anybody else passing that way—had to do was to walk in. Nobody, however—and by nobody I mean the criminally intentioned, briefly burglars—walks into houses perched as ours is. They would be very breathless burglars by the time they got to our garden gate. We should hear their stertorous breathing as they laboured up well in time to lock the door; and Papa, ever pitiful and polite, would as likely as not unlock it again to hasten out and offer them chairs and lemonade. It was not, then, with any misgivings of that sort that we went into our deserted house and felt about for matches; but I was surprised that Johanna, when she could sit comfortably level on the seat by the door, should rather choose to go and stroll in the garden. You cannot stroll in my garden. You can do very few of the things in it that most people can do in most gardens, and certainly strolling is not one of them. It is no place for lovers, or philosophers, or leisurely persons of the sort. It is an unrestful place, in which you are forced to be energetic, to watch where you put your feet, to balance yourself to a nicety, to be continually on the alert. I lit a lantern, and went out in search of Johanna strolling. I stood on the back door steps and looked right and looked left. No Johanna. No sounds of Johanna. Only the crickets, and the soft darting by of a bat. I went down the steps—they are six irregular stones embedded one beneath the other in the clay and leading to the pump from which, in buckets, we supply our need for water—and standing still again, again heard only crickets. I went to the mignonette beds I have made—mignonette and nasturtiums; mignonette for scent and nasturtiums for beauty, and I hope you like nasturtiums—and standing still again, again heard only crickets. The night was dark and soft, and seemed of a limitless vastness. The near shrill of the crickets made the silence beyond more intense. A cat prowled past, velvet-footed, silent as the night, a vanishing grey streak, intent and terrible, concentrated wholly on prey. I went on through the grass, my shoes wet with dew, the lantern light fitfully calling out my possessions from the blackness— the three apple-trees, the currant-bush, the pale group of starworts, children of some accidental wind-dropped seed of long ago; and beside the starworts I stopped again and listened. Still only the crickets; and presently very far away the whistle of the night express from Berlin to Munich as it hurried past the little station in the Paradies valley. It was extraordinarily quiet. Once I thought my own heart-beats were the footsteps of a late wanderer on the road. I went further, down to the very end, to the place where my beautiful, untiring monthly-rose bush unfolds pink flower after pink flower against the fence that separates us from our neighbour's kingdom, and stopped again and listened. At first still only crickets, and the anxious twitter of a bird towards whose nest that stealthy, murderous streak of grey was drawing. It began to rain; soft, warm drops from the motionless clouds spread low across the sky. I forgot Johanna, and became wholly possessed by the brooding spirit of the night, by the feeling of oneness, of identity with the darkness, the silence, the scent. My feet were wet with dew; my hair with the warm and gentle rain. I lifted up my face and let the drops fall on it through the leaves of the apple-trees, warm and gentle as a caress. Then the sudden blare of a trumpet made me start and quiver. I quivered so much that the lantern fell down and went out. The blare was the loudest noise I thought I had ever heard, ripping up the silence like a jagged knife. The startled hills couldn't get over it, but went on echoing and re-echoing it, tossing it backwards and forwards to each other in an endless surprise, and had hardly settled down again with a kind of shudder when they were roused to frenzy by another. After that there was blare upon blare. The man only stopped to take breath. They were louder, more rollicking than any I had heard him produce. And they came from the neighbour's house, from the very dwelling of him of the easily tortured ears, of him for whom Wagner is not good enough. Well, do you know what he had done? I ran down to question, and to extract Johanna and explain the trumpeter, and I met the poor genius, very pale and damp-looking, his necktie struggled up behind to the top of his collar, its bow twisted round somehow under his left ear. He was hurrying out into the night as I arrived, panting, on the doorstep.

'Why in the world——' I began; but a blast drowned further speech.

He flung up his hands, and the darkness engulfed him.

'It's raining,' I tried to cry after his hatless figure.

I thought I heard him call back something about Pilsner—'It's the Pilsner,' I thought I heard him say; but the noise coming from the kitchen was too violent for me to be sure.

His father was in the passage, walking up and down it, his hands in his pockets, his shoulders up to his ears as though he were shrinking from blows. He told me what his unhappy son had done. Not able to endure the trumpet when it was being blown up at our house earlier in the evening, not able to endure it even softened, chastened, subdued by distance and the intervening walls, he had directed his mother to go up and invite the player down

142

to her kitchen, where he was to be cajoled into eating and drinking, because, as the son explained, full of glee at his sagacity, no man who is eating and drinking can at the same time be blowing a trumpet.

'Thus,' said his father, in jerks coincident with the breath-takings of the trumpeter, 'did he hope to obtain peace.'

'But he didn't,' said I.

'No. For a period there was extreme, delicious quiet. Mother'—so he invariably describes his wife—'sacrificed her best sausage, for how shall we permit our son to be tortured? The bread was spread with butter three centimeters deep. The trumpeter and his *Schatz* sat quietly in the kitchen eating it. We sat quietly on the verandah discussing great themes. Then that good beer my son so often praises, that excellent, barrel-kept, cellar-lodged Pilsner beer, bright as amber, clear as ice, cool as—cool as——'

'A cucumber,' I assisted.

'Good. Very good. As a cucumber—as a salad of cucumbers.'

'No, no—there's pepper in a salad. You'd better just keep to plain cucumber,' I interrupted, always rather nice in the matter of images.

'Cool, then, as plain cucumber—this usually admirable stuff instead of, as we had expected, sending him gradually and pleasantly to sleep—I mean, of course, making him gradually and pleasantly so sleepy that thoughts of his bed, growing in affection with every glass, would cause him to arise and depart to his barracks—woke him up. And, my dear Fräulein, you yourself heard—you are hearing now—how completely it did it.'

'Is he—is he——?' I inquired nervously.

The neighbour nodded. 'He is,' he said; 'he has consumed fourteen glasses.'

And indeed he was; and I should say from the tumult,

143

from the formlessness of it, the tunelessness, the rollicksomeness, that never was anybody more so.

'I fear my son will leave us for some quieter spot before his holiday is over,' said the neighbour, looking distressed.

And perhaps it will convince you more than anything else I have said of the extreme value of our Johannas, when I tell you that, goaded by the noise and by his disappointed face to rash promises, I declared I would dismiss the girl unless she broke off such an engagement, and he stared at me for a moment in astonishment, and then resignedly shook his head and said, with the weary conviction of a householder of thirty years' standing, '*Das geht doch nicht.*'

Yours sincerely,

ROSE-MARIE SCHMIDT.

XLIII

DEAR MR ANSTRUTHER,—But it is true. Our servants do not get more than from one hundred to two hundred and fifty marks a year, and indeed I think it is a great deal, and cannot see why, because you spend as much (you say you do, so I must believe it) in a month on gloves and ties, it should make you hate yourself. Do not hate yourself. Your doing so doesn't make us pay our servants more. Why, how do you suppose we could get all we need out of our hundred pounds a year—I translate our marks into your pounds for your greater convenience—if we had to give a servant more than eight of them and for our house more than fifteen? Papa and I do not like to be kept hungry in the matter of books, and we shall probably spend every penny of our income; but I know a number of families with children who live decently and have occasional coffee-parties, and put by for their daughters' *trousseaux* on the same sum. As for the servants themselves, have I not described Johanna's splendid appearance on her Sundays, her white dress and gloves, and the pink ribbons round her waist? She finds her wages will buy these things and still leave enough for the savings-bank. She is quite content. Only I don't know if she would remain so if you were to come and lament over her and tell her what a little way you make the same money go. You see, she would probably not grasp the true significance of the admission, which is, I take it, not that she has too little, but that you spend too much. Yet how can I from my Galgenberg judge what is necessary in gloves and ties for a splendid young man like yourself? The sum seems to me terrific. There must be stacks of gloves and ties constantly growing higher about your path. You, then, spend on these two things alone almost exactly what we three spend in a year on everything. But my astonishment is only the measure of my ignorance. Do not hate yourself. Either spend the money without compunction, or, if you have compunction, don't spend it. A sinner should always, I think, sin gaily or not at all. I don't mean that you in this are a sinner; I only mean that as a general principle half-hearted sinners are contemptible. It is a poor creature who while he sins is sorry. If he must sin, let him at least do it with all his heart, and having done it waste no time in whimpers, but try to turn his back on it and his face towards the good. Please do not hate yourself. I am sure you have to have the things. Your letter is more than usually depressed. Please do not hate yourself. It does no good and lowers your vitality. It is as bad as sorrow, which surely is very bad. I think nothing great was done by any one who wasted time peering about among his faults; but if ever you meet the pastor who prepared me for confirmation, don't tell him I said so. I don't know how it is with yours in England, but here the pastors seem altogether unable to bear listening to descriptions of plain facts. When they come to doctor my soul, why may I not tell them its symptoms as baldly as I tell my body's symptoms to the physician who would heal it? He is not shocked or angry when I show him my sore places; he recommends a plaster or a dose, encourages, and goes away. But your spiritual doctor takes your spiritual sore places as a kind of personal affront; at least, his manner often shows indignation in proportion as you are frank. Instead of being patient, he hardly lets you speak; instead of prescribing, he denounces;

instead of helping, he passionately scolds; and so you do not go to him again, but fight through your later miseries alone. Just at the time of my preparation for confirmation my mother died. My heart, blank with sorrow, was very fit for religious impressions and consolations. The preparation lasts two years, and three times every week during that time I went to classes. For two years I was not allowed to dance or to go to even the mildest parties. For two years, from sixteen to eighteen, I was earnest, prayerful, humbly seeking after righteousness. Then one day, when questionings had come upon me that my conscience could not approve, I went to the pastor who had prepared me as confidently as I would go with a toothache to a dentist, and bared my sensitive conscience to him, and begged to have my thoughts arranged and my doubts and questionings settled. To my amazement and extreme fright I beheld him shocked, angry, hardly able to endure hearing me tell all I had been wondering. It seemed very strange. I sat at last with downcast eyes, silent, ashamed, my heart shrunk back into reserve and frost. I was not being helped; I was being scolded, and bitterly scolded. At last at the door some special word of blame stung me to heat, and I cried, 'Herr Pastor, when my tongue is bad and I show it to a doctor, he gives me a pill. Are you not the doctor of my spirit? Why, then, when I come to you to be healed, do you, instead of giving me medicine, so cruelly rate me?'

And he, staring at me a moment aghast, struck his hands together above his head. 'Thy father!' he cried, 'Thy father! It is he who speaks—it is he speaking in thee. Such words come not unaided from the mouth of eighteen, from the mouth of one confirmed by these very hands. *Ach*, miserable maiden, it is not with such as thee that Paradise is peopled. The taint of thy parentage is heavy upon thee.

Thou art not, thou canst not be, thou hast never been a child of God.'

And that was all I got for my pains.

Tell me, what mood were you in when you wrote? Was it not, apart from its dejection, one rather inclined to peevishness? You ask, for instance, why I write so much about a tipsy trumpeter when I know you are anxious to hear about the other things I never tell you. I can't imagine what they are. You must let me write how and what I like—bear with me while I discourse of roses and nasturtium-beds, of rain and sunshine, clouds and wind, cats, birds, servants, even trumpeters. My life holds nothing greater than these. If you want to hear from me you must hear also of them. And why have you taken so bitter a dislike to our gifted young neighbour down the hill, calling him contemptuously a fiddler? He is certainly a fiddler, if to fiddle in one's hours of ease produces one, and perhaps you would be twice as happy as you are if you could fiddle half so wonderfully as he does. He is gone. His holiday either came to an end or was put to an end by Johanna's *fiancé*. Now, in these early September days, this season of mists and mellow fruitfulness, of cloudy mornings and calm evenings and golden afternoons, he has turned his back on the hills and forests, on the reddening creepers and sweetening grapes, on the splash of water among ferns and rocks, on all those fresh, quiet things that make life worth having, and is sitting at a desk somewhere in Berlin doggedly bent on becoming, by means of a great outlay of days and years, a *Landrath*, a *Regierungsrath*, a *Geheimrath,* and a *Wirklicher Geheimrath mit dem Prädikat Excellenz*. When he has done that he will take down his hat and go forth at last to enjoy life, and will find to his surprise that it isn't there, that it is all behind him, a heap of dusty days piled in the corners of offices, and that his knees shake as he goes about looking for it, and that he can no longer even tune his fiddle by himself but has to have it done for him by the footman.

Isn't that what happens to all you wise men, so prudently determined to make your way in the world? You must be very sure of another life, or how could you bear to squander this? The things you are missing—oh, the things you are missing! while you so carefully add little gain to little gain, or what I would rather call little loss to little loss. I see no point in slaving day after day through one's best years. Suppose you do not, in the end, have a footman to open your door—the footman is merely a symbol, conveniently expressing the multitude of superfluities that gather about the declining years of the person who has got on, things bought with the sacrifice of his life, and none of them giving him back the lost power, gone with youth, to enjoy them—suppose, then, you do not end gloriously with a footman, what of that? I must be blind, for I never can see the desirability of these trappings. Yet they surely are of an immense desirability, since everybody, really everybody, is willing to give so much in payment for them. Our elder neighbour down the hill has actually given his eyes and his back; he peers at life through spectacles, and walks about like Wordsworth's leech-gatherer, bent double through poking about for years in the muddy pools of little boys' badly written exercises; and here he is at fifty still not satisfied with what he has earned, still going on drudging the whole year round, except for his six short weeks in summer. His wife is thrifty; they have only the one son; they live frugally; long ago they must have put by enough to keep them warm and fed and clothed without his doing another stroke of work.

I was interrupted there by a message from him asking if I would come down and help him gather up the windfalls in his orchard, his wife being busy pickling beans. I went, my head full of what I had just been writing to you, and I gathered up together with the apples a little lesson in the foolishness of officious and hasty criticism. It was this way.

Our baskets being full, and our backs rested, he groaned and said that in another week he must leave for Weimar.

'But you like your work,' said I.

'I detest my work,' he said peevishly. 'I detest teaching. I detest little boys.'

'Then why——' I began, but stopped.

'Why? Why? Because I detest it is no reason I should not do it.'

'Yes, it is.'

'What, and at my age begin another?'

'No, no.'

'You would not have me idle?'

'Yes, I would.'

He stared at me gravely through his spectacles. 'This is unprincipled,' he said.

I laughed. It is years since I have observed that the principled groan a good deal and make discontented criticisms of life, and I don't think I care to be one of them.

'It is,' he persisted, seeing that I only laughed.

'Is it?' said I.

'It is man's lot to work,' said he.

'Is it?' said I.

'Certainly,' said he.

'All day?'

'If he cannot get it done in less time, certainly.'

'Every day?'

'Certainly.'

'All through the years of his life?'

'All through the years of his strength, certainly.'

'What for?'

'My dear young lady, have you been living again on vegetables lately?'

'Why?'

'Your words sound as though your thoughts were watery.'

A nettled silence fell upon me, and while I was arranging how best to convince him of their substance he was shaking his head and saying that it was strange how the most intelligent women are unable really to think. 'Water,' he continued, 'is indispensable in its proper place and good in many others where, strictly, it might be done without. I have nothing to say against watery emotions, watery sentiments, even watery affections, especially in ladies, who would be less charming in proportion as they were more rigid. Ebb and flow, uncertainty, instability, unaccountableness, are becoming to your sex. But in the region of thought, of the intellect, of pure reason, everything should be very dry. The one place, my dear young lady, in which I will endure no water is on the brain.'

I had no answer ready. There seemed to be nothing left to do but to go home. I did go a few steps up the orchard, reflecting on the way men have of telling you you cannot think, or are not logical, at the very moment when you appear to yourself to be most unanswerable—a regrettable habit that at once puts a stop to interesting conversation—and presently, as I was nearing our fence, he called after me. 'Fräulein Rose-Marie,' he called pleasantly.

'Well?' said I, looking down at him over a displeased shoulder.

'Come back.'

'No.'

'Come back and dine with us.'

'No.'

'There is mutton for dinner, and before that a soup full of the concentrated strength of beasts. Up there I know you will eat carrots and stewed apples, and I shall never be able to make you see what I see.'

'Heaven forbid that I ever should.'

'What, you do not desire to be reasonable?'

'I don't choose to argue with you.'

'Have I done anything?'

'You are not logical enough for me,' said I, anxious to be beforehand with the inevitable remark.

'Come, come,' said he, his face crinkling into smiles.

'It's true,' said I.

'Come back and prove it.'

'Useless.'

'You cannot.'

'I will not.'

'It is the same thing.'

I went on up the hill.

'Fräulein Rose-Marie!'

'Well?'

'Come back.'

'No.'

'Come back, and tell me why you think I ought to give up my work and sit for the rest of my days with hanging hands.'

I turned and looked down at him. 'Because,' I said, 'are you not fifty? And is not that high time to begin and get something out of life?'

He adjusted his spectacles, and stared up at me attentively. 'Continue,' he said.

'I look at your life, at all those fifty years of it, and I see it insufferably monotonous.'

'Continue.'

'Dull.'

'Continue.'

'Dusty.'

'Continue.'

'Dreary.'

'Continue.' He nodded his head gently at each adjective and counted them off on his fingers.

'I see it full of ink-spots, dog-eared grammars, and little boys.'

'Continue.'

'It is a constant going over the same ground—in itself a maddening process. No sooner do the boys reach a certain age and proficiency and become slightly more interesting than they go on to somebody else, and you begin again at the beginning with another batch. You teach in a bare-walled room with enormous glaring windows, and the ring of the electric tram-bell in the street below makes the commas in your sentences. You have been doing this every day for thirty years. The boys you taught at first are fathers of families now. The trees in the playground have grown from striplings into big shady things. Everything has gone on, and so have you—but you have only gone on getting drier and more bored.'

'Continue,' said he, smiling.

'Your intelligence,' said I, coming down a little nearer, 'restless at first, and for ever trying to push green shoots through the thick rind of routine——'

'Good. Quite good. Continue.'

'——through to a wider space, a more generous light——'

'Poetic. Quite poetic. My compliments.'

'Thank you. Your intelligence, then, for ever—for ever—you've interrupted me, and I don't know where I'd got to.'

'You had got to my intelligence having green shoots.'

'Oh yes. Well, they're not green now. That's the point I've been stumbling towards. They ought to be if you had taken bigger handfuls of leisure and had not wholly wasted your time drudging. But now they ought to be more than shoots—great trees, in whose shade we all would sit gratefully, and you enjoying free days, with the pleasant memory of free years behind you and the cheerful hope of roomy years to come. And during all that time of your imprisonment in a classroom the world outside went on its splendid way, the seasons filled it with beauty which you were not there to see, the sun shone and warmed other people, the winds blew and made other people's flesh tingle and their blood dance—you, of course, were cramped up with cold feet and a headache—the birds sang to other people tunes of heaven, while in your ears buzzed only the false quantities of reluctant little boys, the delicious rain——'

'Stop, stop. You forget I had to earn a living.'

'Of course you had. But you know you earned your *living* long ago. What you are earning now is much more like your dying—the dying, the atrophy of your soul. What does it matter if your wife has one bonnet less a year, and no silk dress——'

'Do not let her hear you,' he said, glancing round.

'—or if you keep no servant, and have less to eat on Sundays than your neighbours, give no parties, and don't cumber yourselves up with acquaintances who care nothing for you? If you gave up these things you could also give up drudging. You are too old to drudge. You have been too old these twenty years. A man of your brains'—he pretended to look grateful—'who cannot earn enough between twenty and thirty to keep him from the necessity of slaving for the rest of his days is not—is not——'

'Worthy of the name of man?'

'I don't know that that's a great thing,' said I doubtfully.

'Let it pass. It is an accepted ending to a sentence beginning as yours did. And now, my dear young lady, you have preached me a sermon——'

'Not a sermon.'

'Permitted me, then, to be present at a lecture——'

'Not a lecture.'

'Anyhow, held forth on the unworthily puny outer conditions of my existence. Tell me, now, one thing. I concede the ink-spots, the little boys, the monotony, the tram-bells, the regrettable number of years; they are all there, and you with your vivid imagination see them all. But tell me one thing: has it never occurred to you that they are the merest shell, the merest husk and envelopment, and that it is possible that, in spite of them'—his voice grew serious—'my life may be very rich within?'

And you, my friend, tell me another thing. Am I not desperately, hopelessly horrid? Shortsighted? Impertinent? The readiest jumper at conclusions? The most arrogant critic of other people? Rich within. Of course. Hidden with God. That is what I have never seen when I have looked on superciliously from the height of my own idleness at these drudging lives. And see how amazing has been my foolishness, for would not my own life judged from outside, this life here alone with Papa, this restricted, poor, solitary life, my first youth gone, my future without prospects, no distractions, few friends, Papa's affection growing vaguer as he grows older,—would it not, looked at as I have been looking at my neighbour's, seem entirely blank and desolate? Yet how sincerely can I echo what he said—My life is very rich within.

Yours sincerely,

ROSE-MARIE SCHMIDT.

XLIV

Galgenberg, Sept. 16.

DEAR MR ANSTRUTHER,—It is kind of you to want to contradict what I said in my last letter about the outward appearance of my life, but really you know I *am* past my first youth. At twenty-six I cannot pretend to be what is known as a young girl, and I don't want to. Not for anything would I be seventeen or eighteen again. I like to be a woman grown, to have entered into the full possession of whatever faculties I am to have, to know what I want, to look at things in their true proportions. I don't know that eighteen has anything that compensates for that. It is such a rudderless sort of age. It may be more charming to the beholder, but it is not half so nice to the person herself. What is the good of loving chocolate to distraction when it only ends by making you sick? And the joy of a new frock or hat is dashed at once when you meet the superior gorgeousness of some other girl's frock or hat. And parties are often disappointing things. And students, though they are deeply interesting, easily lead to tiresome complications if they admire you, and if they don't that isn't very nice either. Why, even the young man in the cake-shop who used so gallantly to serve us with lemonade and had such wonderful curly eyelashes was not much good really, for he couldn't be invited to tea, and whenever we wanted to look at his eyelashes we had to buy a cake, and cakes are dreadfully expensive for persons who have no money. Yes, it is a silly, tittering, calf-like age, and I am glad it can't come back again. Please do not think that I need comforting because it is gone, or because of any of the other items in the list I gave you. The future looks quite pleasant to me—quite bright and sunny. It is only empty of what people call prospects, by which I take them to mean husbands, but I shall fill it with pigs instead. I have great plans. I see what can be done with even one pig from my neighbour's example, who has dug out a sort of terrace and put a sty on it: simply wonders. And how much more could be done with two. I mean to be a very happy old maid. I shall fix my attention in the mornings on remunerative objects like pigs, and spend beautiful afternoons, quite idle physically but with my soul busy up among the poets. Later on in distant years, when Papa doesn't want me any more, I shall try to find a little house somewhere where it is flat, so that I can have other creatures about me besides bees, which are the only live-stock I can keep here. And you mustn't think I shall not be happy, because I shall. *So happy.* I am happy now, and I mean to be happy then; and when I am very old and have to die I shall be happy about that too. I shall 'lay me down with a will,' as the bravest of your countrymen sang.

Do my plans seem to you selfish? I expect they do. People so easily call those selfish who stand a little aside and look on at life. We have a poet of whom we are proud, but whose fame has not, I think, reached across to England, a rugged, robust poet, not very far below Goethe, a painter on large canvases, best at mighty scenes, perhaps least good in small things, in lyrics, in the things in which Heine was so exquisite; and he for my encouragement has said—

> Bei sich selber fängt man an,
> Da man nicht Allen helfen kann.

Isn't it a nice jingle? The man's name is Hebbel, and he lived round about the forties, and perhaps you know more of him than I do, and I have been arrogant again; but it is a jingle that has often cheered me when I was afraid I ought to be teaching somebody something, or making clothes for somebody, or paying somebody domiciliary visits and talking fluently of the *lieber Gott*. I shrink from these things; and a shrinking visitor, shy and uncertain, cannot be so nice as no visitor at all. Is it very wrong of me? When my conscience says it is—it does not say so often—I try to make up by going into the kitchen and asking Johanna kind questions about her mother. I must say she is rather odd when I do. She not only doesn't meet me halfway, she doesn't come even part of the way. She clatters her saucepans with an energy very like fury, and grows wholly monosyllabic. Yet it is not her stepmother; it is her very own mother, and it ought to be the best way of touching responsive chords in her heart and making her feel I am not merely a mistress but a friend. Once, struck by the way the lids of the saucepans were falling about, I tried her with her father, but the din instantly became so terrific that I was kept silent quite a long time, and when it left off felt instinctively that I had better say something about the weather. I don't think I told you that after that trumpeting Sunday, moved to real compassion by the sufferings of him you call the fiddler man, I took my courage in both hands and told Johanna with the pleasantest of smiles—I dare say it was really a rather ghastly one—that her trumpeter must not again bring his instrument with him when he called. 'It can so very well stay at home,' I explained suavely.

She immediately said she would leave on the first of October.

'But, Johanna!' I cried.

She repeated the formula.

'But, Johanna! How can a clever girl like you be so

unreasonable? He is to visit you as often as before. All we beg is that it shall be done without music.'

She repeated the formula.

'But, Johanna!' I expostulated again—eloquent exclamation, expressing the most varied sentiments.

She once again repeated the formula; and next day I was forced to descend into Jena, shaking an extremely rueful fist at the neighbour's house on the way, and set about searching in the obscurity of a registry office for the pearl we are trying all our lives to find.

This office consists of two rooms, the first filled with servants looking for mistresses, and the second with mistresses looking for servants. A Fräulein of vague age but determined bearing sits at a desk in the second room, and notes in a ledger the requirements of both parties. They are always the same: the would-be mistress, full of a hopefulness that crops up again and again to the end of her days, causing attributes like *fleissig, treu, ehrlich, anständig, arbeitslieb, kinderlieb*, to be written down together with her demands in cooking, starching, and ironing, and often adding the information that though the wages may appear small they are not really so, owing to the unusually superior quality of the treatment; and the would-be maid, briefer because without illusions, dictates her firm resolve to go nowhere where there is cooking, washing, or a baby.

'*Gott, diese Mädchen,*' exclaimed a waiting lady to me as I arrived, hot and ruffled after my long tramp in the sun. I dropped into a chair beside her; and hot and ruffled as I was, she, who had been sitting there hours, was still more so. In her agitation she had cried out to the first human being at hand, the Fräulein at the desk having something too distinctly inhuman about her—strange as a result of her long and intimate intercourse with human beings—to be lightly applied to for sympathy. Then, looking at me again, she cried, 'Why, it is the good Rose-Marie!' And I saw she was an old friend of my stepmother's, Frau Meyer, the wife of one of the doctors at the Lunatic Asylum, who used to come in often while you were with us, and whenever she came in you went out.

'Not married yet?' she asked, as we shook hands, smiling as though the joke were good.

I smiled with an equal conviction of its goodness, and said I was not.

'Not even engaged?'

'Not even engaged,' said I, smiling more broadly, as if infinitely tickled.

'You must be quick,' said she.

I admitted the necessity by a nod.

'You are twenty-six—I know your age because poor Emilie'—Emilie was my stepmother—'was married ten years, and when she married you were sixteen. Twenty-six is a great age for a girl. When I was your age I had already had four children. What do you think of that?'

I didn't know what to think of it, so smiled vaguely, and turning to the waiting machine at the desk began my list. 'Hard-working, clean, honest——'

'Yes, yes, if we could but find such treasures,' interrupted Frau Meyer, with a reverberating sigh. 'Here am I engaged to give the first coffee-party of the season——'

'What, in summer?'

'It is not summer in September. If the weather chooses to pretend it is I cannot help it. It is autumn, and I will no longer endure the want of social gatherings. Invariably I find the time between the last Coffee of spring and the first of autumn almost unendurable. What do you do,

Rose-Marie, up there on that horrible mountain of yours, to pass the time?'

Pass the time? I who am so much afraid of Time's passing me that I try to catch at him as he goes, pull him back, make him creep slowly while I squeeze the full preciousness out of every minute? I gazed at her abstractedly, haunted by the recollection of flying days, days gone so quickly, vanished before I well knew how happy I was being. 'I really couldn't tell you,' I said.

'Hard-working, clean, honest——' read out the Fräulein, reminding me that I was busy.

'Moral,' I dictated, 'able to wash——'

'You will never find one,' interrupted Frau Meyer again. 'At least, never one who is both moral and able to wash. Two good things don't go together with these girls, I find. The trouble I am in for want of one! They are as scarce and as expensive as roses in December. Since April I have had three, and all had to leave by the merest accident— nothing at all to do with the place or me; but the ones in there seem to know there have been three in the time, and make the most extravagant demands. I have been here the whole morning, and am in despair.'

She stopped to fan herself with her handkerchief.

'Able to wash,' I resumed, 'iron, cook, mend—have you any one suitable, Fräulein?'

'Many,' was the laconic answer.

'I'm afraid we cannot give more than a hundred and sixty marks,' said I.

'Pooh,' said Frau Meyer; and there was a pause in the scratching of the pen.

'But there are no children,' I continued.

The pen went on more glibly. Frau Meyer fanned herself harder.

'And only two *Herrschaften*.'

The pen skimmed over the paper.

'We live up—we live up on the Galgenberg.'

The pen stopped dead.

'You will never find one who will go up there,' cried Frau Meyer, triumphantly. 'I need not fear your taking a good one away from me. They will not leave the town.'

The Fräulein rang a bell and called out a name. 'It is another one for you, Frau Doctor,' she said; and a large young lady came in from the other room. 'The general servant Fräulein Ottilie Krummacher—Frau Doctor Meyer,' introduced the Fräulein. 'I think you may suit each other.'

'It is time you showed me some one who will,' groaned Frau Meyer. 'Six have I already interviewed, and the demands of all are enough to make my mother, who was Frau Gutsbesitzer Grosskopf of the Grosskopfs of Grosskopfsecke, born Knoblauch, and a lady of the most exact knowledge in household matters, turn in her grave.'

'Town?' asked the large girl, quickly, hardly allowing Frau Meyer to get to a full stop, and obviously callous as to the Grosskopfs of Grosskopfsecke.

'Yes, yes—here, overlooking the marketplace and the interesting statue of the electoral founder of the University. No way to go, therefore, to market. Enlivening scenes constantly visible from the windows——'

'Which floor?'

'Second. Shallow steps, and a nice balustrade. Really hardly higher than the first floor, or even than an ordinary ground floor, the rooms being very low.'

'Washing?'

'Done out of the house. Except the smallest, fewest trifles such as—such as—ahem. The ironing, dear Fräulein, I will do mostly myself. There are the shirts, you know—husbands are particular——'

'How many?'

'How many?' echoed Frau Meyer. 'How many what?'

'Husbands.'

'*Aber*, Fräulein,' expostulated the secretary.

'She said husbands,' said the large girl. 'Shirts, then—how many? It's all the same.'

'All the same?' cried Frau Meyer, who adored her husband.

'In the work it makes.'

'But, dear Fräulein, the shirts are not washed at home.'

'But ironed.'

'I iron them.'

'And I heat the irons and keep up the fire to heat them with.'

'Yes, yes,' cried Frau Meyer, affecting the extreme pleasure of one who has just received an eager assurance, 'so you do.'

The large girl stared. 'Cooking?' she inquired, after a slightly stony pause.

'Most of that I will do myself, also. The Herr is very particular. I shall only need a little—quite a little assistance. And think of all the new and excellent dishes you will learn to make.'

The girl waved this last inducement aside as unworthy of consideration. 'Number of persons in the household?'

Frau Meyer coughed before she could answer. 'Oh,' said she, 'oh, well—there is my husband, and naturally myself, and then there are—there are—are you fond of children?' she ended hastily.

The girl fixed her with a suspicious eye. 'It depends how many there are,' she said cautiously.

Frau Meyer got up and leaned over the Fräulein at the desk, and whispered into her impassive ear.

The Fräulein shook her head. 'I am afraid it is no use,' she said.

Frau Meyer whispered again. The Fräulein looked up, and, fastening her eyes on a point somewhere below the large girl's chin, said, 'The wages are good.'

'What are they?' asked the girl.

'Considering the treatment you will receive——' the girl's eyes again became suspicious—'they are excellent.'

'What are they?'

'Everything found, and a hundred and eighty marks a year.'

The girl turned and walked towards the door.

'Stop! Stop!' cried Frau Meyer desperately. 'I cannot see you throw away a good place with so little preliminary reflection. Have you considered that there would be no trudging to market, and consequently you will only require half the boots and stockings and skirts those poor girls have to buy who live up in the villas that look so grand and pretend to give such high wages?'

The girl paused.

'And no steep stairs to climb, laden with heavy baskets? And hardly any washing—hardly any washing, I tell you!' she almost shrieked in her anxiety. 'And no cooking to speak of? And every Sunday—mind, *every* Sunday evening free? And I never scold, and my husband never scolds, and with a hundred and eighty marks a year there is nothing a clever girl cannot buy. Why, it is an ideal, a delightful place—one at which I would jump if I were a girl, and this lady'—indicating me—'would jump, too, would you not, Rose-Marie?'

The girl wavered. 'How many children are there?' she asked.

'Children? Children? Angels, you mean. They are perfect

angels, so good and well behaved—are they not, Rose-Marie? Fit to go at once to heaven—*unberufen*—without a day's more training, so little would they differ in manner when they got there from angels who have been used to it for years. You are fond of children, Fräulein, I am sure. Naturally you are. I see it in your nice face. No nice Fräulein is not. And these, I tell you, are such unusual——'

'How many are there?'

'*Ach Gott*, there are only six, and so small still that they can hardly be counted as six—six of the dearest——'

The girl turned on her heel. 'I cannot be fond of six,' she said; and went out with the heavy tread of finality.

Frau Meyer looked at me. 'There now,' she said, in tones of real despair.

'It is very tiresome,' said I, sympathizing the more acutely that I knew my turn was coming next.

'Tiresome? It is terrible. In two days I have my Coffee, and no—and no—and no——' She burst into tears, hiding her face from the dispassionate stare of the Fräulein at the desk in her handkerchief, and trying to conceal her sobs by a ceaseless blowing of her nose.

'I am so sorry,' I murmured, touched by this utter melting.

An impulse seized me on which I instantly acted. 'Take Johanna,' I cried. 'Take her for that day. She will at least get you over that. She is excellent at a party, and knows all about Coffees. I'll send her down early, and you keep her as late as you like. She would enjoy the outing, and we can manage quite well for one day without her.'

'Is that—is that the Johanna you had in the Rauchgasse?'

'Yes—trained by my stepmother—really good in an emergency.'

Frau Meyer flung her arms round my neck. '*Ach danke, danke, Du liebes, gutes Kind!*' she cried, embracing me with a warmth that showed me what heaps of people she must have asked to her party.

And I, after the first flush of doing a good deed was over and cool reflection had resumed its sway, which it did by the time I was toiling up the hill on the way home after having been unanimously rejected as mistress by the assembled maidens, I repented; for was not Johanna now my only hope? 'Frau Meyer,' whispered Reflection in my despondent ear, 'will engage her to go to her permanently on the 1st, and she will go because of the twenty marks more salary. You have been silly. Of course she would have stayed with you with a little persuasion rather than have to look for another place and spend her money at a registry-office. It is not likely, however, that she will refuse a situation costing her nothing.'

But see how true it sometimes is that virtue is rewarded. Johanna went down as I had promised, and worked all day for Frau Meyer. She was given a thaler as a present, as much cake and coffee as she could consume, and received the offer of a permanent engagement when she should leave us. This she told me standing by my bedside late that night, the candle in her hand lighting up her heated, shining face, and hair dishevelled by exertion. 'But,' said she, 'Fräulein Rose-Marie, not for the world would I take the place. Such a restless lady, such a nervous gentleman, such numbers of spoilt and sprawling children. If I had not been there today and beheld it from the inside I would have engaged myself to go. But after this'—she waved the candle—'never.'

'What are you going to do, then, Johanna?' I asked, thinking wistfully of the four years we had passed together.

'Stay here,' she announced defiantly.

I put my arms round her neck and kissed her.

Yours sincerely,

ROSE-MARIE SCHMIDT.

XLV

DEAR MR ANSTRUTHER,—Today I went down to Jena with the girl from next door, who wanted to do such mild shopping as Jena is prepared for, mild shopping suited to mild purses, and there I drifted into the bookshop in the market-place where I so often used to drift, and there I found a book dealing with English poetry from Chaucer onwards, with pictures of the poets who had written it. But before I go on about that—and you'll be surprised at the amount I have to say—I must explain the girl next door. I don't think I ever told you that there is one. The neighbour let his house just before he left, and let it unexpectedly well, the people taking the upper part of it for a whole year, and this is their daughter. The neighbour went off jubilant to his little inky boys.

'See,' said he, at parting, 'my life actually threatens to become rich without as well as within.'

'Don't,' I murmured, turning as hot as people do when they are reminded of past foolishness.

The new neighbours have been here ten days, and I made friends at once with the girl over the fence. She saw me gathering together into one miserable haycock the September grass Johanna and I had been hacking at in turns with a sickle for the last week, and stood watching me with so evident an interest that at last I couldn't help smiling at her.

'This is our crop for the winter,' I said, pointing to the haycock; 'I protest I have seen many a mole-hill bigger.'

'It isn't much,' said the girl.

'No,' I agreed, raking busily.

'Have you a cow?' she asked.

'No.'

'A pig?'

'No.'

'No animals?'

'Bees.'

The girl was silent; then she said bees were not animals.

'But they're live-stock,' I said. 'They're the one link that connects us with farming.'

'What do you make hay for, then?'

'Only to keep the grass short, and then we try to imagine it's a lawn.'

Raking, I came a little nearer; and so I saw she had been, quite recently, crying.

I looked at her more attentively. She was pretty, with the prettiness of twenty; round and soft, fair and smooth. She had on an elaborately masculine shirt, and high stiff collar, and tie, and pin, and belt; and from under the edge of the hard straw hat, tilted up at the back by masses of burnished coils of hair, I saw a pulpy red mouth, the tip of an indeterminate nose, and two unhappy eyes, tired with crying.

'How early to begin,' I said.

'Begin what?'

'It's not nine yet. Do you always get your crying done by breakfast-time?'

She flushed all over her face.

'Forgive me,' I said, industriously raking. 'I'm a rude person.'

The girl was silent for a few moments, considering, I suppose, whether she should turn her back on the impertinent stranger once and for all, or forgive the indiscretion and make friends.

Well, she made friends. She and I, alone up on the hill, the only creatures of anything like the same age, sure to see each other continually in the forests, on the road, over the fence, certainly we were bound either to a tiresome system of pretending to be unaware of each other's existence or to be friends. We are friends. It is the wisest thing to be at all times. In ten days we have become fast friends, and after the first six she left off crying.

Now I'll tell you why we have done it so quickly. It is not, as perhaps you know, my practice to fall easily on the stranger's neck. I am too lumbering, too slow, too acutely conscious of my shortcomings for that; really too dull and too awkward for anything but a life almost entirely solitary. But this girl has lately been in love. It is the common fate. It happens to us all. That in itself would not stir me to friendship. The man, however, in defiance of German custom, so strong on this point that the breaking of it makes a terrific noise, after being publicly engaged to her, after letting things go so far that the new flat was furnished, and the wedding-guests bidden, said he was afraid he didn't love her enough, and gave her up.

When she told me that my heart went out to her with a rush. I shall not stop to explain why, but it did rush, and from that moment I felt that I must put my arms round her, I, the elder and quieter, take her by the hand, help her to dry her poor silly eyes, pet her and make her happy again. And really after six days there was no more crying, and for the last three she has been looking at life with something of the critical indifference that lifts one over so many tiresome bits of the road. Unfortunately her mother doesn't like me. Don't you think it's dreadful of her not to?

She fears I am emancipated, and knows that I am Schmidt. If I were a Wedel, or an Alvensleben, or a Schulenburg, or of any other ancient noble family, even an obscure member of its remotest branch, she would consider my way of living and talking merely as a thing to be smiled at with kind indulgence. But she knows that I am Schmidt. Nothing I can say or do, however sweet and sane, can hide that horrid fact. And she knows that my father is a careless child of nature, lamentably unimpressible by birth and office; that my mother was an Englishwoman with a name inspiring little confidence; and that we let ourselves go to an indecent indifference to appearances, not even trying to conceal that we are poor. How useless it is to be pleasant and pretty—I really have been very pleasant to her, and the daughter kindly tells me I am pretty—if you are both Schmidt and poor. Though I speak with the tongues of angels and have no family it avails me nothing. If I had family and no charity I would get on much better in the world, in defiance of St Paul. Frau von Lindeberg would take me to her heart, think me distinguished where now she thinks me odd, think me witty where now she thinks me bold, listen to my speeches, laugh at my sallies, be interested in my gardening and in my efforts to live without meat; but here I am, burning, I hope, with charity, with love for my neighbours, with ready sympathy, eager friendliness, desire to be of use, and it all avails me nothing because my name is Schmidt.

It is the first time I have been brought into daily contact with our nobility. In Jena there were very few: rare bright spots here and there on the sober background of academic middle class; little stars whose shining even from a distance made us blink. Now I see them every day, and find them very chilly and not in the least dazzling. I no longer blink. Perhaps Frau von Lindeberg feels that I do not, and cannot, forgive an unblinking Schmidt. But really, now, these pretensions are very absurd. The free blood of the Watsons surges within me at the sight of them. I think of things like Albion's daughters, and Britannia ruling waves, and I feel somehow that it is a proud thing to be partly Watson and to have had progenitors who lived in a house called The Acacias in a street called Plantagenet Road, which is what the Watsons did. What claims have these Lindebergs to the breathless, nay, sprawling respect they apparently demand? Here is a retired Colonel who was an officer all his life, and, not clever enough to go on to the higher military positions, was obliged to retire at fifty. He belongs to a good family, and married some one of slightly better birth than his own. She was a Freiin—Free Lady—von Dammerlitz, a family, says Papa, large, unpleasant, and mortgaged. It has given Germany no great warriors or statesmen. Its sons have all been officers who did not turn that corner round which the higher honours lie, and its daughters either did not marry at all, being portionless, or married impossible persons, said Papa, such as——

'Such as?' I inquired, expecting to hear they married postmen.

'Pastors, my dear,' said Papa, smiling.

'Pastors?' I said, surprised, pastors having seemed to me, who view them from their own level, eminently respectable and desirable as husbands.

'But not from the Dammerlitz point of view, my dear,' said Papa.

'Oh,' said I, trying to imagine how pastors would look seen from that.

Well, here are these people freezing us into what they consider our proper place whenever we come across them, taking no pains to hide what undesirable beings we are in their sight, staring at Papa's hat in eloquent silence when it is more than usually tilted over one ear, running eyes that chill my blood over my fustian clothes—I'm not sure what fustian is, but I'm quite sure my clothes are made of it— oddly deaf when we say anything, oddly blind when we meet anywhere unless we actually run into them, here they are, doing all these things every day with a repeated gusto, and with no reason whatever that I can see to support their pretensions. Is it so wonderful to be a *von?* For that is all, look as I will, that I can see they have to go on. They are poor, as the retired officer invariably is, and they spend much time pretending they are not. They know nothing; he has spent his best years preoccupied with the routine of his calling, which leaves no room for anything approaching study or interest in other things, she in bringing up her son, also an officer, and in taking her daughter to those parties in Berlin that so closely resemble, I gather from the girl Vicki's talk, the parties in Jena—a little wider, a little more varied, with more cups and glasses, and with, of course, the chance we do not have in Jena of seeing some one quite new, but on the whole the same. He is a solemn, elderly person in a black-rimmed *pince-nez*, dressed in clothes that give one the impression of always being black. He vegetates as completely as any one I have ever seen or dreamed of. Prolonged coffee in the morning, prolonged newspaper-reading, and a tortoise-like turn in the garden kill his mornings. Dinner, says Vicki, kills another hour and a half; then there is what we call the Dinner Sleep on the sofa in his darkened room, and that brings him to coffee-time. They sit over the cups till Vicki wants to scream, at least she wants to since she has known me, she says; up to then, after her miserable affair, she sat as sluggishly as the others, but huddled while they were straight, and red-eyed, which they

172

were not. After coffee the parents walk up the road to a certain point, and walk back again. Then comes the evening paper, which he reads till supper-time, and after supper he smokes till he goes to bed.

'Why, he's hardly alive at all,' I said to Vicki, when she described this existence.

She shrugged her shoulders. 'It's what they all do,' she said, 'all the retired. I've seen it a hundred times in Berlin. They're old, and they never can start anything fresh.'

'We won't be like that when we're old, will we?' I said, gazing at her wide-eyed, struck as by a vision.

She gazed back into my eyes, misgiving creeping into hers.

'Sleep, and eat, and read the paper?' she murmured.

'Sleep, and eat, and read the paper?' I echoed.

And we stared at each other in silence, and the far-away dim years seemed to catch up what we had said, and mournfully droned back, 'Sleep, and eat, and read the paper. . . .'

But what is to be done with girls of good family who do not marry and have no money? They can't go governessing, and indeed it is a dreary trade. Vicki has learned nothing except a little cooking and other domestic drudgery, only of use if you have a house to drudge in and a husband to drudge for; of those pursuits that bring in money and make you independent and cause you to flourish and keep green and lusty she knows nothing. If I had a daughter I would bring her up with an eye fixed entirely on a husbandless future. She should be taught some trade as carefully as any boy. Her head should be filled with as much learning as it would conveniently hold side by side with a proper interest in ribbons. I would spend my days impressing her with the gloriousness of independence, of having her time entirely at her own disposal, her life free and clear, the world open before her, as open as it was to Adam and Eve when they turned their backs once and for all on the cloying sweetness of Paradise, and far more interesting than it was to them, for it would be full of inhabitants eager to give her the hearty welcome always awaiting those rare persons, the cheery and the brave.

'Oh,' sighed Vicki, when with great eloquence and considerable elaboration I unfolded these views, 'how beautiful!'

Papa was nearer the open window under which we were sitting than I had thought, for he suddenly popped out his head.

'It is a merciful thing, Rose-Marie,' he said, 'that you have no daughter.'

We both jumped.

'She would be a most dreary young female,' he went on, smiling down as from a pulpit on our heads, and wiping his spectacles. 'Offspring continually goaded and galvanized by a parent, hammered upon, chiselled, beaten out flat——'

'Dear me, Papachen,' I murmured.

'Beaten out flat,' said Papa, waving my interruption aside with his spectacles, 'by the dead weight of opinions already stale, the victims of a system, the subjects of an experiment, the prisoners of prejudice, are bound either to flare into rank rebellion on the first opportunity or to grow continually drearier and more conspicuously stupid.'

Vicki stared first up at Papa, then at me, her soft, crumpled sort of mouth twisted into troubled surprise.

Papa leaned further out and hit the windowsill with his hand for all the world like a parson hitting his pulpit's cushion.

'One word,' he said, 'one word of praise or blame, one

single word from an outsider will have more effect upon your offspring than years of trouble taken by yourself, mountains of doctrine preached by you, rivers of good advice, oceans of exhortations, cautions as numerous as Abraham's posterity, well known to have been as numerous as the sea sand, private prayers, and public admonition.'

And he disappeared with a jerk.

'*Ach*,' said Vicki, much impressed.

Papa popped out his head again. 'You may believe me, Rose-Marie,' he said.

'I do, Papachen,' said I.

'You have to thank me for much.'

'And I do,' said I, heartily, smiling up at him.

'But for nothing more than for leaving you free to put forth such shoots as your nature demanded in whatever direction your instincts propelled you.' And he disappeared and shut the window.

Vicki looked at me doubtfully. 'You said beautiful things,' she said, 'and he said just the opposite. Which is true?'

'Both,' said I, promptly, determined not to be outdone as a prophet by Papa.

Poor Vicki. It is so hard to have life turned into a smudge when one is only twenty. She adored this man, was so proud of him, so proud of herself for being chosen by him. She grew, in the year during which they were engaged, into a woman, and can never now retrace her steps back to that fairy place of sunshine and carelessness in which we so happily wander if we are left alone for years and years after we are supposed to be grown up. Do you realize what a blow in the face she has received, as well as in her unfortunate little heart? All her vanities, without which a girl is but a poor thing, shrivelled up, her self-respect gone, her conceit, if there was any, and I suppose there was because there always is, gone headlong after it. A betrothal here is almost as binding and quite as solemn as a marriage. It is announced in the papers. It is abundantly celebrated. And the parents on both sides fall on each other's necks and think highly of one another till the moment comes for making settlements. The Lindebergs spent all they had laid by and borrowed more to buy the trousseau and furnish the house. Vicki cried bitterly when she talked of her table-napkins. She says there were twelve dozen in twelve different patterns, and each twelve was tied up with a pink ribbon fastened by a buckle and a bow. They had to be sold again at a grievous loss, and the family fled from Berlin and the faces of their acquaintances, faces crooked with the effort to sympathize when what they really wanted to do, says Vicki, was to smile, and came to this cheap place where they can sit in obscurity darning up the holes in their damaged fortunes. Frau von Lindeberg, who has none of the torment of rejected love to occupy her feelings and all the bitterness of the social and financial blow, cannot help saying hard things to Vicki, things pointed and poisoned with reproaches that sometimes almost verge on taunts. The man was a good *parti* for Vicki; little money, but much promise for the future, a good deal older than herself and already brilliant as an officer; and during the engagement the satisfied mother overflowed, as mothers will, with love for the creditable daughter.

'It was so nice,' said Vicki, dolefully sniffing. 'She seemed to love me almost as much as she loves my brother. I was so happy. I had so much. Then everything went at once. Mamma can't bear to think that no one will ever want to marry me now, because I have been engaged.'

Well, love is a cruel, horrible thing. Hardly ever do both the persons love with equal enthusiasm, and if they do, what is the use? It is all bound to end in smoke and nothingness, put out by the steady drizzle of marriage. And for the others, for the masses of people who do not love equally, of whom one half is at a miserable disadvantage, at the mercy absolutely of the other half, what is there but pain in the end? And yet—and yet it is a pretty thing in its beginnings, a sweet, darling thing. But, like a kitten, all charm and delicious ways at first, innocent, soft, enchanting, it turns into a cat with appalling rapidity and cruelly claws you. I'd like to know if there's a single being on earth so happy and so indifferent that he has not got hidden away beneath a brave show of clothes and trimmings the mark of Love's claws. And I think most of the clawings are so ferocious that they are for a long time ghastly tears that open and bleed again; and when with years they slowly dry up there is always the scar, red and terrible, that makes you wince if by any chance it is touched. That is what I think. What do you think?

Good-bye.

No, don't tell me what you think. I don't want to know.

XLVI

Galgenberg, Sept. 24.

DEAR MR ANSTRUTHER,—Yesterday I was so much
absorbed by Vicki's woes that I never got to what I really
wanted to write about. It's that book I found in the Jena
bookshop. It was second-hand and cheap, and I bought it,
and it has unkindly revenged itself by playing havoc with
my illusions. It is a collection of descriptions of what is
known of the lives of the English poets, beginning with
Chaucer, who is luckily too far away to provide much tattle,
and coming down the centuries growing bigger with gossip
as it comes, till it ends with Rossetti and Fitzgerald and
Stevenson. Each poet has his portrait. It was for that I bought
it. I cannot tell you how eagerly I looked at them. At last
I was going to see what Wordsworth looked like, and
Coleridge, and Keats, and Shelley. One of my dreams has
been to go to the National Portrait Gallery of yours in
London, described in an old *Baedeker* I once saw, and gaze
at the faces of those whose spirits I know so well. Now I
don't want to. Can you imagine what it is like, what an
extremely blessed state it is, only to have read the works of
a poet, the filtered-out best of him, and to have lived so far
from his country and from biographies or collections of his
letters that all gossip about his private life and criticisms of
his morals are unknown to you? Milton, Wordsworth, Keats,
Shelley, Burns, have been to me great teachers, great
examples, before whose shining image, built up out of the
radiant materials their works provided, I have spent glorious
hours in worship. Not a cloud, not a misgiving has dimmed

my worship. We need altars—anyhow, we women do—and they were mine. I have not been able to be religious in the ordinary sense, and they have taken the place of religion. Our own best poets, Goethe, Schiller, Heine, and the rest, do not appeal to me in the same way. Goethe is wonderful, but he leaves you sitting somehow in a cold place from which you call out at intervals with conviction that he is immense the while you wish he would keep the feet of your soul a little warmer. Schiller beats his patriotic drum, his fine eyes rolling continually towards the gallery, too unintermittently for perfect delight. Heine the exquisite, the cunning worker in gems, the stringer of pearls on frailest golden threads, is too mischievous, too malicious, to be set up in a temple; and then you can't help laughing at his extraordinary gift for maddening the respectable, at the extraordinary skill and neatness with which he deposits poison in their tenderest places, and how can he worship who is being made to laugh? If I knew little about our poets' lives—inevitably I know more than I want to—I still would feel the same. There is, I think, in their poetry nothing heavenly. It is true, I bless God for them, thank Him for having let them live and sing, for having given us such a noble heritage, but I can't go all the way Papa goes, and melt in a bath of rapture whenever Goethe's name is mentioned. I remember what you said about Goethe. It has not influenced me. I do think you were wrong. But I do, too, think that everything really heavenly in our nation, everything purely inspired, manifestly immortal, has gone, not into our poetry but into our music. That has absorbed our whole share of divine fire, and left our poets nothing but the cool and conscious exercise of their intellects.

Well, I am preaching. I would make a very arrogant parson, wouldn't I, laying down the law more often than the prophets from that safe citadel a pulpit; but please have patience, for I want you to comfort me. The book really has made me unhappy. It is the kind of book you must go on reading—angry, rebelling at every page, but never leaving it till you've reached the last word. Then you throw it as hard as you can into the furthest corner of the room, and shake yourself as a dog does come up out of muddy water, and think to shake it off as easily as he does his mud; but you can't, because it has burned itself into your soul. I don't suppose you will understand what I feel. When a person possesses very few things those few things are terribly precious. See the mother of the only child, and compare her conduct, when it coughs, to the conduct of the mother of six, all coughing. See how one agonizes; and see with what serenity the other brings out her bottle of mixture and pours it calmly down her children's throats. Well, I'm like the first mother, and you are like the second. I expect you knew long ago, and have never minded knowing, the littlenesses of my gods; but I, I felt as unsettled while I read about them, as uneasy, as fidgety, as frightened as a horse being driven by somebody cruel, which knows that every minute the lash will come down in some fresh place. Think: I knew nothing about Harriet Westbrook and her tragic life and death; I had never heard of Emilia Viviani; of Mary; of her whose name was Eliza, but who soared aloft in the sunshine of Shelley's admiration re-christened Portia, only presently to descend once more into the font and come out luridly as the Brown Demon. I never knew that Keats loved somebody called Brawne, and that she was unwilling, that she saw little in him, in Endymion the god-like, the divinely gifted, and that he was so persistent, so unworthily persistent, that the only word I can find that at all describes it is the German *zappelnd*. I had never heard of Jean Armour, of the headlong descent from being 'him who walked in glory and in joy, Following his plough along the mountainside' to hopeless black years spent in public-houses at the beck and call—think of it, think of the divine spirit forced to it by its body—of any one who would pay for a drink. I never knew about Coleridge's opium, or that to Carlyle he appeared as a helpless Psyche overspun with Church of England cobwebs, as a weak, diffusive, weltering, ineffectual man. I never knew that Wordsworth's greeting was a languid handful of numb, unresponsive fingers, that his speech was prolix, thin, endlessly diluted. I never knew that Milton had three wives, that the first one ran away from him a month after their marriage, that he was hard to his daughters, so hard that they wished him dead. All these things I never knew; and for years I have been walking with glorious spirits, and have been fed on honey-dew, and drunk the milk of Paradise. When first I saw Wordsworth's portrait I turned cold. Don't laugh; I did actually turn cold. He had been so much in my life. I had pictured him so wonderful. Calm; beautiful, with the loftiest kind of beauty; faintly frosty at times, and detached, yet gently cheery and always dignified. It is the picture from a portrait by some one called Hancock. Very bitterly do I dislike Hancock. It is a profile. It would, if I had seen it in the flesh, completely have hidden from my silly short sight the inner splendours. I'm afraid—oh, I'm afraid, and I shiver with shame to think it—that I would have regarded him only as an elderly gentleman of irreproachable character, out of whose way it was as well to get because he showed every sign of being a bore. Will you think me irretrievably silly when I tell you that I cried over that picture? For one dreadful moment I stared at it in startled horror; then I banged the book to and fled up into the forest to cry. There was a smugness—but no, I won't think of it. I'll upset all my theories about the face being the mirror of the soul. It can't be. If it is, *Peter Bell* and *The Thorn* are accounted for; but who shall account for the bleak nobility, the communings with nature on lofty heights in the light of setting suns? Or, when he comes down nearer, for that bright world he unlocks of things dear to memory, of home, of childhood, of quiet places, of calm affections? And for the tenderness with which it is done? And for its beautiful, simple goodness?

Coleridge's picture was another disillusionment, but not so great a shock, because I have loved him less. He was so rarely inspired. I don't think you need more than the fingers of one hand for the doing of sums with Coleridge's inspirations. Still, it saddened me to be told he was a helpless Psyche. I didn't like to hear about his cobwebs. I hated being forced to know of his weakness, of his wasted life growing steadily dingier the farther he travelled from that East that had seen him set out so bright with morning radiance. Really, the world would be a peaceful place if we could only keep quiet about each other's weak points. Why are we so restless till we have pulled down, belittled, besmudged? You'll say that without a little malice talk would grow very dull; you'll tell me it is the salt, the froth, the sparkle, the ginger in the ginger-beer, the mustard in the sandwich. But you must admit that it becomes only terrible when it can't leave the few truly great spirits alone, when it must somehow drag them down to our lower level, pointing out—in writing, so that posterity too shall have no illusions—the spots on the sun, the weak places in the armour, and pushing us, who want to be left alone praying in the forecourt of the temple, down the area steps into the kitchen. Two nights and two days have I spent feverishly with that book. I dare not hope that I shall forget it. I have never yet forgotten undesirable, bad things. Now, when I take my poets up with me into the forest, and sit on one of those dusky pine-grown slopes where the light is subdued to a mysterious grey green and the world is quieted into a listening silence, and far away below the roofs of Jena glisten in the sun, and the white butterflies, like white flowers come to life, flutter after each other across the blue curtain of heat that hangs beyond the trees,—now, when I open them and begin to read the noble, familiar words, will not those other words, those anecdotes, those personal descriptions, those suggestions, those buttonholings, leer at me between the lines? Shall I, straining my ears after the music, not be shown now for ever only the instrument, and how pitifully the ivory has come off the keys? Shall I, hungering after my spiritual food, not have pushed upon my notice, so that I am forced to look, the saucepan, tarnished and not quite clean, in which it was cooked? Please don't tell me you can't understand. Try to imagine yourself in my place. Come out of that gay world of yours where you are talking or being talked to all day long, and suppose yourself Rose-Marie Schmidt, alone, in Jena, on a hill, with books. Suppose yourself for hours and hours every day of your life with nothing particular that you must do, that you have no shooting, no hunting, no newspapers, no novels. Suppose you are passionately fond of reading, and that of all reading you most love poetry. Suppose you have inherited from a mother who loved them as much as you do a precious shelf-full of the poets, cheap editions, entirely free from the blight of commentaries, foot-notes, and introductory biographies. And suppose these books in the course of years have become your religion, your guide, the source of your best thoughts and happiest moments;—would you look on placidly while some one scrawled malicious truths between their lines? No, you would not. You would feel as I do. Think what the writers are to me, how I have built up their personalities entirely out of the materials they gave me in their work. They never told me horrid things about themselves. Their spirits, which alone they talked about, were serene and white. I knew Milton was blind, because he chose beautifully to tell me so. I knew he must have been an appreciative and regretful husband, because no husband who did not appreciate and regret would go so far as to talk of his deceased wife as his late espoused saint. I knew he was a tender friend, a friend capable of deepest love and sorrow, for, in spite of Johnson's 'It is not to be considered as the effusion of real passion,' I was convinced by the love and sorrow of Lycidas. I knew he was a man whose spirit was dissolved continually into the highest ecstasies, who lived with all heaven before his eyes,—briefly, I said Amen to Wordsworth's 'His soul was like a star, and dwelt apart.' And now a series of sordid little pictures rises up before me and chokes my Amen. I cannot bear to think of him having two or three olives for supper and a little cold water, and then being cross to his daughters. Of course he must be cross on such a supper. I can't conceive it kind to drill the daughters so strictly in languages they did not understand that they could read them aloud to him with extraordinary correctness. I shrink from the thought of the grumbling there was in that house of heavenly visions, grumbling and squabbling stamped out, it is true, by the heavy parental foot wherever noticed, but smouldering on from one occasion to the other. I cannot believe—I wish I could—that a child will dislike a parent without cause; the cause may be small things, a series of trifles each of little moment, snubs too often repeated, chills too often applied, stern looks, short words, sarcasms,—and these, as you and I both know, are quite ordinary dulnesses, often daily ingredients of family life; but they sit with a strange and upsetting grace on the poet of Paradise, and I would give anything never to have heard of them.

And then you know I loved Fitzgerald. He had one of my best altars. You remember you read *Omar Khayyam* twice aloud to me—once in the spring (it was the third of April, a sudden hot day, blue and joyous, slipped in to show God had not forgotten us between weeks of hopeless skies and icy winds) and once last September, that afternoon we drifted down the river past the town, away from houses, and people, and work, and lessons, out to where the partridges scuttled across the stubble and all the world was golden. (That was the eleventh of September; I am rather good, you see, at dates.) Well, now I call him Fitz, and laugh at the description of him going about Suffolk lanes in a battered tall hat tied on in windy weather by a handkerchief, and trailing behind him, instead of clouds of glory, a shawl of green and black plaid. It isn't, of course, in any way a bad thing to trail shawls after you on country walks; there is nothing about it or him that shocks or grieves; he is very lovable. But I don't want to laugh. I don't want to call him Fitz. He is one of the gods in my temple, a place from which I rigorously exclude the sense of humour. I don't like gods who are amusing. I cannot worship and laugh simultaneously. I know that laughter is good, and I know that even derision in small quantities is as wholesome as salt; but I like to laugh and deride outside holy places, and not be forced to do it while I am on my knees.

Now, don't say what on earth does the woman want, because it seems to me so plain. What the woman wants is that present and future poets should wrap themselves sternly in an impenetrable veil of anonymity. They won't, but she can go on praying that they will. They won't, because of the power of the passing moment, because of the pleasantness of praise, of recognition, of personal influence, and, I suppose, but I'm not sure, of money. Do you remember that merry rhymer Prior, how he sang

> 'Tis long ago
> Since gods came down incognito?

Well, I wish with all my heart they had gone on doing it a little longer. He wasn't, I think, deploring what I deplore, the absence of a sense for the anonymous in gods, of a sense of the dignity of separation, of retirement, of mystery, wherever there is even one spark of the Divine; I think he thought they had all been, and that neither incognito nor in any other form would they appear again. He implied, and so joined himself across the centuries to the Walrus and the Carpenter, that there were no gods to come. Well, he has been dead over a hundred and eighty years, and they have simply flocked since then. I'd like to write the great names on this page, the names of the poets, first and greatest of the gods, to raise it to dignity and confound the ghost of Prior, but I won't out of consideration for you.

Does not my enthusiasm, my mountain energy, make you groan with the deadly fatigue of him who has to listen and cannot share? I'll leave off. My letter is growing unbecomingly fat. The air up here is so bracing that my very unhappinesses seem after all full of zest, very vocal, healthy griefs, really almost enjoying themselves. I'll go back to my pots. I'm busy today, though you mightn't think it, making apple jelly out of our very own apples. I'll go back to my pots and forget—no, I won't make a feeble joke I was just going to make, because of what I know your face would look like when you read it. After all, I believe I'm more than a little bit frightened of you.

Yours sincerely,
ROSE-MARIE SCHMIDT.

XLVII

Galgenberg, Sept. 30.

DEAR MR ANSTRUTHER,—How nice of you to be so kind,
to write so consolingly, to be so patient in explaining where
I am thinking wrong. I burned the book in the kitchen
fire, and felt great satisfaction in clearing the house of its
presence. You are right; I have no concern with the body
of a poet—all my concern is with his soul, and the two
shall be severely separated. I am glad you agree with me
that poets should be anonymous, but you seem to have even
less hope that they ever will be than I have. At least, I pray
that they may; you apparently take no steps whatever to
bring it about. You say that experience teaches that we must
not expect too much of gods; that the possible pangs of
posterity often leave them cold; that they are blind to the
merits of bushels, and discern neither honour nor profit
in the use of those vessels of extinguishment; you fear that
they will not change, and you exhort me to see to it
that their weakness shall not be an occasion for my
stumbling. That is very sensible advice. But before your kind
letter came a few fresh autumn mornings had cleared a
good deal of my first dejection away. If the gods won't hide
themselves I can, after all, shut my eyes. If I may not rejoice
in the divine in them with undistracted attention I will try
at least to get all the warmth I can from its burning. And
I can imitate my own dainty and diligent bees, and take
care to be absorbed only in their honey. You make me
ashamed of my folly in thinking I could never read Burns
again now that I know about his sins. I did secretly think

188

so. I was sure of it. I felt quite sick to see him tumbled from his altar into the mud. Your letter shows me that once again I have been foolish. Why, it has verged on idiocy. I myself have laughed at people in Jena, strictly pious people, who will not read Goethe, who have a personally vindictive feeling against him because of his different love-affairs, and I have listened astonished to the fury with which the proposal of a few universal-minded persons to give Heine a statue was opposed, and to the tone almost of hatred with which one man whenever his name is mentioned calls out *Schmutzfink*. About our poets I have been from the beginning quite sane. But yours were somehow more sacred to me; sacred, I suppose, because they were more mysterious, more distant—glorious angel-trumpets through which God sent His messages. I was so glad, I whose tendency is, I am afraid, to laugh and criticize, to possess one thing at which I could not laugh, to have a whole tract of beauty in which I could walk seriously, with downcast eyes; and I thought I was never going to be able to be serious there again. It was a passing fit, a violent revulsion. If I like carefully to separate my own soul and body, why should I not do the same with those of other sinners? It has always seemed to me so quaint the way we admit, the good nature with which we reiterate, that we are all wretched sinners. We do it with such an immense complacency. We agree so heartily, with such comfortable, regretful sighs, when anybody tells us so; but with only one wretched sinner are we of a real patience. With him, indeed, our patience is boundless. I know this, I have always known it, and I will not now, at an age when it is my hope to grow every year a little better, forget it and be as insolently intolerant as the man who shudders at the name of Heine, will not read a line of him and calls him *Schmutzfink*. That writer's books you tell me about, the books the virtuous in England will not read because his private life was disgraceful, beautiful books, you say, into which went his best, in which his spirit showed how bright it was, how he had kept it apart and clean, I shall get them all and read them all. No sinner, cursed with a body at variance with his soul and able in spite of it to hear the music of heaven and give it exquisite expression, shall ever again be identified by me with what at such great pains he has kept white. I know at least three German writers to whom the same thing happened, men who live badly and write nobly. My heart goes out to them. I think of them lame and handicapped, leading their muse by the hand with anxious care so that her shining feet, set among the grass and daisies along the roadside, shall not be dimmed by the foulness through which they themselves are splashing. They are caked with impurities, but with the tenderest watchfulness they keep her clean. She is their gift to the world, the gift of their best, of their angel, of their share of divinity. And the respectable, afraid for their respectability, turn their backs in horror and go and read without blinking ugly things written by other respectables. Why, no priest at the altar, however unworthy, can hinder the worshipper from taking away with him as great a load of blessings as he will carry. And a rose is not less lovely because its roots are in corruption. And God Himself was found once in a manger. Thank you, and good-bye.

ROSE-MARIE SCHMIDT.

XLVIII

DEAR MR ANSTRUTHER,—We are very happy here just
now because Papa's new book, at which he has been
working two years, is finished. I am copying it out, and
until that is done we shall indulge in the pleasantest day-
dreams. It is our time, this interval between the finishing
of a book of his and its offer to a publisher, for being
riotously happy. We build the most outrageous castles in
the air. Nothing is certain, and everything is possible. The
pains of composition are over, and the pains of rejection
are not begun. Each time we suppose they never will, and
that at last ears will be found respectfully ready to absorb
his views. Few and far between have the ears been till now.
His books have fallen as flat as books can fall. Nobody
wanted to hear all, or even half, that he could tell them
about Goethe. Jena shrugged its shoulders, the larger world
was blank. The books have brought us no fame, no money,
some tragic hours, but much interest and amusement. Always
tragic hours have come when Papa clutched at his hair and
raved rude things about the German public; and when the
money didn't appear there have been uncomfortable
moments. But these pass; Papa leaves his hair alone; and the
balance remains on the side of nice things. We don't really
want any more money, and Papa is kept busy and happy,
and just to see him so eager, so full of his work, seems to
warm the house with pleasant sunshine. Once, for one book,
a cheque did come; and when we all rushed to look we
found it was for two marks and thirty pfennings—'being

the amount due,' said the accompanying stony letter, 'on royalties for the first year of publication.' Papa thought this much worse than no cheque at all, and took it round to the publisher in the molten frame of mind of one who has been insulted. The publisher put his thumbs in the armholes of his waistcoat, leaned back in his chair, gazed with refreshing coolness at Papa, who was very hot, and said that as trade went it was quite a good cheque, and that he had sent one that very morning to another author—a Jena celebrity who employs his leisure writing little books of riddles—for ninety pfennings.

Papa came home beaming with the delicious feeling that money was flowing in and that he was having a boom. The riddle man was a contemptuous acquaintance who had been heard to speak lightly of Papa's books. Papa felt all the sweetness of success, of triumph over a disagreeable rival; and since then we have looked upon that special book as his *opus magnum*.

While I copy he comes in and out to ask me where I have got to and if I like it. I assure him that I think it delightful, and so honestly I do in a way, but I don't think it will be the public's way. It begins by telling the reader, presumably a person in search of information about Goethe, that Jena is a town of twenty thousand inhabitants, of whom nineteen thousand are apparently professors. The town certainly does give you that impression as you walk about its little streets, and at every corner meet the same battered-looking persons in black you met at the corner before; but what has that to do with Goethe? And the pages that follow have nothing to do with him either that I can see, being a disquisition on the origin and evolution of the felt hats the professors wear—dingy, slouchy things—winding up with an explanation of their symbolism and inevitableness, based on a carefully drawn parallel between them and the kind of brains they have to cover. From this point, the point of the head-wear of the learned in our present year, he has to work back all the way to Goethe in Jena a century ago. It takes him several chapters to get back, for he doesn't go straight, being constitutionally unable to resist turning aside down the green lanes of moralizing that branch so seductively off the main road and lead him at last very far afield; and when he does arrive he is rather breathless, and flutters for some time round the impassive giant waiting to be described, jerking out little anecdotes, very pleasant little anecdotes, but quite unconnected with his patient subject, before he has got his wind and can begin.

He is rosy with hope about this book. 'All Jena will read it,' he says, 'because they will like to hear about themselves'—I wonder if they will—'and all Germany will read it because it will like to hear about Goethe.'

'It has heard a good deal about him already, you know, Papachen,' I say, trying gently to suggest certain possibilities.

'England might like to have it. There has been nothing since that man Lewes, and never anything really thorough. A good translation, Rose-Marie—what do you think of that as an agreeable task for you during the approaching winter evenings? It is a matter worthy of consideration. You will like a share in the work, a finger in the literary pie, will you not?'

'Of course I would. But let me copy now, darling. I'm not half through.'

He says that if those blind and prejudiced persons publishers won't risk bringing it out he'll bring it out at his own expense sooner than prevent the world's rightly knowing what Goethe said and did in Jena; so there's a serious eventuality ahead of us! We really will have to live on lettuces, and in grimmest earnest this time. I hope he won't want to keep racehorses next. Well, one thing has happened that will go a little way towards meeting new expenses,—I go down every day now and read English with Vicki, at the desire of her mother, for two hours, her mother having come to the conclusion that it is better to legalize, as it were, my relations with Vicki, who flatly refused to keep away from us. So I am a breadwinner, and can do something to help Papa. It is true I can't help much, for what I earn is fifty pfennings each time, and as the reading of English on Sundays is not considered nice, I can only altogether make three marks a week. But it is something, and it is easily earned, and last Sunday, which was the end of my first week, I bought the whole of the Sunday food with it, dinner and supper for us, and beer for Johanna's lover, who says he cannot love her unless the beer is a particular sort and has been kept for a fortnight properly cold in the coal-hole.

Since I have read with Vicki Frau von Lindeberg is quite different. She is courteous with the careful courtesy decent people show their dependents; kindly; even gracious at times. She is present at the reading, darning socks and ancient sheets with her carefully kept fingers, and she treats me absolutely as though I were attached to her household as governess. She is no longer afraid we will want to be equals. She asks me quite often after the health of him she calls my good father. And when a cousin of hers came last week to stay a night, a female Dammerlitz on her way to a place where you drink waters and get rid of yourself, she presented me to her with pleasant condescension as the *kleine Engländerin* engaged as her daughter's companion. '*Eine recht liebe Hausgenossin,*' she was pleased to add, gently nodding her head at each word; and the cousin went away convinced I was a resident official, and that the tales she had heard about the Lindebergs' poverty couldn't be true.

'It's not scriptural,' I complained to Vicki, stirred to honest indignation.

'You mean, to say things not quite—not quite?' said Vicki.

'Such big ones,' I fumed. 'I'm not little. I'm not English. I'm not a *Hausgenossin*. Why such unnecessary ones?'

'Now, Rose-Marie, you do know why Mamma said "little."'

'It's a term of condescension.'

'And *Engländerins* are rather grand things to have in the house, you know—expensive, I mean. Always dearer than natives. Mamma only wants Cousin Mienchen to suppose we are well off.'

'Oh,' said I.

'You don't mind?' said Vicki, rather timidly, taking my hand.

'It does hurt me,' said I, putting a little stress on the 'me,' a stress implying infinite possible hurt to Frau von Lindeberg's soul.

'It is horrid,' murmured Vicki, her head drooping over her book. 'I wish we didn't always pretend we're not poor. We are. Poor as mice. And it makes us so sensitive about it, so afraid of anything's being noticed. We spend our lives on tenterhooks—not nice things at all to spend one's life on.'

'Wriggly, uncomfortable things,' I agreed.

'I believe Cousin Mienchen isn't in the least taken in, for all our pains.'

'I don't believe people ever are,' said I; and we drifted into a consideration of the probable height of our temperatures and colour of our ears if we could know how much the world we pose to really knows about us, if we could hear with what thoroughness those of our doings and even of our thoughts that we believed so secret are discussed.

Frau von Lindeberg wasn't there, being too busy arranging comforts for her cousin's journey to preside, and so it was that we drifted unhindered from Milton into the foggier regions of private wisdom. We are neither of us wise, but it is surprising how talking to a friend, even to a friend as unwise as yourself, clears up your brains and lets in new light. That is one of the reasons why I like writing to you and getting your letters; only you mustn't be offended at my bracketing you, you splendid young man, with poor Vicki and poor myself in the class Unwise. Heaven knows I mean nothing to do with book-learning, in which, I am aware, you most beautifully excel.

Yours sincerely,

ROSE-MARIE SCHMIDT.

XLIX

DEAR MR ANSTRUTHER,—I am very sorry indeed to hear
that your engagement is broken off. I feared something
of the sort was going to happen because of all the things
you nearly said and didn't in your letters lately. Are you
very much troubled and worried? Please let me turn
into the elder sister for a little again and give you the
small relief of having an attentive listener. It seems to
have been rather an unsatisfactory time for you all along. I
don't really quite know what to say. I am, anyhow, most
sincerely sorry, but I find it extraordinarily difficult to
talk about Miss Cheriton. It is, of course, lamentable that
our writing to each other should have been, as you say it
was, so often the cause of quarrels. You never told me
so, or I would at once have stopped. You fill several
pages with surprise that a girl of twenty-two can be so
different from what she appears, that so soft and tender an
outside can have beneath it such unfathomable depths of
hardness. I think you have probably gone to the other
extreme now, and because you admired so much are all
the more violently critical. It is probable that Miss
Cheriton is all that you first thought her, unusually
charming and sympathetic and lovable, and your characters
simply didn't suit each other. Don't think too unkindly in
your first anger. I am so very sorry; sorry for you, who must
feel as if your life had been convulsed by an earthquake,
and all its familiar features disarranged; sorry for your father's
disappointment; sorry for Miss Cheriton, who must have

been wretched. But how infinitely wiser to draw back in time and not, for want of courage, drift on into that supreme catastrophe marriage. You mustn't suppose me cynical in calling it a catastrophe—perhaps I mean it only in its harmless sense of *dénouement*; and if I don't I can't see that it is cynical to recognize a spade when you see it as certainly a spade. But do not let yourself go to bitterness, and so turn into a cynic yourself. You say Miss Cheriton apparently prefers a duke, and are very angry. But why if, as you declare, you have not really loved her for months past, are you angry? Why should she not prefer a duke? Perhaps he is quite a nice one, and you may be certain she felt at once, the very instant, when you left off caring for her. About such things it is as difficult for a woman to be mistaken as it is for a barometer to be hoodwinked in matters meteorologic. It was that, and never the duke, that first influenced her. I am as sure of it as if I could see into her heart. Of course she loved you. But no girl with a spark of decency would cling on to a reluctant lover. What an exceedingly poor thing in girls she would be who did. I can't tell you how much ashamed I am of that sort of girl, the girl who clings, who follows, who laments—as if the world, the splendid, amazing world, were empty of everything but one single man, and there were no sun shining, no birds singing, no winds blowing, no hills to climb, no trees to sit under, no books to read, no friends to be with, no work to do, no heaven to go to. I feel now for the first time that I would like to know Miss Cheriton. But it is really almost impossibly difficult to write this letter; each thing I say seems something I had better not have said. Write to me about your troubles as often as you feel it helps you, and believe that I do most heartily sympathize with you both, but don't mind, and forgive me, if my answers are not satisfactory. I am unpractised and ill at ease, clumsy, limited, in this matter of frank writing about feelings, a matter in which you so far surpass me. But I am always most sincerely your friend

Rose-Marie Schmidt.

L

DEAR MR ANSTRUTHER,—It's not much use for the absent
to send bland advice, to exhort to peace and a putting aside
of anger, when they have only general principles to go on.
You know more about Miss Cheriton than I do, and I am
obliged to believe you when you tell me you have every
reason to be bitter. But I can make few comments. My
mouth is practically shut. Only, as you told me you long
ago left off caring for her, the smart you are feeling now
must be, it seems to me, simply the smart of wounded vanity,
and for that I'm afraid I have no soothing lotion ready. Also,
I am bound to say that I think she was quite right to give
you up once she was sure you no longer loved her. I am
all for giving up, for getting rid of things grown rotten
before it is too late, and the one less bright spot I see on
her otherwise correct conduct is that she did not do it
sooner. Don't think me hard, dear friend. If I were your
mother I would blindly yearn over my boy. As it is, you
must forgive my unfortunate trick of seeing plainly. I wish
things would look more adorned to me, less palpably
obvious and ungarnished. These tiresome eyes of mine have
often made me angry. I would so much like to sympathize
wholly with you now, to be able to be indignant with Miss
Cheriton, call her a minx, say she is heartless, be ready with
all sorts of healing balms and syrups for you, poor boy, in
the clutches of a cruel annoyance. But I can't. If you could
love her again and make it up, that indeed would be a happy
thing. As it is—and your letter sets all hopes of the sort

aside once and for ever—you have had an escape; for if she had not given you up, I don't suppose you would have given her up—I don't suppose that is a thing one often does. You would have married her, and then Heaven knows what would have become of your unfortunate soul.

After all, you need not have told me you had left off loving her. I knew it. I knew it at the time. I knew it within a week of when it happened. And I have always hoped—I cannot tell you how sincerely—that it was only a mood, and that you would go back to her again and be happy.

Yours sincerely,
ROSE-MARIE SCHMIDT.

LI

DEAR MR ANSTRUTHER,—This is a world, it seems to me, where everybody spends their time falling out of love and making their relations uncomfortable. I have only two friends, the rest of my friends being acquaintances, and both have done it or had it done to them. Is it then to be wondered at that I should argue that if it happens to both my friends in a set where there are only two, the entire world must be divided into those who give up and those who are given up, with a Greek chorus of lamenting and explanatory relatives as a finish? Really one might think that love, and its caprices, and its tantrums—you see, I'm in my shrewish mood—makes up the whole of life. Here's Vicki groaning in the throes of a relapse because some one has written that she met her late lover at a party and that he ate only soup; here she is overcome by this picture, which she translates as a hankering in spite of everything after her, and wanting to write to him, and ready to console him, and crying her eyes all red again, and no longer taking the remotest interest in *Comus* or in those frequent addresses of mine to her on Homely Subjects, to which up to yesterday she listened with such flattering respect; and here are you writing me the most melancholy letters, longer and drearier than any letters ever were before, filled with yearnings after something that certainly is not Miss Cheriton—but beyond that certainty I can make out nothing. It is a strange and wonderful world. I stand bewildered, with you on one side and Vicki on the other, and fling exhortations at you in turn. I try scolding, to brace you, but neither of you will be braced. I try sympathy, to soothe you, but neither of you will be soothed. What am I to do? May I laugh? Will that give too deep offence? I'm afraid I did laugh over your father's cable from America when the news of your broken engagement reached him. You ask me what I think of a father who just cables 'Fool' to his son at a moment when his son is being horribly worried. Well, you must consider that cabling is expensive, and he didn't care to put more than one word, and if there had been two it might have made you still angrier. But, seriously, I do see that it must have annoyed you, and I soon left off being so unkind as to laugh. It is odd how much older I feel than either of you lamenters—quite old and quite settled, and so objective somehow. I hope being objective doesn't make one unsympathetic, but I expect it really rather tends that way; and yet if it were so, and I were as hard and husky as I sometimes dimly fear I may be growing, would you and Vicki want to tell me your sorrows? And other people do too. Think of it, Papa Lindeberg, hitherto a long narrow person buttoned up silently in black, mysterious simply because he held his tongue, a reader of rabid Conservative papers through black-rimmed glasses, and as numb in the fingers as Wordsworth when he shakes my respectful hand, has began to unbend, to unfold, to expand like those Japanese dried flowers you fling into water; and having started with good mornings and weather-comments and politics, and from them proceeded to the satisfactorily confused state of the British army, has gone on imperceptibly but surely to confidential criticisms of the mistakes made here at head-quarters in invariably shelving the best officers at the very moment when they have arrived at what he describes as their prime, and has now reached the stage when he comes up through the orchard every morning at the hour I am due for my lesson to help me over the fence. He comes up with much stateliness and deliberation, but he does come up; and we walk down together, and every day the volume of his confidences increases, and he more and more minutely describes his grievances. I listen and nod my head, which is easy, and apparently all he wants. His wife stops him at once, if he begins to her, by telling him with as much roundness as is consistent with being born a Dammerlitz that the calamities that have overtaken them are entirely his fault. Why was he not as clever as those subordinates who were put over his head? she asks with dangerous tranquillity; and nobody can answer a question like that.

'It makes me twenty years younger,' he said yesterday as he handed me over the fence with the same politeness I have seen in the manner of old men handing large dowagers to their places in a set of quadrilles, 'to see your cheerful morning face.'

'If you had said shining morning face you'd have been quoting Shakespeare,' said I.

'Ah yes. I fear my Shakespeare days are done. I am now at the time of life when serious and practical considerations take up the entire attention of a man. Shakespeare is more suitable now for my daughter than for me.'

'But clever men do read him.'

'Ah yes.'

'Quite grown-up ones do.'

'Ah yes.'

'With beards.'

'Ah yes.'

'Real men.'

'Ah yes, yes. Professors. Theatre people. People of no

family. People who have no serious responsibilities on their shoulders. People of the pen, not men of the sword. But officers—and who in our country of the well-born is not, was not, or will not be an officer?—have no time for general literature. Of course,' he added, with a slight bow, for he regards me as personally responsible for everybody and everything English, 'we have all heard of him.'

'Indeed?' said I.

'When I was a boy,' he said this morning, 'I read at school of a young woman—a mythological person—called Hebe.'

'She was the daughter of Juno and wild lettuce,' said I.

'It may be,' he said. 'The parentages of the mythological period are curiously intricate. But why is it, dear Fräulein Schmidt, that though I can recollect nothing of her but her name, whenever I see you you remind me of her?'

Now, was not that very pleasant? Hebe, the restorer of youth to gods and men; Hebe, the vigorous and wholesome. Thoreau says she was probably the only thoroughly sound-conditioned and robust young lady that ever walked the globe, and that whenever she came it was spring. No wonder I was pleased.

'Perhaps it's because I'm healthy,' said I.

'Is that it?' he said, obviously fumbling about in his brain for the reason. And when he got to the house he displayed the results of his fumbling by saying, 'But many people are healthy.'

'Yes,' said I; and left him to think it out alone.

So now there are two nice young women I've been compared to—you once said I was like Nausicaa, and here a year later, a year in which various rather salt and stinging waves have gone over my head, is somebody comparing me to Hebe. Evidently the waves did me no harm. It is true, on the other hand, that Papa Lindeberg is short-sighted. It is also true that last night I found a beautiful shining silvery hair insolently flaunting in the very front of my head. 'Yes, yes, my dear,' said Papa—my Papa—when I showed it him, 'we are growing old.'

'And settled. And objective,' said I, carefully pulling it out before the glass. 'And yet, Papachen, inside me I feel quite young.'

Papa chuckled. 'Insides are no safe criterion, my dear,' he said. 'It is the outside that tells.'

'Tells what?'

'A woman's age.'

Evidently I have not yet reminded my own Papa of Hebe.

ROSE-MARIE SCHMIDT.

LII

DEAR MR ANSTRUTHER,—Well, yes, I do think you must
get over it without much help from me. You have a great
deal of my sympathy, I assure you; far more than you think.
I don't put it into my letters because there's so much of it
that it would make them overweight. Also, it would want
a great deal of explaining. You see, it's a different sort from
what you expect, and given for other reasons than those
you have in your mind; and it is quite impossible to account
for in any way you are likely to understand. But do consider
what, as regards the broken-off engagement, you must look
like from my point of view. Candidly, are you a fit object
for my compassion? I see you wandering now through Italy
in its golden autumn looking at all your dear Luinis and
Bellinis and Botticellis and other delights of your first
growing up, and from my bleak hilltop I watch you hungrily
as you go. November is nearly upon us, and we shiver under
leaden clouds and driving rain. The windows are loose, and
all of them rattle. The wind screams through their chinks
as though somebody had caught it by the toes and was
pinching it. We can't see out for the raindrops on the panes.
When I go to the door to get a breath of something fresher
than house air I see only mists, and wreaths of clouds, and
mists again, where a fortnight ago lay a little golden town
in a cup of golden hills. Do you think that a person with
this cheerless prospect can pity you down there in the sun?
I trace your bright line of march on the map and merely
feel envy. I am haunted by visions of the many beautiful

207

places and climates there are in the world that I shall never see. The thought that there are people at this moment sitting under palm-trees or in the shadow of pyramids fanning themselves with their handkerchiefs while I am in my clammy room—the house gets clammy, I find, in persistent wet weather—not liking to light a lamp because it is only three o'clock, and yet hardly able to see because of the streaming panes and driving mist, the thought of these happy people makes me restive. I too want to be up and off, to run through the wet pall hanging over this terrible grey North down into places where sunshine would dry the fog out of my hair, and brown my face, and loosen my joints, and warm my poor frozen spirit. I would change places with you this minute if I could. Gladly would I take the burden of your worries on to my shoulders, and, carrying them like a knapsack, lay them at the feet of the first Bellini Madonna I met and leave them there for good. It would give me no trouble to lay them down, those worries produced by other people. One little shake, and they'd tumble off. Always things and places have been more to me than people. Perhaps it is often so with persons who live lonely lives. Anyhow, don't at once cry out that I'm unnatural and inhuman, for things are, after all, only filtered out people—their ideas crystallized into tangibleness, their spirit taking visible form; either they are that, or they are, I suppose, God's ideas—after all, the same thing put into shapes we can see and touch. So that it's not so dreadful of me to like them best, to prefer their company, their silent teaching, although you will, I know, lecture me and perhaps tell me I am petrifying into a mere thing myself. Well, it is only fair that you should lecture me, who so often lecture you.

Yours quite meekly,

ROSE-MARIE SCHMIDT.

LIII

DEAR MR ANSTRUTHER,—I won't talk about it any more.
Let us have done with it. Let us think of something else. I
shall get tired of the duke if you are not careful, so please
save me from an attitude so unbecoming. This is All Saints'
Day: the feast of white chrysanthemums and dear memories.
My mother used to keep it as a day apart, and made me
feel something of its mysticalness. She had a table in her
bedroom, the nearest approach that was possible to an altar,
with one of those pictures hung above it of Christ on the
Cross that always make me think of Swinburne's

> God of this grievous people, wrought
> After the likeness of their race—

do you remember?—and candles, and jars of flowers, and
many little books; and she used on her knees to read in the
little books, kneeling before the picture. She explained to
me that the Lutheran whitewash starved her soul, and that
she wanted, however clumsily, to keep some reminder with
her of the manner of prayer in England. Did I ever tell you
how pretty she was? She was so very pretty, and so adorably
nimble of tongue. Quick, glancing, vivid, she twinkled in
the heavy Jena firmament like some strange little star. She
led Papa and me by the nose, and we loved it. I can see
her now expounding her rebellious theories, sitting
limply—for she was long and thin—in a low chair, but with
nothing limp about her flower-like face and eyes shining

with interest in what she was talking about. She was great on the necessity, a necessity she thought quite good for everybody but absolutely essential for a woman, of being stirred up thoroughly once a week at the very least to an enthusiasm for religion and the life of the world to come. She said there was nothing so good for one as being stirred up, that only the well stirred ever achieve great things, that stagnation never yet produced a soul that had shot up out of reach of fogs on to the clear heights from which alone you can call out directions for the guidance of those below. The cold, empty Lutheran churches were abhorrent to her. 'They are populated on Sundays,' she said, 'solely by stagnant women—women so stagnant that you can almost see the duckweed growing on them.'

She could not endure, and I, taught to see through her eyes, cannot endure either, the chilly blend of whitewash and painted deal pews in the midst of which you are required here once a week to magnify the Lord. Our churches—all those I have seen—are either like vaults or barns, the vault variety being slightly better and also more scarce. Their aggressive ugliness, and cold, repellent service, keeping the congealed sinner at arm's length, nearly drove my mother into the Roman Church, a place no previous Watson had ever wanted to go to. The churches in Jena made her think with the tenderest regard of the old picturesque pre-Lutheran days, of the light and colour and emotions of the Catholic services, and each time she was forced into one she said she made a bigger stride towards Rome. 'Luther was a most mischievous person,' she would say, glancing half defiantly through long eyelashes at Papa. But he only chuckled. He doesn't mind about Luther. Yet in case he did, in case some national susceptibility should have been hurt, she would get up lazily—her movements were as lazy as her tongue was quick—and take him by the ears and kiss him.

She died when she was thirty-five: sweet and wonderful to the last. Not did her beauty suffer in the least in the sudden illness that killed her. 'A lily in a linen-clout She looked when they had laid her out,' as your Meredith says; and on this day every year, this day of saints so dear to us, my spirit is all the time in those long ago happy years with her. I have no private altar in my room, no picture of a 'piteous Christ'—Papa took that—and no white flowers in this drenched autumnal place to show that I remember; nor do I read in the little books, except with gentle wonderment that she should have found nourishment in them, she who fed so constantly on the great poets. But I have gone each All Saints' Day for ten years past to church in Jena in memory of her, and tried by shutting my eyes to imagine I was in a beautiful place without whitewash, or hideous, almost brutal, stained glass.

This morning, knowing that if I went down into the town I would arrive spattered with mud up to my ears and so bedraggled that the pew-opener might conceivably refuse me admission on the ground that I would spoil her pews, I set out for the nearest village across the hills, hoping that a country congregation would be more used to mud. I found the church shut, and nobody with the least desire to have it opened. The rain beat dismally down on my umbrella as I stood before the blank locked door. A neglected fence divided the graves from the parson's front yard, protecting them, I suppose, as much as in it lay, from the depredations of wandering cows. On the other side of it was the parson's manure heap, on which stood wet fowls mournfully investigating its contents. His windows, shut and impenetrable, looked out on to the manure heap, the fowls, the churchyard, and myself. It is a very ancient church, picturesque, and with beautiful lancet windows with delicate traceries carefully bricked up. Not choosing to have walked five miles for nothing, and not wishing to break a habit ten years' old of praying in a church for my darling mother's soul on this day of souls and darling saints, I gathered up my skirts and splashed across the parson's pools and knocked modestly at his door for the key. The instant I did it two dogs from nowhere, two infamous little dogs of that unpleasant breed from which I suppose Pomerania takes its name, rushed at me, furiously barking. The noise was enough to wake the dead; and since nobody stirred in the house or showed other signs of being wakened, it became plain to my deductive intelligence that its inmates couldn't be dead. So I knocked again. The dogs yelled again. I stood looking at them in deep disgust, quite ashamed of the way in which the dripping stillness was being rent because of me. A soothing umbrella shaken at them only increased their fury. They seemed, like myself, to grow more and more indignant the longer the door was kept shut. At last a servant opened it a few inches, eyed me with astonishment, and when she heard my innocent request eyed me with suspicion. She hesitated, half shut the door, hesitated again, and then, saying she would go and see what the Herr Pastor had to say, shut the door quite. I do not remember ever having felt less respectable. The girl clearly thought I was not; the dogs clearly were sure I was not. Properly incensed by the shutting of the door and the expression on the girl's face, I decided that the only dignified course was to go away; but I couldn't because of the dogs.

The girl came back with the key. She looked as though she had a personal prejudice against me. She opened the door just wide enough for a lean person to squeeze through, and bade me, with manifest reluctance, come in. The hall had a brick floor and an umbrella-stand. In the umbrella-stand stood an umbrella, and as the girl, who walked in front of me, passed it, she snatched out the umbrella and carried it with her, firmly pressed to her bosom. I did not at once grasp the significance of this action. She put me into an icy shut-up room and left me to myself. It was the *gute Stube*—good room—room used only on occasions of frigid splendour. Its floor was shiny with yellow paint, and to meet the difficulty of the paint being spoiled if people walked on it, and that other difficulty of a floor being the only place you can walk on, strips of cocoanut matting were laid across it from one important point to another. There was a strip from the door to the window; a strip from the door to another door; a strip from the door to the sofa; and a strip from the sofa on which the caller sits to the chair on which sits the callee. A baby of apparently brand newness was crying in an adjoining room. I waited, listening to it for what seemed an interminable time, not daring to sit down because it is not expected in Germany that you shall sit in any house but your own until specially requested to do so. I stood staring at the puddles my clothes and umbrella were forming on the strip of matting, vainly trying to rub them out with my feet. The wail of the unfortunate in the next room was of an uninterrupted and haunting melancholy. The rain beat on the windows forlornly. As minute after minute passed and no one came, I grew very restless. My fingers began to twitch and my feet to tap. And I was cooling down after my quick walk with a rapidity that meant a cough and a sore throat. There was no bell, or I would have rung it and begged to be allowed to go away. I did turn round to open the door and try to attract the servant's notice and tell her I could wait no longer, but I found to my astonishment that the door was locked. After that the whole of my reflections were resolved into one chaotic Dear me, from which I did not emerge till the parson appeared through the other door, bringing with him a gust of wailing from the unhappy baby within and of the characteristic smell of infant garments drying at a stove.

He was cold, suspicious, inquisitive. Evidently unused to being asked for permission to go into his church, and equally evidently unused to persons passing through a village which was, for most persons, on the way to nowhere, he endeavoured with some skill to discover what I was doing there. With equal skill I evaded answering his questions. They included inquiries as to my name, my age, my address, my father's profession, the existence or not of a husband, the number of my brothers and sisters, and distinct probings into the size of our income. It struck me that he had a great deal of time and very few visitors, except thieves. Delicately I conveyed this impression to him, leaving out only the thieves, by means of implications of a vaguely flattering nature. He shrugged his shoulders, and said it was too wet for funerals, which were the only things doing at this time of the year.

'What, don't they die when it is wet?' I asked, surprised.

'Certainly, if it is necessary,' said he.

'Oh,' said I, pondering. 'But if some one does he has to be buried?'

'We put it off,' said he.

'Put it off?'

'We put it off,' he repeated firmly.

'But——' I began, in a tone of protest.

'There's always a fine day if one waits long enough,' said he.

'That's true,' said I, struck by a truth I had not till then consciously observed.

He did not ask me to sit down, a careful eye, I suppose, having gauged the probable effect of my wet clothes on his dry chairs, so we stood facing each other on the strip of matting throwing questions and answers backwards and forwards like a ball. And I think I played quite skilfully, for at the end of the game he knew little more than when we began.

And so at last he gave me the key, and having with a great rattling of its handle concealed that he was unlocking the door, and further cloaked this process by a pleasant comment on the way doors stick in wet weather, which I met with the cold information that ours didn't, he whistled off the dogs, and I left him still with an inquiry in his eye.

The church is very ancient and dates from the thirteenth century. You would like its outside—I wonder if in your walks you ever came here—but its inside has been spoilt by the zealous Lutherans and turned into the usual barn. In its first state of beauty in those far-off Catholic days what a haven it must have been for all the women and most of the men of that lonely turnip-growing village; the one beauty spot, the one place of mystery and enthusiasm. No one, I thought, staring about me, could possibly have their depths stirred in the middle of so much whitewash. The inhabitants of these bald agricultural parishes are not sufficiently spiritual for the Lutheran faith. Black gowns and bareness may be enough for those whose piety is so exalted that ceremonies are only a hindrance to the purity of their devotions; but the ignorant and the dull, if they are to be stirred, and especially the women who have entered upon that long series of grey years that begins for those worked gaunt and shapeless in the fields somewhere about twenty-five and never leaves off again, if they are to be helped to be less forlorn need many ceremonies, many symbols, much show, and mystery and awfulness. You will say that it is improbable that the female inhabitants of such a poor parish should know what it is to feel forlorn; but I know better. You will, turning some of my own words against me, tell me that one does not feel forlorn if one is worked hard enough; but I know better about that too— and I said it only in reference to young men like yourself. It is true, the tragedy of the faded face combined with the uncomfortably young heart, which is the tragedy that every woman who has had an easy life has to endure for quite a number of years, finds no place in the existence of a drudge; it is true, too, that I never yet saw, and I am sure you didn't, a woman of the labouring classes make efforts to appear younger than she is; and it is also true that I have seldom seen, and I am sure you haven't, women of the class that has little to do leave off making them. Ceaseless hard work and the care of many children do away very quickly with the youth both of face and heart of the poor man's wife, and with the youth of heart go the yearnings that rend her whose heart, whatever her face may be doing, is still without a wrinkle. But drudgery and a lost youth do not make your life less, but more dreary. These poor women have not, like their husbands, the solace of the public-house *Schnaps*. They go through the bitterness of the years wholly without anaesthetics. Really I don't think I can let you go on persisting that they feel nothing. Why, we shall soon have you believing that only you in this groaning and travailing creation suffer. Please divest yourself of these illusions. Read, my young friend, read the British poet Crabbe. Read him much; ponder him more. He knew all about peasants. He was a plain man, with a knack for rhyme and rhythm that sets your brain ajingling for weeks, who saw peasants as they are. They must have been the very ones we have here. In his pages no honeysuckle clambers picturesquely about their path, no simple virtues shine in their faces. Their hearth is not snowy, their wife not neat and nimble. They do not gather round bright fires and tell artless tales on winter evenings. Their cheer is certainly homely, but that doesn't make them like it, and they never call down blessings upon it with moist uplifted eyes. Grandsires with venerable hair are rather at a discount; the young men's way of trudging cannot be described as elastic; and their talk, when there is any, does not consist of praise of the local landowner. Do you think they do not know that they are cold and underfed? And do not know they have grown old before their time through working in every sort of weather? And do not know where their rheumatism and fevers come from?

I walked back through the soaking, sighing woods thinking of these things and of how unfairly the goods of life are distributed and of the odd tendency misfortunes have to collect themselves together in one place in a heap. Old thoughts, you'll say; old thoughts are stale as life, thoughts that have drifted through countless heads, and after a while drifted out of them again, leaving no profit behind them. But one can't help thinking them and greatly marvelling. Make the most, you fortunate young man, of freedom, and Italy, and sunshine, and your six and twenty years. If I could only persuade you to let yourself go quite simply to being happy! Our friendship, in spite of its sincerity, has up to now been of so little use to you; and a friendship which is not helpful might just as well not exist. I wish I knew what words of mine would help you most. How gladly would I write them. How gladly would I see you in untroubled waters, forging straight ahead towards a full and fruitful life. But I am a foolish, ineffectual woman, and write you waspish letters when I might, if I had more insight, have found out what those words are that would set you tingling with the joy of life.

Yours sincerely,
ROSE-MARIE SCHMIDT.

I've been reading some of the very beautiful prayers in my mother's English Prayer-book to make up for not having prayed in church today. Its margins are thickly covered with pencilled comments. In parts like the Psalms and Canticles they overflow into the spaces between the verses. They are chiefly notes on the beauties of thought and language, and comparisons with similar passages in the Bible. Here and there between the pages are gummed little pictures of Madonnas and 'piteous Christs.' But when the Athanasian Creed is reached the tone of the comments changes. Over the top of it is written, 'Some one has said there is a vein of dry humour running through this Creed that is very remarkable.' And at the end of each of those involved clauses that try quite vainly, yet with an air of defying criticism, to describe the undescribable, my mother has written with admirable caution 'Perhaps.'

LIV

DEAR MR ANSTRUTHER,—So you are coming to Berlin
next month. I thought you told me in one of your letters
that Washington was probably going to be your first
diplomatic post. Evidently you are glad it is not; but if I
were going to be an *attaché* I'd much rather be it at
Washington than Berlin, the reason being that I've not been
to Washington and I have been to Berlin. Why are you so
pleased—forgive me, I meant so much pleased, but it is
strange how little instinct has to do with grammar—about
Berlin? You didn't like it when you were here and went for
two days to look at it. You said it was a hard white place,
full of broad streets with nobody in them. You said it was
barren, soulless, arid, pretentious, police-ridden; that
everybody was an official, and that all the officials were
rude. You were furious with a policeman who stared at you
without answering when you asked him the way. You were
scandalized by the behaviour of the men in the local trains,
who sat and smoked in the faces of the standing women,
and by those men who walked with their female relations
in the streets and caused their parcels to be carried by them.
You came home to us saying that Jena was best, and you
were thankful to be with us again. I went to Berlin once,
a little while before you came to Germany, and didn't like
it either. But I didn't like it because it was so full, because
those streets that seemed to you so empty were bewildering
to me in their tumultuous traffic—so you see how a place
is what your own eye makes it, your Jena or your London

eye; and I didn't like it, besides, because we spent a sulphuric night and morning with relations. The noise of the streets all day and the sulphur of the relations at night spoilt it for me. We went there for a jaunt, to look at the museums and things, and stay the night with Papa's brother who lives there. He is Papa's younger brother, and spends his days in a bank, handing out and raking in money through a hole in a kind of cage. He has a pen behind his ear—I know, because we were taken to gaze upon him between two museums—and wears a black coat on weekdays as well as on Sundays, which greatly dazzled my stepmother, who was with us. I believe he is eminently respectable, and the bank values him as an old and reliable servant, and has made him rich. His salary is eight thousand marks a year—four hundred pounds, sir; four times as much as what we have—and my stepmother used often and fervently to wish that Papa had been more like him. I thought him a terrifying old uncle, a parched, machine-like person, whose soul seemed withdrawn into unexplorable vague distances, reduced to a mere far-off flicker by the mechanical nature of his work. He is ten years younger than Papa, but infinitely more faded. He never laughs. He never even smiles. He is rude to his wife. He is withering to his daughters. He made me think of owls as he sat at supper that night in his prim clothes, with round gloomy eyes fixed on Papa, whom he was lecturing. Papa didn't mind. He had had a happy day, ending with two very glorious hours in the Royal Library, and Tante Else's herring salad was much to his taste. 'Hast thou no respect, Heinrich,' he cried at last, when my uncle, warmed by beer, let his lecture slide over the line that had till then divided it from a rating; 'hast thou then no respect for the elder brother, and his white and reverend hairs?'

But Onkel Heinrich, aware that he is the success and

example of the family, and as intolerant as successes and examples are of laxer and poorer relations, waved Papa's banter aside with contempt, and proposed that instead of wasting any more of an already appallingly wasted life in idle dabblings in so-called literature he too should endeavour to get a post, however humble, in a bank in Berlin, and mend his ways, and earn an income of his own, and cease from living on an income acquired by marriages.

My stepmother punctuated his words with nods of approval.

'What, as a doorkeeper, eh, thou cistern filled with wisdom?' cried Papa, lifting his glass and drinking gaily to Tante Else, who glanced uneasily at her husband, he not yet having been, to her recollection, called a cistern.

'It is better,' said my stepmother, to whom a man so punctual, so methodical, and so well-salaried as Onkel Heinrich seemed wholly ideal, 'it is better to be a doorkeeper in—in——'

She was seized with doubt as to the applicability of the text, and hesitated.

'A bank?' suggested Papa, pleasantly.

'Yes, Ferdinand, even in a bank rather than dwell in the tents of wickedness.'

'That,' explained Papa to Tante Else, leaning back in his chair and crossing his hands comfortably over what, you being English, I will call his chest, 'is my dear wife's poetic way——'

'Scriptural way, Ferdinand,' interrupted my stepmother. 'I know no poetic ways.'

'It is the same thing, *meine Liebste*. The scriptures are drenched in poetry. Poetic way, I say, of referring to Jena.'

'*Ach so*,' said Tante Else, vague because she doesn't know her Bible any better than the rest of us Germans; it is only you English who have it at your fingers' ends; and, of course, my stepmother had it at hers.

'Tents,' continued Tante Else, feeling that as *Hausfrau* it was her duty to make herself conversationally conspicuous, and anxious to hide that she was privately at sea, 'tents are unwholesome as permanent dwellings. I should say a situation somewhere as doorkeeper in a healthy building was much to be preferred to living in nasty draughty things like tents.'

'*Quatsch*,' said Onkel Heinrich, with sudden and explosive bitterness; you remember, of course, that *quatsch* is German for silly, or nonsense, and that it is far more expressive, and also more rude, than either.

My stepmother opened her mouth to speak, but Tante Else, urged by her sense of duty, flowed on.

'You cannot,' she said, addressing Papa, 'be a doorkeeper unless there is a door to keep.'

'Let no one,' cried Papa, beating approving hands together, 'say again that ladies are not logicians.'

'*Quatsch*,' said Onkel Heinrich.

'And a door is commonly a—a———' She cast about for the word.

'A necessity?' suggested Papa, all bright and pleased attention.

'A convenience?' suggested my cousin Lieschen, the rather pretty unmarried daughter, a girl with a neat head, an untidy body, and plump red hands.

'An ornament?' suggested my cousin Elschen, the rather pretty married daughter, another girl with a neat head, an untidy body, and plump red hands.

'A thing you go in at?' I suggested.

'No, no,' said Tante Else, impatiently, determined to run down her word.

'A thing you go out at, then?' said I, proud of the resourcefulness of my intelligence.

'No, no,' said Tante Else, still more impatiently. '*Ach Gott*, where do all the words get to?'

'Is it something very particular for which you are searching?' asked my stepmother, with the sympathetic interest you show in the searchings of the related rich.

'Something not worth the search, we may be sure,' remarked Onkel Heinrich.

'*Ach Gott*,' said Tante Else, not heeding him, 'where do they——' She clasped and unclasped her fingers; she gazed round the room and up at the ceiling. We all sat silent, feeling that here there was no help, and watched while she chased the elusive word round and round her brain. Only Onkel Heinrich continued to eat herring salad with insulting emphasis.

'I have it,' she cried at last, triumphantly.

We at once revived into a brisk attention.

'A door is a characteristic——'

'A most excellent word,' said Papa, encouragingly. 'Continue, my dear.'

'It is a characteristic of buildings that are massive and that have windows and chimneys like other buildings.'

'Excellent, excellent,' said Papa. 'Definitions are never easy.'

'And—and tents don't have them,' finished Tante Else, looking round at us with a sort of mild surprise at having succeeded in talking so much about something that was neither neighbours nor housekeeping.

'*Quatsch*,' said Onkel Heinrich.

'My dear,' protested Tante Else, forced at last to notice these comments.

'I say it is *quatsch*,' said Onkel Heinrich, with a volcanic vehemence startling in one so trim.

'Really, my dear,' said Tante Else.

'I repeat it,' said Onkel Heinrich.

'Do you not think, my dear——'

'I do not think, I know. Am I to sit silent, to have no opinion, in my own house? At my own table?'

'My dear——'

'If you do not like to hear the truth, refrain from talking nonsense.'

'My dear Heinrich—will you not try—in the presence of—of relations, and of—of our children——' Her voice shook a little, and she stopped, and began with great haste and exactness to fold up her table-napkin.

'*Ach*—*quatsch*,' said Onkel Heinrich again, irritably pushing back his chair.

He waddled to a cupboard—of course he doesn't get much exercise in his cage, so he can only waddle—and took out a box of cigars.

'Come, Ferdinand,' he said, 'let us go and smoke together in my room and leave the dear women to the undisturbed enjoyment of their wits.'

'I do not smoke,' said Papa, briefly.

'Come, then, while I smoke,' said Onkel Heinrich.

'Nay, I fear thee, Heinrich,' said Papa. 'I fear thy tongue applied to my weak places. I fear thine eye, measuring their deficiencies. I fear thy intelligence, known to be great——'

'Worth exactly,' said Onkel Heinrich, suddenly facing us, the cigar-box under his arm, his cross owl's eyes rounder than ever, 'worth exactly, on the Berlin brain market, eight thousand marks a year.'

'I know, I know,' cried Papa, 'and I admire—I admire. But there is awe mingled with my admiration, Heinrich— awe, respect, terror. Go, thou man of brains and marketableness, thou man of worth and recognition, go and leave me here with these lesser intellects. I fear thee, and I will not watch thee smoke.'

And he got up and raised Tante Else's hand to his lips with great gallantry, and wished her, after our pleasant fashion at the end of meals, a good digestion.

But Tante Else, though she tried to smile and return his wishes, could not get back again into her *role* of serene and conversational *Hausfrau*. My uncle waddled away, shooting a sniff of scorn over his shoulder as he went, and my aunt endeavoured to conceal the fact that she was wiping her eyes. Lieschen and Elschen began to talk to me both at once. My stepmother cleared her throat, and remarked that successful public men often had to pay for their successes by being the victims at home of nerves, and that their wives, whose duty it is always to be loving, might be compared to the warm and soothing iron passed over a shirt newly washed, and deftly, by its smooth insistence, flattening away each crease.

Papa gazed at my stepmother with admiring astonishment while she elaborated this image. He had hold of Tante Else's hand and was stroking it. His bright eyes were fixed on his wife, and I could see by their expression that he was trying to recall the occasions on which his own creases had been ironed out.

With the correctness with which one guesses most of a person's thoughts after you have lived with him ten years, my stepmother guessed what he was thinking.

'I said public men,' she remarked, 'and I said successes.'

'I heard, I heard, *meine Liebste*,' Papa assured her, 'and I also completely understand.'

He made her a little bow across the table. 'Do not heed him, Else, my dear,' he added, turning to my aunt. 'Do not heed thy Heinrich—he is but a barbarian.'

'Ferdinand!' exclaimed my stepmother.

'Oh no,' sighed Tante Else, 'it is I who am impatient and foolish.'

'I tell thee he is a barbarian. He always was. In the nursery he was, when, yet unable to walk, he crawled to that spot on the carpet where stood my unsuspecting legs the while my eyes and hands were busy with the playthings on the table, and fastening his youthful teeth into them made holes in my flesh and also in my stockings, for which, when she saw them, my mother whipped me. At school he was, when, carefully stalking the flea gambolling upon his garments, he secured it between a moistened finger and thumb, and, waiting with the patience of the savage sure of his prey, dexterously transferred it, at the moment his master bent over his desk to assure himself of his diligence, to the pedagogue's sleeve or trouser, and then looked on with that glassy look of his while the victim, returned to his place on the platform, showed an ever-increasing uneasiness, culminating at last in a hasty departure and a prolonged absence. As a soldier he was, for I have been told so by those comrades who served with and suffered from him, but whose tales I will not here repeat. And as a husband— yes, my dear Else, as a husband he has not lost it—he is, undoubtedly, a barbarian.'

'Oh no, no,' sighed Tante Else, yet listening with manifest fearful interest.

'Ferdinand,' said my stepmother, angrily, 'your tongue is doing what it invariably does, it is running away with you.'

'Why are married people always angry with each other?' asked Lieschen, the unmarried daughter, in a whisper.

'How can I tell, since I am not married?' I answered in another whisper.

'They are not,' whispered Elschen, with all the authority

of the lately married. 'It is only the old ones. My husband and I do not quarrel. We kiss.'

'That is true,' said Lieschen, with a small giggle which was not without a touch of envy. 'I have repeatedly seen you doing it.'

'Yes,' said Elschen, placidly.

'Is there no alternative?' I inquired.

'No what?'

'Alternative.'

'I do not know what you mean by alternative, Rose-Marie,' said Elschen, trying to twist her wedding-ring round on her finger, but it couldn't twist because it was too deeply embedded. 'Where do you get your long words from?'

'Must one either quarrel or kiss?' I asked. 'Is there no serene valley between the thunderous heights on the one hand and the swampy enervations on the other?'

To this Elschen merely replied, while she stared at me, '*Grosser Gott.*'

'You are a queer cousin,' said Lieschen, giggling again, the giggle this time containing a touch of contempt, her giggles never being wholly unadulterated. 'I suppose it is because Onkel Ferdinand is so poor.'

'I expect it is,' said I.

'He has hardly any money, has he?'

'I believe he has positively none.'

'But how do you live at all?'

'I can't think. It must be a habit.'

'You don't look very fat.'

'How can I, when I'm not?'

'You must come and see my baby,' said Elschen, apparently irrelevantly, but I don't think it really was; she thought a glimpse of that, I am sure, refreshing baby would cure most heart-sicknesses.

'Yes, yes, it is a splendid baby,' said Lieschen, brightening, 'and its wardrobe is trimmed throughout with the best Swiss embroidery threaded with beautiful blue ribbons. It cost many hundred marks, I assure you. There is nothing that is not both durable and excellent. Elschen's mother-in-law is a very rich lady. She gave it all. She keeps two servants, and they wear washing dresses and big white aprons, just like English servants. Elschen's mother-in-law says it is a great expense because of the laundry bills, but that she doesn't mind. If you were going to stay longer, and had got the necessary costumes, we might have taken you to see her, and she might perhaps have asked you to stay to coffee.'

'Really?' said I, in a voice of concern.

'Yes. It is a pity for you. You would then see how elegant Berlin people are. I expect this'—she waved her hand—'is quite different from Jena, and seems strange to you, but it is nothing, I assure you, nothing at all, compared to Elschen's mother-in-law's furniture and food.'

'Really?' said I, again with concern.

I did a dreadful thing next morning at breakfast: I broke a jug. Never shall I forget the dismay and shame of that moment. Really, I am rather a deft person, used to jugs, and not, as a rule, of hasty or unconsidered movements. It was, I think, the electric current streaming out of Onkel Heinrich that had at last reached me too and galvanized me into a nervous and twitching behaviour. He came in last, and the moment he appeared words froze, smiles vanished, eyes fell, and Papa's piping alone continued to be heard in the cheerless air. I don't know what had passed between him and Tante Else since last we had seen him, but his opaque black eyes were crosser and blacker than ever. Perhaps it was only that he had smoked more than was good for him, and the whole family was punished for that over-indulgence. I could not help reflecting how lucky it was that we were his relations and not hers; what must happen to hers if they ever come to see her I dare not think. It was while I was reflecting on their probable scorched and shrivelled condition, and at the same time was eagerly passing him some butter that I don't think he wanted but that I was frantically afraid he might want, that my zealous arm swept the milk-jug off the table, and it fell on the varnished floor, and with a hideous clatter of what seemed like malicious satisfaction smashed itself to atoms.

'There now,' cried my stepmother, casting up her hands, 'Rose-Marie all over.'

'I am very sorry,' I stammered, pushing back my chair and gathering up the pieces, and mopping up the milk with my handkerchief.

'Dear niece, it is of no consequence,' faltered Tante Else, her eyes anxiously on her husband.

'No consequence?' cried he—and his words sounded the more terrific from their being the first, beyond a curt good morning, that he had uttered. 'No consequence?'

And when my shameful head reappeared above the table and I got on to my feet and carried the ruins to a sideboard, murmuring hysterical apologies as I went, he pointed with a lean finger to what had once been a jug, and said, with an owlish solemnity and weightiness of utterance I have never heard equalled—

'It was very expensive.'

I can't tell you how glad, how thankful I was to get home.

Yours sincerely,

ROSE-MARIE SCHMIDT.

LV

DEAR MR ANSTRUTHER,—I shall send this to Jermyn
Street, as it can no longer catch you in Italy. Jena is not on
the way from London to Berlin, and I don't know what
map persuaded you that it was. It is very faithful and devoted
of you to want so much to see Professor Martens again, but
you know he is a busy man, and for five minutes with him
as he rushes from a lecture to a private lesson it hardly
seems worth while to make such a tremendous *détour*. Why,
you would be hours pottering about on branch lines and
at junctions, and would never, I am certain, see your luggage
again. Still, it is not for me to refuse your visit to Professor
Martens on his behalf, who as yet knows nothing about it.
I merely advise; and you know I do not easily miss an
opportunity of doing that.

What another odd idea of yours to want to call on our
Berlin relations. Has Italy put these various warm genialities
into your head? I did not think I had made the Heinrich
Schmidts attractive. I was shivering while I wrote with
renewed horror, as the remembrance of that evening with
them and of that morning rose up again before me. That
the result should be a thirst on your part for their address
fills me with astonishment. Do you want to go and do them
good? Soften Onkel Heinrich, and teach him to cherish
kind Tante Else with the meek blue eyes and claret-coloured
silk dress? You cannot seriously intend to set up regular
social intercourse with them. It is certain you will never
meet them at any party you go to—no, not even Elschen's

mother-in-law. The classes are with us divided so rigorously that the needle's eye was child's play to the camel compared to this other entering. You will, very properly, remembering my cloistered life, inquire what I know about it; but it seems to me—only please don't laugh—that I have seen and known quite a good deal. When Experience leaves gaps, quick Imagination fills them up. The straws I have noticed have been enough to show me which way the wind was blowing; and women, pray remember, are artists at putting two and two together. Therefore I prophesy that if you are at the English Embassy in Berlin fifty years and meet fresh people every day of them, among those people will never be Onkel Heinrich and Tante Else. What, then, is the use of giving you their address? I will, if you really seriously wish it; but I must warn you that they would be intensely surprised by a call from you, and it would in no way add to their comfort. The connecting thread is altogether too slender. Papa is not a relation whose introductions they value, and to come from him is a handicap rather than a recommendation. Do you know the only possible conclusion they would come to?—and come to it they certainly would—that somehow, somewhere, in a tram, or a shop, or walking, you had seen Lieschen, and had fallen in love with her. And before you knew where you were you would be married to Lieschen.

How sad to have to come away from the flaming Spanish chestnuts of Italy and turn your face towards London fogs. You don't seem to mind. You never do seem to mind the things that would fill my heart with leaden despair, and over other things that should not matter you cry out. Indeed, far from minding, you seem eager to be off. Yet London can't be nice in November, and Berlin, where you so soon will be, is simply horrid. It was in November that we were there, and we splashed about in a raw, wet cold—rain on the verge of sleet and snow, a bitter wind at the corners, the omnibuses all full (we could not afford the dearer and more respectable tram), and everybody we met had an unkind strange face that stared at us, in spite of hurry and umbrellas, with a thoroughness and comprehensiveness that must be peculiar to Berlin. Papa's galoshes didn't fit and kept coming off, and they always did it at the most difficult moment, generally when we were crossing a street, and there they would lie, scattered beneath hoofs and wheels, till I had rescued them again. Also his umbrella, being old and never having been very strong, turned inside out at extra gusty corners, and we, who had come to look and wonder, found that the Berlin people thought we had come to be looked and wondered at. But do not let me damp your ardour with these gloomy tales. It is such an excellent thing that you should be ardent at all, after this long while of dissatisfaction with life, that I ought to cheer you on and not talk dreary. Besides, your umbrella won't mind corners, and you do not wear galoshes. I wish you joy, then, of your new post, and hope you will be very happy in it. Papa was most interested to hear you were coming so near us, and sends you many messages, whose upshot is that you are to be a good boy and do him credit. He doesn't know about the unfortunate ending to your engagement, and I shall not tell him, for he would be sorry; and more and more, as the days and months melt away into a dream, I am anxious that he should not be made sorry. Do you not think that old people should never be made sorry?

Yours sincerely,

ROSE-MARIE SCHMIDT.

I hope you will waste no precious time coming to Jena to see Professor Martens. I heard a rumour that he was ill, or away or something, so that you would have your long and *extremely* tiresome journey positively for nothing.

LVI

DEAR MR ANSTRUTHER,—Was it so short? I don't remember. This one shall be longer, then. Tell me, do you think there is any use in trying to cure a person of being in love? I have come to the conclusion that it's hopeless. Such cures must be made from the inside outwards, and not from the outside inwards. I thought I was going to stir Vicki to a noble independence, and you should have heard the speeches I made her. Sometimes I had to laugh at them myself, they were such extraordinarily heroic and glowing things for one dripping Fräulein with none too brave a heart to hurl at another dripping Fräulein with no brave heart at all, as they trotted along with shortened skirts and umbrellas through wind-racked, howling forests. Vicki has gone all to pieces again, and her eyes are redder than ever. I don't know whether it is these November mists that have done it, but certainly after all my hauling of her up the rocks of proud self-sufficiency she has flopped back again deeper than before into the morass in which I found her. It's a perfect bog of sentiment she's sunk in now. I make her go for ten-mile walks, and aim at doing them in two hours, thus hoping to bring out her love-sickness in the form of healthy perspiration, but it's no good. 'Oh,' gasps Vicki, when we start off up the sombre aisles of pines, and see them stretching away before us into a grey infinity, and mark their reeking trunks, black with damp, hoar with lichen, and hear their sighings and their creakings through the patter of rain on our umbrellas, and feel their wet breath on our cheeks, 'oh, what an empty, frightening world it is!'

Then I tell her, with what enthusiasm I may, that it's not, that it's beautiful, that we are young and strong, that our life can be made just exactly as glorious as we are energetic enough to make it. And she doesn't believe a word; she simply shakes her head, and moans that she isn't energetic.

'But you are,' I say, with a fine show of confidence. 'Come, let us walk faster. Who would dare say you were not who saw you now?'

'Oh!' wails Vicki; and trots along blowing her nose.

Poor little soul. I've tried kissing her, and it did no good either. I petted her for a whole day; sat with my arms round her; had her head on my shoulder; whispered every consolation I could think of; but unfortunately the only person who has ever petted her was the faithless one, and it made her think of him with renewed agony, and opened positive sluices of despair. I've tried scolding her—the 'My dear Vicki, really for a woman grown' tone, but she gets so much of that from her mother, and, besides, she isn't a woman grown, but only a poor, unhappy, cheated little child. But how dull, how dry, how profitless are the comfortings of one woman for another. I feel it in every nerve the whole time I am applying them. One kiss from the wretched man himself and the world blazes into radiance. A thousand of the most beautiful and eminent verities enunciated by myself only collect into a kind of frozen pall that hangs about her miserable little head and does nothing more useful than suffocate her. She has been inclined to feel bad ever since the fatal letter about the soup, but there were intervals in which with infinite haulings I did get her up on to the rocks again, those rocks she finds so barren, but from whose tops she can at least see clearly and be kept dry. Now that this terrible weather has come upon us, and every day is wetter and sadder than the last, she has collapsed entirely.

If I could write as well as Papa I would like to write an essay on the connection between a wet November and the renewed buddings of love. Frau von Lindeberg is dreadfully angry, and came up, and actually came in, a thing she has not done yet, and sat on the sofa, carefully enthroned in its middle and well spread out in case I should so far forget myself as to want to sit upon it too, and asked me what nonsense I had been putting into the child's head.

'Nonsense?' I exclaimed, remembering my noble talk.

'She was getting over it. You must have said something.'

'Said something? Yes, indeed I said something. Never has one person said so many things before.'

She stared in amazement. 'What,' she cried, 'you actually— you dared—you have the effrontery——'

'Shall I tell you what I said?'

And for an hour I gave the astonished lady, hemmed in on the sofa by the table and by my chair, the outlines of my views on ideals and conduct. I made the most of the hour. The outlines were very thick. No fidgeting or attempts to stop me were considered. She had come to scold; she should stay to learn.

'Well, well,' she said, when I, tired of talking, got up and removed the impeding table with something of the brisk politeness of a dentist unhooking the patient's bib and screwing down his chair after he has done his worst, 'you seem to be a good sort of girl. You have, I see, meant no harm.'

'Meant no harm? I neither meant it nor did I do it. Allow me to make the point clearer——' And I prepared to push back the table upon her and begin again.

'No, no—it is quite clear, thank you. Kindly go on endeavouring, then, to influence my unhappy child for good. I trust your excellent father is well. Good morning.'

But influence as I may, Vicki has given up wearing those starched shirts with the high linen collars and neat ties in which she first dazzled me, and has gone into nondescript woollen clothes something like mine. She says it is because of the washing bills, but I know it to be but a further symbol of her despair. The one remnant of her first trimness is her beautifully brushed hair. Stooping over her to see that her English exercises are correct, I like to lay my cheek a moment on it, so lightly that she does not notice, for it is wonderful stuff—soft, wavy, shining, and ought alone, without the little ear and curve of the young cheek, without the silly pretty mouth and kind straightforward eyes, to have immeshed that stupid man beyond all possibility of disentangling himself. She was not made for Milton and the Muses. Nature, carving her out, moulding her body and her mind, putting in a dimple here and giving an eyelash an extra curl there, had a pleasant eye on a firelit future for Vicki, a cosy, sheltered future with a fender for her feet, a baby for each arm, and an adored husband coming in at the end of the day to be fed and kissed. But this man has outwitted Nature. He weighed, with true German caution, Vicki and her dimples against the tiny portion which was all he could extract from her parents, and found them not heavy enough to make up for the alarming emptiness of that other scale. Now Vicki's fender and babies and busy happy life have vanished into the land of Never Will Be's. She will not find some one else to take his place. She has a story attached to her: a fatal thing here for a girl. Unlike your Miss Cheriton, who gently waves you aside and engages herself without the least difficulty to a duke, Vicki is a marked person, and will be avoided by our careful and calculating young men. She is doomed never to spoil and tease those babies, never to spoil and worship that husband.

Instead, she will, for a year, continue to range the hills here with me, trying to listen politely to my admonishments while inwardly she shudders at the loneliness and vastness of the forests and of life, and then her parents' lease will be up, and they and she will drift down into some little town in the Harz where retired officers finish lives grown vegetable, and the years will pounce upon her and strip her one by one of her little stock of graces. Don't suppose I blame the man, because I don't; I only resent that he should have so much the best of it. There is no law obliging a man to marry because some lovesick girl wants him to—if I were a man I would never marry—but I do deplore the exceeding number of the girls who want him to. If each girl would say her prayers and go her own way, go about her business, her parents having seen to it that she should have a business to go about, what a cheerful, tearless place the world would be. And you must forgive my vociferousness, but really I have had a woeful morning with Vicki, who cried so bitterly into the pages of my Milton that the best part of *Samson Agonistes* is stuck together, and all the red has come off the edges.

Papa Lindeberg came in at the end of the lesson to offer me his umbrella to go home with.

'It is a wet day, Fräulein Hebe,' said he, looking round.

'It is,' said I, gazing ruefully at my poor Milton.

'Even the daughters of the gods,' said he—thus mildly do we continue to joke together—'must sometimes use umbrellas.'

'Yes,' said I, smiling at this pleasant old man, this old man I thought at first so disagreeable; and he went with me to the door, and asked me in an anxious whisper what I thought of Vicki. 'It lasts long—it lasts long,' said he, helplessly.

'Yes,' said I, standing under the umbrella in the rain, while he in the porch rubbed one hand mechanically over the other and stared at me.

'You are a very fortunate young lady,' he said wistfully.

'I?'

'Our poor Vicki—if she were more like you——'

'Like me?'

'It is so clear that you have never known this terrible malady of love. You have the face of a joyful *Backfisch*.'

'Oh!'—I began to laugh; and laughed and laughed till the umbrella shook showers of raindrops off each of its points.

He stood watching me thoughtfully. 'It is true,' he said.

'Oh!' was all I could ejaculate; for, indeed, the idea made me very merry.

'No member of our sex,' said he, 'has ever even for a moment caught what is still a bright and untouched maiden fancy.'

'There was a young man once,' I began, 'in the Jena cake-shop——'

'*Ach*,' he interrupted, waving the young man and his cakes away with an impatient movement of the hand.

'I didn't know,' said I, 'that you could read people's pasts.'

'Yours is easy enough to read. It is shining so clearly in your eyes, it is reflected so limpidly in your face——'

'How nice!' said I, interrupting in my turn, for my feet were getting grievously wet; and you note, I hope, with what industriousness I preserve and record anything of a flattering nature that any one ever says to me.

But you shall hear the other side too; for I turned away, and he turned away, and before I had gone a yard my shoelace came undone and I had to go back to the shelter of the porch to tie it up, and while I had my foot on the scraper and was bending down tying a bow and a knot that should last me till I got home, I heard Frau von Lindeberg from the parlour off the passage make him the following speech:—

'I am constantly surprised, Ludwig, at the amount of time and conversation I see you bestow on Fräulein Schmidt. I can hardly call it impertinence, but there is something indescribable about her manners—an unbecoming freedom, an almost immodest frankness, an almost naked naturalness, that is perilously near impertinence. People of that class do not understand people of ours; and she will, if you are kinder than is absolutely necessary, certainly take advantage of it. Let me beg you to be careful.'

And Ludwig, beginning then and there, never answered a word.

Yours sincerely,
ROSE-MARIE SCHMIDT.

What do you think? Papa's book has been refused by the Jena publisher, by three Berlin publishers, by two in Stuttgart, and one in Leipzig. It is now journeying round Leipzig to the remaining publishers. The first time it came back we felt the blow and drooped; the second time we felt it but did not droop; the third time we felt nothing; the fourth time we laughed.

'Foolish men,' chuckled Papa, tickled by such blindness to their own interests, 'if none will have it we will translate it and send it to England, what?'

'Who is we, darling?' I asked anxiously.

'We is you, Rose-Marie,' said Papa, pulling my ear.

'Oh,' said I.

Scene closes.

LVII

DEAR MR ANSTRUTHER,—It is strange to address this letter to Berlin, and to know that by the time it gets there you will be there too. Well, let it welcome you very heartily back to the Fatherland. I think I know the street you are in; it is facing the Thiergarten, isn't it, and looks north? Quite close to the Brandenburg Thor? I remember it because we trudged, among other places, also about the Thiergarten on our memorable visit, and Papa's eye caught the name of your street, and he stood for ten minutes in the rain giving us a spirited sketch of the man's life and claims to have a street called after him. My stepmother waited with a grim patience, her skirts firmly clutched in each hand. She had come to sight-see and to have things explained to her, so that it would be waste of a railway fare not to look and listen. Papa was in great splendour that day, so obviously superior, in the universality of his knowledge, to either of us damp womenfolk. You won't get much sun there unless your rooms are at the back, but, on the other hand, it is undoubtedly a street for the exclusive and well-to-do, as even I could see as to whom marble steps and wrought-iron gates convey the usual lesson. I, however, would sooner live in a kennel facing south than in a palace where the sun never came; but then, as you know, my tendencies are incurably kennelwards.

Today I am humble and hanging my head, for I have discovered to my pain and horror that Papa and I are living well beyond our income. I expect we have bought too many books, and spent too much in stamps to be used by publishers; but it is certain that we've already consumed over seventy pounds of our yearly hundred, and that we only took five months to do it in. What do you think of that? We have been squandering money right and left somehow. There were no clothes to buy, for what we have will last us at least two years, and where it has all gone to I can't imagine. Indeed, I am a useless person if I cannot even manage a tiny house like this and make such sufficient means do. Papa has written to Professor Martens to tell him he is willing to take in a young man again. Willing? He is eager, hungry for a young man, for he sees that without one things will go badly with us. And I, remembering the wealth we enjoyed while Mr Collins was with us, have written to him to ask if he cares to come back and finish learning German. I don't know if he still wants to, or rather if his father still wants him to, for German to Joey was as the fly in the apothecary's ointment, in its extreme offensiveness, nor have I told Papa that I wrote, because of the peculiar horror with which he regards Joey; but I couldn't resist when I know that six months of Joey would deliver us for two whole years from all young men whatever, and I hope, when the time comes, if it ever does, and Joey with it, to persuade Papa by judicious argument of the eminent desirability of this particular young man.

There are, however, certain difficulties in the way. Our house has two bedrooms, two sitting-rooms, an attic, a kitchen, and a coal-hole. Johanna inhabits the attic. One sitting-room is sacred to Papa and his work. The other is a scrap-room in which we have our meals and receive Frau von Lindeberg when she calls, and I write letters and read books and darn stockings. Where, then, will Joey sleep? The answer is as clear as daylight and very startling: Joey must sleep with Papa. Now that this truth has dawned upon me I spend hours lost in thoughts of things like screens and dividing curtains, besides preparing elaborate speeches for the bringing of Papa to reason. He himself was the first to declare we must positively take in a young man again, and he surely will see, when it is pointed out to him, that any one we have must sleep at the intervals appointed by Nature. I'm afraid he'll see it in the case of every one except the fruitful Joey. It is most unfortunate that Joey should be so foolish about Goethe, for we really do want somebody who doesn't mind about money, and I remember several poor boys in the past who were so very poor that on the days when my stepmother demanded payment I used to have to go out early and wander among the hills till evening, unable to endure the sound of the thalers being wrung out of them. Oh, money is the most horrid of all necessities! I am ashamed to think of the many bright hours of life soiled by anxieties about it, by meannesses about it. Wherever even a question of it arises Love and the Graces fly affrighted, followed closely by the entire troop of equally terrified Muses, out of the nearest window. I detest it. I do not want it. But with all my defiance of it I am crushed beneath the yoke of the penny as completely as everybody else. Well do I know that penny, and how much it is when there's one over, and what worlds away when there's one too few.

Here comes Johanna to lay the dinner. We are rankly vegetarian again, Papa leading the way with immense determination, for he has set his heart at this unfortunate juncture on a new biography of Goethe that must needs come out just now, a big thing in two volumes costing a terrible number of marks, very well done, full of the result of original digging among archives; but he dare not buy it, he says, in the present state of our affairs. 'Dost thou not think, Rose-Marie,' he said, his face in grievous puckers at the prospect, 'that a renewed and careful course of herbage may quickly set the matter right?'

'Not quickly,' said I, shaking my head, and pondering privately what, exactly, he meant by the word renewed.

He looked crestfallen.

'But ultimately,' I said, wishing to cheer him.

'Ultimately—ultimately,' he echoed peevishly. 'The word has a knell-like sound about it that I do not like. When we have reached thy Ultimately I shall no longer be in a state to desire or appreciate Bielschowsky's *Goethe*. My brain, by then, will be clothed with grass, and my veins be streams of running water.'

'Well, darling,' said I, putting my arm through his, 'you'll be at least very nice and refreshing, and extraordinarily like a verse of the Psalms.'

And for two days he has held out undaunted, and here comes our lentil soup and roast apples, so good-bye.

Yours sincerely,

Rose-Marie Schmidt.

LVIII

Galgenberg, Dec. 4.

DEAR MR ANSTRUTHER,—This morning I woke up and
wondered at the strange hush that had fallen on our house,
set so near to a sighing, restless forest; and I looked out of
the window and it was the first snow. All night it must have
snowed, for there was the most beautiful smooth bank of
it without a knob anywhere to show where lately I had
been digging, from beneath my window up into the
forest. Each pine tree was a fairy tree, its laden branches
one white sparkle. The clouds were gone, and by the time
I had done breakfast there was a brilliant blue sky, and the
hills round Jena stood out so sharply against it that they
looked as if somebody had been at them with a hatchet.
Never was there such a serene and silent world as the one
I stepped out into, shovel in hand. I had come to clear a
pathway from the kitchen to the pump; instead, I stood as
silent as everything else, the shovel beneath my arm, gazing
about me and drinking in the purity in a speechless ecstasy.
Oh, the air, Mr Anstruther, the air! Unhappy young man,
who did not breathe it. It was like nothing you've got in
Berlin, of that you may be very certain. It was absolutely
calm; not a breath stirring. It was icy, yet crisp and *frappé
du soleil*. And then how wonderful the world looked after
the sodden picture of yesterday still in my mind. Each twig
of the orchard trees had its white rim on the one side, exact
and smooth, drawn along it by the finger of the north wind.
The steps down from the back door had vanished beneath
the loveliest, sleekest white covering. The pump, till the day

before and ever since I have known it, a bleakly impressive object silhouetted in all its lankness and gauntness against a background of sky and mountain, was grown grotesque, bulky, almost playful, its top and long iron handle heaped with an incredible pile of snow, its spout hung about with a beard of icicles. Frau von Lindeberg's kitchen smoke went up straight and pearly into the golden light. The roofs of Jena were in blue shadow. Our neighbour's roof flashed with a million diamonds in the sun. Two rooks cawed to each other from the pine tree nearest our door; and Rose-Marie Schmidt said her morning prayers then and there, still clinging to her shovel. Then she pulled off her coat, hung her hat on the door-handle, and began in a sort of high rapture to make a pathway to the pump. What are the joys of summer to these? There is nothing like it, nothing, nothing in the world. I know no mood of Nature's that I do not love—or think I do when it is over—but for keenness of feeling, for stinging pleasure, for overflowing life, give me a winter's day with the first snow, a clear sky, and the thermometer ten degrees Réaumur below zero.

Vicki called out from her doorway—you could hear the least call this morning at an extraordinary distance—to ask if I were snowed up too much to come down as usual.

'I'm coming down, and I'm making the path to do it with,' I called back, shovelling with an energy that set my hair dancing about my ears.

She shouted back—her very shout was cheerful, and I did not need to see her face to know that today there would be no tears—that she too would make a path up to meet mine; and presently I heard the sounds of another joyful shovel.

Underneath, the ground was hard with frost; it had frozen violently for several hours before the snow came up on the huge purple wings of the north wind. The muddy roads, the soaked forest, the plaintive patter of the rain, were wiped out of existence between a sleeping and a waking. This was no world in which to lament. This was no place in which sighs were possible. The thought that a man's marrying one or not could make so much as the faintest smudge across the bright hopefulness of life made me laugh aloud with healthiest derision. Oh, how my shovel rang against the frozen stones! The feathery snow was scattered broadcast at each stroke. My body glowed and tingled. My hair grew damp about my forehead. The sun smiled broadly down upon my back. Papa flung up his window to cheer me on, but shut it again with a slam before he had well got out his words. Johanna came for an instant to the door, peeped out, gasped that it was cold—*unheimlich kalt* was her strange expression: *unheimlich* = dismal, uncanny; think of it!—and shut the door as hurriedly as Papa had shut the window. An hour later two hot and smiling young women met together on the path they had shovelled, and straightened themselves up, and looked proudly at the results of their work, and laughed at each other's scarlet faces and at the way their noses and chins were covered with tiny beads. 'As if it were August and we'd been reaping,' said Vicki; and the big girl laughed at this, and the small girl laughed at this, with an excessiveness that would have convinced a passer-by that somebody was being very droll.

But there was no passer-by. You don't pass by if snow lies on the roads three feet deep. We are cut off entirely from Jena and shops. This letter won't start for I haven't an idea how long. Milk cannot come to us, and we cannot go to where there is a cow. I have flour enough to bake bread with for about ten days unless the Lindebergs should have none, in which case it will last less than five. The coal-hole is stored with cabbages and carrots, buried, with cunning circumvention of decay, in sand. Potatoes abound in earth-covered heaps out of doors. Apples abound in Johanna's attic. We vegetarians come off well on occasions like this, for the absence of milk and butter does not afflict the already sorely afflicted, and of course the absence of meat leaves us completely cold.

Vicki and I have been mending a boy's sledge we found in the lumber-room of their house—I suppose the sledge used in his happier days by the *Assessor* now chained to a desk in Berlin—and with this we are going out after coffee this afternoon when the sky turns pale green and stars come out and blink at us, to the top of the road where it joins the forest, dragging the sledge up as best we can over the frozen snow, and then, tightly clutching each other, and I expect not altogether in silence, we intend to career down again as far as the thing will career, flashing, we hope, past her mother's gate at a speed that will prevent all interference. Perhaps we shall not be able to stop, and will be landed at last in the middle of the market-place in Jena. I'll take this letter with me in case that happens, because then I can post it. Good-bye. It's going to be glorious. Don't you wish you had a sledge and a mountain too?

Yours sincerely,
ROSE-MARIE SCHMIDT.

LIX

DEAR MR ANSTRUTHER,—We are still in sunshine and frost up here, and are all very happy, we three Schmidts—Johanna is the third—because Joey arrives tomorrow and we shall once more roll in money. I hasten to tell you this, for there were signs in your last two letters that you were taking our position to heart. It is wonderfully kind, I think, the way you are interested in our different little pains and pleasures. I am often more touched than I care to tell you by the sincerity of your sympathy with all we do, and feel very grateful for so true a friend. I was so glad you gave up coming to Jena on your way to Berlin, for it showed that you try to be reasonable, and then you know Professor Martens goes to Berlin himself every now and then to take sweet counsel with men like Harnack, so you will be sure to see him sooner or later, and see him comfortably, without a rush to catch a train. You say you did not come because I urged you not to, and that in all things you want to please me. Well, I would prefer to suppose you a follower of that plain-faced but excellent guide, Common Sense. Still, being human, the less lofty and conscientious side of me does like to know there is some one who wishes to please me. I feel deliciously flattered—when I let myself think of it; nearly always I take care to think of something else—that a young man of your undoubted temporal and spiritual advantages should be desirous of pleasing an obscure person like me. What would Frau von Lindeberg say? Do you remember Shelley's wife's sister, the Miss Westbrook who brushed her hair so much, with her constant 'Gracious Heavens, what would Miss Warne say?' I feel inclined to exclaim the same thing about Frau von Lindeberg, but with an opposite meaning. And it is really very surprising that you should be so kind, for I have been a shrew to you often, and have been absorbed in my own affairs, and have not erred on the side of over-sympathy about yours. Some day, when we are both very old, perhaps you will get a few hours' leave from the dowager duchess you'll marry when you are forty, and will come and look at my pigs and my garden, and sit with me before the fire and talk over our long friendship and all the long days of our life. And I, when I hear you are coming, shall be in a flutter, and will get out my best dress, and will fuss over things like asparagus and a salad, and tell the heated and awe-stricken maid that His Britannic Majesty's Ambassador at the Best Place to be an Ambassador in in the World is coming to supper; and we shall feel how sweet it is to be old dear friends.

Meanwhile we are both very busy with the days we have got to now. Today, for instance, has been so violently active that every bone I possess is aching. I'll tell you what happened, since you so earnestly assure me that all we do interests you. The snow is frozen so hard that far from being cut off as I had feared from shops and food, there is the most glorious sledging road down to Jena; and at once, on hearing of Joey's imminence, Vicki and I coasted down on the sledge, and I bought the book Papa has been wanting and a gigantic piece of beef. Then we persuaded a small but strong boy, a boy of open countenance and superior manners whom we met in the market-place, to drag the sledge with the beef and the book up the hill again for us; and so we set out homewards, walking gaily one on each side of him, encouraging him with loud admiration of his prowess. 'See,' said I, when I knew a specially steep bit was coming, 'see what a great thing it is to be able to draw so much so easily.'

A smirk and renewed efforts were the result of this speech at first; but the smirk grew smaller as the hill grew steeper, and the efforts dwindled to vanishing point with the higher windings of the road. At last there was no smirk at all, and at my sixth repetition of the encouragement he stopped dead. 'If it is such a great thing,' he said, wiping his youthful forehead with a patched sleeve, and looking at me with a precociousness I had not till then observed in his eyes, 'why do you not do it yourself?'

Vicki and I stared at each other in silent wonder.

'Because,' I said, turning a reproachful gaze on him, 'because, my dear little boy, I desire you to have the chance of earning the fifty pfennings we have promised to give you when we get to the top.'

He began to pull again, but no longer with any pride in his performance. Vicki and I walked in silence behind, and at the next steep bit, instead of repeating a form of words I felt had grown vain, I skilfully unhooked the parcel of meat hanging on the right-hand runner and carried it, and Vicki, always quick to follow my example, unhooked the biography of Goethe from the left-hand runner and carried that. The sledge leaped forward, and for a space the boy climbed with greater vigour. Then came another long steep bit, and he flagged again.

'Come, come,' said I, 'it is quite easy.'

He at once stopped and wiped his forehead. 'If it is easy,' he asked, 'why do you not do it yourself?'

'Because, my dear little boy,' said I, trying to be patient, but meat is heavy, and I knew it to be raw, and I feared every moment to feel a dreadful dampness oozing through the paper, and I was out of breath, and no longer completely calm, 'you engaged to pull it up for us, and having engaged to do it, it is your duty to do it. I will not come between a boy and his duty.'

The boy looked at Vicki. 'How she talks,' he said.

Vicki and I again stared at each other in silent wonder, and while we were staring he pulled the sledge sideways across the road and sat down.

'Come, come,' said I, striving after a brisk severity.

'I am tired,' he said, leaning his chin on his hand and studying first my face and then Vicki's with a detached, impartial scrutiny.

'We too are tired,' said I, 'and see, yet we carry the heavy parcels for you. The sledge, empty, is quite light.'

'Then why do you not pull it yourself?' he asked again.

'Anyhow,' said Vicki, 'while he sits there we needn't hold these great things.' And she put the volumes on the sledge, and I let the meat drop on it, which it did with a horrible, soft, heavy thud.

The boy sat motionless.

'Let him get his wind,' said Vicki, turning away to look over the edge of the road at the view.

'I'm afraid he's a bad little boy,' said I, following her and gazing too at the sparkling hills across the valley. 'A bad little boy, encased in an outer semblance of innocence.'

'He only wants his wind,' said Vicki.

'He shows no symptoms of not having got it,' said I; for the boy was very calm, and his mouth was shut sweetly in a placid curve.

We waited, looking at the view, humanely patient as became two highly civilized persons. The boy got up after a few minutes and shook himself.

'I am rested,' he announced, with a sudden return to the politeness that had charmed us in Jena.

'It certainly was rather a long pull up,' said I, kindly, softened by his manner.

'Yes,' said he, 'but I will not keep the ladies waiting longer.'

And he did not, for he whisked the sledge round, sat himself upon it, and before we had in the least understood what was happening, he and it and the books for Papa and the beef for Joey were darting down the hill, skimming along the track with the delicious swiftness none knew and appreciated better than we did. At the bend of the road he gave a joyful whoop and waved his cap. Then he disappeared.

Vicki and I stared at each other once more in silent wonder.

'What an abandoned little boy,' she gasped at last—he must have been almost in Jena by the time we were able to speak.

'The poor beef,' said I, very ruefully, for it was a big piece and had cost vast sums.

'Yes, and the books,' said Vicki.

'Yes, and the *Assessor's* sledge,' said I.

There was nothing for it but to hurry down after him and seek out the authorities and set them in pursuit; and so we hurried as much as can be hurried over such a road, tired, silent, and hungry, and both secretly nettled to the point of madness at having been so easily circumvented by one small boy.

'Little boys are more pestilential than almost anything I know,' said Vicki, after a period of speechless crunching over the snow.

'Far more than anything I know,' said I.

'I'm thankful I did not marry,' said she.

'So am I,' said I.

'The world's much too full of them as it is,' said she.

'Much,' said I.

'Oh,' she cried suddenly, stamping her foot, 'if I could only get hold of him—wicked, wicked little wretch!'

'What would you do?' I asked, curious to see if her plans were at all like mine.

'Gr—r—r—r,' said Vicki, clenching all those parts of her, such as teeth and fists, that would clench.

'Oh, so would I!' I cried.

We were almost at the bottom; the road was making its final bend; and, as we turned the corner, behold the boy, his cap off, his head bent, his shoulders straining at the rope, pulling the sledge laboriously up again. And there was the beef hung on one runner, and there were the books hung on the other. We both stopped dead, arrested by this spectacle. He was almost upon us before he saw us, so intent was he on his business, his eyes on the ground, the sun shining on his yellow hair, the drops of labour rolling down his crimson cheeks.

'What?' he panted, pausing when he saw our four boots in a row in his path, and had looked up and recognized the rest of us, 'what, am I there already?'

'No,' I cried, in the voice of justified anger, 'you are not there—you are here, at the very beginning of the mountain. Now, what have you to say for yourself?'

'Nothing,' said he, grinning and wiping his face with his sleeve. 'But it was a good ride.'

'You have only just escaped the police and prison,' I said, still louder. 'We were on our way to hand you over to them.'

'If I had been there to hand,' said he, winking at Vicki, to whom he had apparently taken a fancy that was in no way encouraged.

'You had stolen our sledge and our parcels,' I continued, glaring down on him.

'Here they are. They are all here. What more do you want?' said he. 'How she talks,' he added, turning to Vicki and thrusting out his underlip with an expression that could only mean disgust.

'You are a very naughty little boy,' said Vicki. 'Give me the rope and be off.'

'Give me my fifty pfennings.'

'Your fifty pfennings?' we exclaimed with one voice.

'You promised me fifty pfennings.'

'To pull the sledge up to the top.'

'I am ready to do it.'

'Thank you. We have had enough. Let the rope go——'

'And get home to your mother——'

'And ask her to give you a thorough——'

'A bargain is a bargain,' said the boy, planting himself squarely in front of me, while I adjusted the rope over my shoulders and prepared to pull.

'Now, run away, you very naughty little boy,' said I, pulling sideways to pass him by.

He stepped aside too, and faced me again.

'You promised me fifty pfennings,' he said.

'To pull the sledge up.'

'I am willing to do it.'

'Yes, and coast down again as soon as you have got to the top. Be off with you. We are not playing games.'

'A promise is a promise,' said the boy.

'Vicki, remove him from my path,' said I.

Vicki took him by the arm and gingerly drew him on one side, and I started up the hill, surprised to find what hard work it was.

'I am coming too,' said the boy.

'Are you?' said Vicki.

'Yes. To fetch my fifty pfennings.'

We said no more. I couldn't, because I was so breathlessly pulling, and Vicki marched by my side in indignant silence, with a jealous eye divided between the parcels and the boy. He, unencumbered, thrust his hands into his pockets and beguiled the way by shrilly whistling.

At each winding of the road when Vicki and I changed places he renewed his offer to fulfil his first bargain; but we, more and more angry as we grew hotter and hotter, refused with an ever-increasing wrath.

'Come, come,' said he, when a very steep bit had forced me to pause and struggle for breath, 'come, come——' and he imitated my earlier manner—'it is quite easy.'

I looked at him with what of majesty I could, and answered not a word.

At Vicki's gate he was still with us. 'I will see you safely home,' Vicki said to me when we got there.

'This where you live?' inquired the boy, peeping through the bars of the gate with cheerful interest. 'Nice little house.'

We were silent.

'I will see her home,' he said to Vicki, 'if you don't want to. But she can surely take care of herself, a great girl like that?'

We were silent.

At my gate he was still with us. 'This where she lives?' he asked Vicki, again peeping through the bars with cheerful interest. 'Funny little house.'

We were silent. In silence we opened the gate and dragged the sledge in. He came too.

'You cannot come in here,' said Vicki. 'This is private property.'

'I only wish to fetch my fifty pfennings,' said he. 'It will save you trouble if I come to the door.'

We went in in silence, and together carried the sledge inside, a thing we had not yet done, and took it with immense exertions into the parlour, and put it under the table, and tied it by each of its four corners to each of the table's four legs.

'There,' said Vicki, scrambling to her feet again, and looking at her knots with satisfaction, 'that's safe if anything is.'

I went with her to the door. The boy was still there, cap in hand, very polite, very patient.

'And my fifty pfennings?' he asked pleasantly.

I cannot explain what we did next. I pulled out my purse and paid him, which was surprising enough, but Vicki, to whom fifty pfennings are also precious, pulled out hers too and gave him fifty on her own account. I am quite unable to explain either her action or mine. The boy made us each the politest bow, his cap sweeping the snow.

'She,' he said to Vicki, jerking his head my way, 'may think she is the prettiest, but you are certainly the best.'

And he left us to settle it between us, and walked away shrilly whistling.

And I am so tired that my very pen has begun to ache, so good-bye.

ROSE-MARIE SCHMIDT.

Oh, I must tell you that Papa refused to have Joey sleep in his room with a flatness that put a stop to my arguments before they were even begun. 'Nay,' he cried, 'I will not.' And when I opened my mouth to produce the arguments— 'Nay,' he cried again, 'I will not.' He drowned my speech. He would not listen. He would not reason. Parrot-like through the house resounded his cry—'Nay, I will not.' I was in despair. But everything has arranged itself. Joey is to have the *Assessor's* room on the ground-floor of our neighbour's house, and will come up here for lessons and meals. He is only to sleep down there, and will be all day here. We telegraphed to Weimar to ask about it, and the ever kind owner immediately agreed. Frau von Lindeberg is displeased, for she says no Dammerlitz has ever yet been known to live in a house where there was a lodger—a common lodger she said first, but corrected herself, and covered up the common with a cough.

LX

DEAR MR ANSTRUTHER,—I must write tonight, though it is late, to tell you of my speechless surprise when I came in an hour ago and found you had been here. I knew you had the moment I came in. At once I recognized the smell of the cigarettes you smoke. I went upstairs and called Johanna, for I was not sure that you were not still here, in the parlour, and frankly I was not going down if you were, for I do not choose to have my fastnesses stormed. She told me of your visit; how you had come up on foot soon after Vicki and Joey and I had started off for an afternoon's tobogganing on the hills, how you had stayed talking to Papa, and talking and talking, till you had to hurry down to catch the last train. 'And he bade me greet you for him,' finished Johanna. 'Indeed?' said I.

Do you like winter excursions into the country? Is Berlin boring you already? I shook my head in grave disapproval as Johanna proceeded with her tale. I am all for a young man's attending to his business and not making sudden wild journeys that take him away for a whole day and most of a night. Papa was delighted, I must say, to have had at last, as he told me with disconcerting warmth, at last after all these months, an intelligent conversation; but with his delight the success of your visit ends, for when I heard of it I was not delighted at all. Why did you go into the kitchen? Johanna says you would go, and then that you went out hatless at the back door and down to the bottom of the garden, and that you stood there leaning against the fence as though it were summer. 'Still without a hat,' said Johanna, in her turn shaking her head, '*bei dieser Kälte.*'

Bei dieser Kälte, indeed. Yes; what made you do it? I am glad I was out, for I do not care to look on while the usually reasonable behave unaccountably. I don't think I can be friends with you for a little after this. I think I really must quarrel, for it isn't very decent to drop unexpectedly upon a person who from time to time has told you, with the frankness that is her most marked feature, that she doesn't want to be dropped upon. No doubt you wished to see Papa as well, and, on your way through Jena, Professor Martens; but I will not pretend to suppose your call was not chiefly intended for me, for it is to me and not to either of those wiser ones that you have written every day for months past. You are a strange young man. Heaven knows what you have accustomed yourself to imagining me to be. I almost wish now that you had seen me when I came in from our violent exercise, a touzled, short-skirted, heated person. It might have cured you. I forgot to look in the glass, but of course my hair and eyelashes were as white with hoar-frost as Vicki's and Joey's, and from beneath them and from above my turned-up collar must have emerged just such another glowing nose. Even Papa was struck by my appearance—after having gazed, I suppose, for hours on your composed correctness—and remarked that living in the country did not necessarily mean a complete return to savage nature.

The house feels very odd tonight. So do I. It feels haunted. So do I. I want to scold you, and yet I cannot. I have the strangest desire to cry. It is the thought that you came this long way, toiled up this long hill, waited those long hours, all to see some one who is glad to have missed you, that makes me want to. The night is so black outside my window, and somewhere through that blackness you are travelling at this moment, disappointed, across the endless frozen fields and forests that you must go through inch by inch before you reach Berlin. Why did you do a thing so comfortless? And here have I actually begun to cry—I think because it is so dark, and you are not yet home.

ROSE-MARIE SCHMIDT.

LXI

DEAR MR ANSTRUTHER,—I don't quite understand. Purely motherly, I should say. Perhaps our notions of the exact meaning of the word 'friend' are different. I include in it a motherly and sisterly interest in bodily well-being, in dry socks, warm feet, regular meals. I do not like my friend to be out on a bitter night, to take a tiring journey, to be disappointed. My friend's mother would have, I imagine, precisely the same feeling. My friend should not, then, mistake mere motherliness for other and less comfortable sentiments. But I am busy today, and have no time to puzzle out your letter. It must have been the outcome of a rather strange mood.

Yours sincerely,

ROSE-MARIE SCHMIDT.

Tell me more about your daily life in Berlin, the people you see, the houses you go to, the attitude, kind or otherwise, of your chief. Tell me these things, instead of swamping me with subtleties of sentiment. I don't understand subtleties, and I fear and despise sentiment as a certain spoiler of plain bread-and-butter happiness. There should be no sentiment between friends. The moment there is they leave off being just friends; and is not that what we both most want to be?

LXII

Galgenberg, Dec. 19.

OH, I can do nothing with you! You are bent, I'm afraid, on losing your friend. Don't write me such letters—don't, don't, don't! My heart sinks when I see you deliberately setting about strangling our friendship. Am I to lose it, then, that too? Your last letters are like bad dreams, so strange and unreasonable, so without the least order or self-control. I read them with my fingers in my ears—an instinctive foolish movement of protection against words I do not want to hear. Dear friend, do not take your friendship from me. Give yourself a shake; come out from those vain imaginings your soul has gone to dwell among. What shall I talk to you about this bright winter's morning? Yes, I will write you longer letters; you needn't beg so hard, as though the stars couldn't get along in their courses if I didn't. See, I am willing to do anything to keep my friend. You are my only one, the only person in the world to whom I tell the silly thoughts that come into my head and so get rid of them. You listen, and you are the only person in the world who does. You help me, and I in my turn want to be allowed to go on helping you. Do not put an end to what is precious—believe me, it will grow more and more precious with years. Do not, in the heat and impatience of youth, kill the poor goose who, if left alone, will lay the most beautiful golden eggs. What shall I talk to you about to turn your attention somewhere else, somewhere far removed from that unhappy bird? Shall I tell you about Papa's book, finally refused by every single publisher, come back battered and draggled to be galvanized by me into fresh life in an English translation? Shall I tell you how I sit for three hours daily doing it, pen in hand, ink on fingers, hair pushed back from an anxious brow, Papa hovering behind with a dictionary in which, full of distrust, he searches as I write to see if it contains the words I have used? Shall I tell you about Joey, whose first disgust at finding himself once more with us has given place by degrees that grow visibly wider to a rollicking enjoyment? Less and less does he come up here. More and more does he stay down there. He hurries through his lessons with a speed that leaves Papa speechless, and is off and hauling the sledge up past our gate with Vicki walking demurely beside him, and is whizzing down again past our gate with Vicki sitting demurely in front of him, before Papa is well through the list of adjectives he applies to him once at least every day. I never see the sledge now nearer than in the distance. Vicki wears her stiff shirts again, and her neat ties again, and the sporting belt that makes her waist look so very trim and tiny. If anything she is more aggressively starched and boyish than before. Her collars seem to grow higher and cleaner each time I see her. Her hat is tilted further forward. Her short skirts show the neatest little boots. She is extraordinarily demure. She never cries. Joey reads *Samson Agonistes* with us, and points out the jokes to Vicki. Vicki says why did I never tell her it was so funny? I stare first at one and then at the other, and feel a hundred years old.

'I say,' said Joey, coming into the kitchen just now.

'Well, what?' said I.

'I'm going to Berlin for a day.'

'Are you indeed?'

'Tell the old man, will you?'

'Tell the who?'

264

'The old man. I shan't be here for the lesson tomorrow, thank the Lord. I'm off by the first train.'

'Indeed,' said I.

There was a silence, during which Joey fidgeted about among the culinary objects scattered around him. I went on peeling apples. When he had fidgeted as much as he wanted to he lit a cigarette.

'No,' said I. 'Not in kitchens. A highly improper thing to do.'

He threw it into the dustbin. 'I say,' he said again.

'Well, what?' said I, again.

'What do you think—what do you think——'

He paused. I waited. As he didn't go on I thought he had done.

'What do I think?' I said. 'You'd be staggered if I told you, it's such a lot, and it's so terrific.'

'What do you think,' repeated Joey, taking no heed of me, but, with his hands in his pockets, kicking a fallen apple aimlessly about on the floor, 'what do you think the little girl'd like for Christmas and that, don't you know?'

I stopped peeling and gazed at him, knife and apple suspended in mid-air.

'The little girl?' I inquired. 'Do you mean Johanna?'

Joey stared. Then he grinned at me monstrously.

'You bet,' was his cryptic reply.

'What am I to bet?' I asked patiently.

Joey gave the fallen apple a kick. Looking down, I observed that it was the biggest and the best, and stooped to rescue it.

'It's not pretty,' said I, rebuking him, 'to kick even an apple when it's down.'

'Oh, I say,' said Joey, impatiently, 'do be sensible. There never was any gettin' much sense out of you, I remember. And you're only pretendin'. You know I mean Vicki.'

'Vicki?'

He had the grace to blush. 'Well, Fräulein What's her name. You can't expect any one decent to get the hang of these names of yours. They ain't got any hang, so how's one to get it? What'd she like for Christmas? Don't you all kick up a mighty fuss here over Christmas? Trees and presents and that? Plummier plum-pudding than we have, and mincier mince-pies; what?'

'If you think you will get even one plum-pudding or mince-pie,' said I, thoughtfully peeling, 'you are gravely mistaken. The national dish is carp boiled in beer.'

Joey looked really revolted. 'What?' he cried, not liking to credit his senses.

'Carp boiled in beer,' I repeated distinctly. 'It is what I'm going to give you on Christmas Day.'

'No, you're not,' he said hastily.

'Yes, I am,' I insisted. 'And before it and after it you will be required, in accordance with German custom, to sing chorales.'

'I'd like to see myself doin' it. You'll have to sing 'em alone. I'm invited to feed down there.'

And he jerked his head towards that portion of the kitchen wall beyond which, if you passed through it and the intervening coal-hole and garden and orchard, you would come to the dwelling of the Lindebergs.

'Oh,' said I; and looked at him thoughtfully.

'Yes,' said he, trying to meet my look with an equal calm, but conspicuously failing. 'That bein' so,' he went on hurriedly, 'and my droppin', so to speak, into the middle of somebody's Christmas tree and that, it seems to me only decent to give the little girl somethin'. What shall I get her? Somethin' to put on, I suppose. A brooch, or a pin, what?'

'Or a ring,' said I, thoughtfully peeling.

'A ring? What, can one—oh, I say, don't let's waste time rottin'——'

And glancing up through cautious eyelashes I saw he was very red.

'It'd be easy enough if it was you,' he said revengefully.

'What would?'

'Hittin' on what you'd like.'

'Would it!'

'All you'd want to do the trick would be a dictionary.'

'Now, Mr Collins, that's unkind,' said I, laying down my knife.

He began to grin again. 'It's true,' he insisted.

'It suggests such an immeasurable stuffiness,' I complained.

'It isn't my fault,' said he, grinning.

'But perhaps I deserve it because I mentioned a ring. Let me tell you, as man to man, that you must buy no brooches for Vicki.'

'A pin, then?'

'No pins.'

'A necklace, then?'

'Nothing of the sort. What would her parents say? Give her chocolates, a bunch of roses, perhaps a book—but nothing more. If you do you'll get into a nice scrape.'

Joey looked at me. 'What sort of scrape?' he asked curiously.

'Gracious heavens, don't you see? Are you such a supreme goose? My poor young man, the parents would immediately ask you your intentions.'

'Oh, would they?' said Joey, in his turn becoming thoughtful; and after a moment he said again, 'Oh, would they?'

'It's as certain as anything I know,' said I.

'Oh, is it?' said Joey, still thoughtful.

'It's a catastrophe young men very properly dread,' said I.

'Oh, do they?' said Joey, sunk in thought.

'Well, if you're not listening——' And I shrugged my shoulders, and went on with my peeling.

He pulled his cap out of the pocket into which it had been stuffed, and began to put it on, tugging it first over one ear and then over the other in a deep abstraction.

'You're in my kitchen,' I observed.

'Sorry,' he said, snatching it off. 'I forgot. You always make me feel as if I were out of doors.'

'How very odd,' said I, interested and slightly flattered.

'Ain't it. East wind, you know—decidedly breezy, not to say nippin'. Well, I must be goin'.'

'I think so too,' said I, coldly.

'Don't be dull while I'm away,' said Joey; and departed with a nod.

But he put in his head again the next moment. 'I say, Miss Schmidt——'

'Well, what?'

'You think I ought to stick to chocolates, then?'

'If you don't there'll be extraordinary complications,' said I.

'You're sure of that?'

'Positive.'

'You'd swear it?'

I threw down my knife and apple. 'Now, what's the matter with the boy!' I exclaimed impatiently. 'Do I ever swear?'

'But if you did you would?'

'Swear what?'

'That a bit of jewellery would bring the complications about?'

'Oh—dense, dense, dense! Of course it would. You'd be surprised at the number and size of them. You can't be too careful. Give her a hymn-book.'

Joey gave a loud whoop.

'Well, it's safe,' said I, severely, 'and it appeals to parents.'

'You bet,' said Joey, screwing his face into a limitlessly audacious wink.

'I wish,' said I, very plaintively, 'that I knew exactly what it is I am to bet. You constantly tell me to do so, but never add the necessary directions.'

'Oh, I'm goin',' was Joey's irrelevant reply; and his head popped out as suddenly as it had popped in.

Or shall I tell you—I am anxious to make this letter long enough to please you—about Frau von Lindeberg, who spent two days elaborately cutting Joey, the two first days of his appearance in their house as lodger, persuaded, I suppose, that no one even remotely and by business connected with the Schmidts could be anything but undesirable, and how, meeting him in the passage, or on his way through the garden to us, the iciest stare was all she felt justified in giving him in return for his friendly grin, and how on the third day she suddenly melted, and stopped and spoke pleasantly to the poor solitary, commiserating with his situation as a stranger in a foreign country, and suggesting the alleviation to his loneliness of frequent visits to them? No one knows the first cause of this melting. I think she must have heard through her servant of the number and texture of those pink and blue silk handkerchiefs, of his amazing piles of new and costly shirts, of the obvious solidity of the silver on everything of his that has a back or a stopper or a handle or a knob. Anyhow, on that third morning she came up and called on us, asking particularly for Papa.

'I particularly wished,' she said to me, spreading herself out as she did the last time on the sofa, 'to see your good father on a matter of some importance.'

'I'll go and call him,' said I, concealing my conviction that though I might call he would not come.

And he would not. 'What, interrupt my work?' he cried. 'Is the woman mad?'

I went back and made excuses. They were very lame ones, and Frau von Lindeberg instantly brushed them aside.

'I will go to him,' she said, getting up. 'Your excellent father will not refuse me, I am sure.'

Papa was sitting in his slippers before the stove, doing nothing, as far as I could see, except very comfortably reading the new book about Goethe.

'I am sorry to disturb so busy a man,' said Frau von Lindeberg, bearing down with smiles on this picture of peace.

Papa sprang up, and, seeing there was no escape, pretended to be quite pleased to see her. He offered her his chair, he prayed for indulgence towards his slippers, and, sitting down facing her, inquired in what way he could be of service.

'I want to know something about the young Englishman who occupies a room in our house,' said Frau von Lindeberg, without losing time. 'You understand that it is not only natural but incumbent on a parent to wish for information in regard to a person dwelling under the same roof.'

'I can give every information,' said Papa, readily. 'His name in English is Collins. In German it is *Esel*.'

'Oh, really!' said Frau von Lindeberg, taken aback.

'It is, madam,' said Papa, looking very pleasant, as became a man in his own house confronted by a female visitor. 'We have rechristened him. And no array of words with which I am acquainted will express the exactness of his resemblance to that useful but unintelligent beast.'

'Oh, really!' said Frau von Lindeberg, not yet recovered.

'The ass, madam, is conspicuous for the narrowness of its understanding. So is Mr Collins. The ass is exasperating to persons of normal brains. So is Mr Collins. The ass is lazy in regard to work, and obstinate. So is Mr Collins. The ass is totally indifferent to study. So is Mr Collins. The ass has never heard of Goethe. Neither has Mr Collins. The ass is useful to the poor. So is Mr Collins. The ass, indeed, is the poor man's most precious possession. So, emphatically, is Mr Collins.'

'Oh, really!' said Frau von Lindeberg again.

'Is there anything more you wish to know?' Papa inquired politely, for she seemed unable immediately to go on.

She cleared her throat. 'In what way—in what way is he useful?' she asked.

'Madam, he pays.'

'Yes—of course, of course. You cannot'—she smiled—'be expected to teach him German for nothing.'

'Far from doing that, I teach him German for a good deal.'

'Is he—do you know anything about his relations? You understand,' she added, 'that it is not altogether pleasant for a private family like ours to have a strange young man living under the same roof.'

'Understand?' cried Papa. 'I understand it so thoroughly that I most positively refused to have him under this one.'

'Ah—yes,' said Frau von Lindeberg, a Dammerlitz expression coming into her face. 'The cases are not—are not quite—pray tell me, who and what is his father?'

'A respectable man, madam, I should judge.'

'Respectable? And besides respectable?'

'Eminently worthy, I should say, from his letters.'

'Ah yes. And—and anything else?'

'Honourable too, I fancy. Indeed, I have not a doubt.'

'Is he of any family?'

'He is of his own family, madam.'

'Ah yes. And did you—did you say he was well off?'

'He is apparently revoltingly rich.'

An electric shock seemed to make Frau von Lindeberg catch her breath.

'Oh, really,' she then said evenly. 'Did he inherit his wealth?'

'Made it, madam. He is an ironmonger.'

Another electric shock made Frau von Lindeberg catch her breath again. Then she again said—'Oh, really!'

There was a pause.

'England,' she said, after a moment, 'is different from Germany.'

'I believe it is,' admitted Papa.

'And ironmongers there may be different from ironmongers here.'

'It is at least conceivable.'

'Tell me, what status has an ironmonger in England?'

'What status?'

'In society.'

'Ah, that I know not. I went over there seven and twenty years ago for the purpose of marrying, and I met no ironmongers. Not consciously, that is.'

'Would they—would they be above the set in which you then found yourself, or would they——' she tried to conceal a shiver—'be below it?'

'I know not. I know nothing of society either there or here. But I do know that money, there as here, is very mighty. It is, I should say, merely a question of having enough.'

'And has he enough?'

'The man, madam, is, I believe, perilously near becoming

that miserable and isolated creature a millionaire. God help the unfortunate Joey.'

'But why? Why should God help him? Why is he unfortunate? Does not he get any share?'

'Any share? He gets it all. He is the only child. Now, I put it to you, what chance is there for an unhappy youth with no brains——'

'Oh, I must really go! I have taken up an unwarrantable amount of your time. Thank you so very much, dear Herr Schmidt—no, no, do not disturb yourself, I beg—your daughter will show me the way——'

'But,' cried Papa, vainly trying to detain this determinedly retreating figure, 'about his character, his morals—we have not yet touched——'

'Ah yes—so kind—I will not keep you now. Another time, perhaps——'

And Frau von Lindeberg got herself out of the room and out of the house. Scarcely did she say good-bye to me, in so great and sudden a fever was she to be gone; but she did turn on the doorstep and give me a curiously intense look. It began at my eyes, travelled upwards to my hair, down across my face, and from there over my whole body to my toes. It was a very odd look. It was the most burningly critical look that has ever shrivelled my flesh.

Now, what do you think of this enormous long letter? It has made me quite cheerful just writing it, and I was not very cheerful when I began. I hope the reading of it will do you as much good. Good-bye. Write and tell me you are happy.

Yours sincerely,
ROSE-MARIE SCHMIDT.

Do, do try to be happy!

LXIII

DEAR MR ANSTRUTHER,—The house is quite good enough for me, I assure you—the 'setting,' I think you call it, suggesting with pleasant flattery that there is something precious to be set. It only has the bruised sort of colour you noticed when its background is white with snow. In summer against the green it looks as white as you please; but a thing must be white indeed to look so in the midst of our present spotlessness. And it is not damp if there are fires enough. And the rooms are not too small for me— 'poky' was the adjective you applied to the dear little things. And I am never lonely. And Joey is very nice, even though he doesn't quite talk in blank verse. I feel a sort of shame when you make so much of me, when you persist in telling me that the outer conditions of my life are unworthy. It makes me feel so base, such a poor thing. Sometimes I half believe you must be poking fun. Anyhow, I don't know what you would be at; do you wish me to turn up my nose at my surroundings? And do you see any good that it would do? And the details you go into! That coffee-pot you saw and are so plaintive about came to grief only the day before your visit, and will, in due season, be replaced by another. Meanwhile it doesn't hurt coffee to be poured out of a broken spout, and it doesn't hurt us to drink it after it has passed through this humiliation. On the contrary, we receive it thankfully into cups, and remain perfectly unruffled. You say, and really you say it in a kind of agony, that the broken spout, you are sure, is symbolic of much that is invisible in

274

my life. You say—in effect, though your words are choicer—
that if you had your way my life would be set about with
no spouts that were not whole. If you had your way? Mr
Anstruther, it is a mercy that in this one matter you have
not got it. What an extremely discontented creature I would
become if I spent my days embedded in the luxury you,
by a curious perverseness, think should be piled around me.
I would gasp ill-natured epigrams from morning till night.
I would wring my hands, and rend the air with cries of *cui
bono*. The broken spout is a brisk reminder of the
transitoriness of coffee-pots and of life. It sets me hurrying
about my business, which is first to replace it, and then by
every possible ingenuity to make the most of the passing
moment. The passing moment is what you should keep
your eye on, my young friend. It is a slippery, flighty thing;
but, properly pounced upon, lends itself fruitfully to
squeezing. The upshot of your last letter is, I gather, that
for some strange reason, some extremity of perverseness,
you would have me walk in silk attire, and do it in halls
made of marble. It suffocates me only to think of it. I love
my freedom and forest trampings, my short skirts and
swinging arms. I want the wind to blow on me, and the
sun to burn me, and the mud to spatter me. Away with
caskets and settings and frames! I am not a picture or a
jewel, whatever your poetic eye, misled by a sly and tricky
Muse, persists in seeing. It would be quite a good plan, and
of distinctly tonic properties, for you to write to Frau von
Lindeberg and beg her to describe me. She, it is certain,
would do it very accurately, untroubled by the deceptions
of any muse.

How kind of you to ask me what I would like for
Christmas, and how funny of you to ask if you might not
give me a trinket. I laughed over that, for did I not write

to you three days ago and give you an account of my conversation with Joey on the subject of trinkets at Christmas? Is it possible you do not read my letters? Is it possible that, having read them, you forget them so immediately? Is it possible that proverbs lie, and the sauce appropriate to the goose is not also appropriate to the gander? Give me a book. There is no present I care about but that. And if it happened to be a volume in the dark blue binding edition of Stevenson to add to my row of him, I would be both pleased and grateful. Joey asked me what I wanted, so he is getting me the *Travels with a Donkey*. Will you give me *Virginibus Puerisque?*

Yours sincerely,

ROSE-MARIE SCHMIDT.

If you'd rather, you may give me a new coffee-pot instead.

Later.

But only an earthenware one, like the one that so much upset you.

LXIV

DEAR MR ANSTRUTHER,—We had a most cheerful Christmas, and I hope you did too. I sent you my blessing lurking in the pages of Frenssen's new and very wonderful book, which ought to have reached you in time to put under your tree. I hope you did have a tree, and were properly festive? The Stevenson arrived, and I found it among my other presents, tied up by Johanna with a bit of scarlet tape. Everything here at Christmas is tied up with scarlet, or blue, or pink tape, and your Stevenson lent itself admirably to the treatment. Thank you very much for it, and also for the little coffee set. I don't know whether I ought to keep that, it is so very pretty and dainty and beyond my deserts, but—it would break if I packed it and sent it back again, wouldn't it? so I will keep it, and drink your health out of the little cup with its garlands of tiny flower-like shepherdesses.

The audacious Joey did give Vicki jewellery, and a necklace if you please, the prettiest and obviously the costliest thing you can imagine. What happened then was in exact fulfilment of my prophecy; Vicki gasped with joy and admiration, he tells me, and before she had well done her gasp Frau von Lindeberg, with, as I gather, a sort of stately regret, took the case out of her hands, shut it with a snap, and returned it to Joey.

'No,' said Frau von Lindeberg.

'What's wrong with it?' Joey says he asked.

'Too grand for my little girl,' said Frau von Lindeberg. 'We are but humble folk.' And she tossed her head, said Joey.

'Ah—Dammerlitz,' I muttered, nodding with a complete comprehension.

'What?' exclaimed Joey, starting and looking greatly astonished.

'Go on,' said I.

'But I say,' said Joey, in tones of shocked protest.

'What do you say?' I asked.

'Why, how you must hate her,' said Joey, quite awestruck, and staring at me as though he saw me for the first time.

'Hate her?' I asked, surprised. 'Why do you think I hate her?'

He whistled, still staring at me.

'Why do you think I hate her?' I asked again, patient as I always try to be with him.

He murmured something about as soon expecting it of a bishop.

In my turn I stared. 'Suppose you go on with the story,' I said, remembering the hopelessness of ever following the train of Joey's thoughts.

Well, there appears to have been a gloom after that over the festivities. You are to understand that it all took place round the Christmas tree in the best parlour, Frau von Lindeberg in her black silk and lace high-festival dress, Herr von Lindeberg also in black with his orders, Vicki in white with blue ribbons, the son, come down for the occasion, in the glories of his dragoon uniform with clinking spurs and sword, and the servant starched and soaped in a big embroidered apron. In the middle of these decently arrayed rejoicers, the candles on the tree lighting up every inch of him, stood Joey in a Norfolk jacket, gaiters, and green check tie.

'I was goin' to dress afterwards for dinner,' he explained plaintively; 'but how could a man guess they'd all have got into their best togs at four in the afternoon? I felt an awful fool, I can tell you.'

'I expect you looked one too,' said I, with cheerful conviction.

There appears, then, to have descended a gloom after the necklace incident on the party, and a gloom of a slightly frosty nature. Vicki, it is true, was rather melting than frosty, her eyes full of tears, her handkerchief often at her nose, but Papa Lindeberg was steeped in gloom, and Frau von Lindeberg was sad with the impressive Christian sadness that does not yet exclude an occasional wan smile. As for the son, he twirled his already much twirled moustache and stared very hard at Joey.

When the presents had been given, and Joey found himself staggering beneath a waistcoat Vicki had knitted him, and a pair of pink bed-socks Frau von Lindeberg had knitted him, and an empty photograph frame from Papa Lindeberg, and an empty purse from the son, and a plate piled miscellaneously with apples and nuts and brown cakes with pictures gummed on to them, he observed Frau von Lindeberg take her husband aside into the remotest corner of the room and there whisper with him earnestly and long. While she was doing this the son, who knew no English, talked with an air of one who proposed to stand no nonsense to Joey, who knew no German, and Vicki, visibly depressed, slunk round the Christmas tree blowing her nose.

Papa Lindeberg, says Joey, came out of the corner far more gloomy than he went in; he seemed like a man urged on unwillingly from behind, a man reluctant to advance, and yet afraid or unable to go back.

'I beg to speak with you,' he said to Joey, with much military stiffness about his back and heels.

'Now, wasn't I right?' I interrupted triumphantly.

'Poor old beggar,' said Joey, 'he looked frightfully sick.'

'And didn't you?'

'No,' said Joey, grinning.

'Most young men would have.'

'But not this one. This one went off with him trippin' on the points of his toes, he felt so fit.'

'Well, what happened then?'

'Oh, I don't know. He said a lot of things. I couldn't understand' em, and I don't think he could either; but he was very game and stuck to it once he'd begun, and went on makin' my head spin, and I dare say his own too. Long and short of it was that in this precious Fatherland of yours the Vickis don't accept valuables except from those about to become their husbands.'

'I should say that the Vickis in your own or any other respectable Fatherland didn't either,' said I.

'Well, I'm not arguin', am I?'

'Well, go on.'

'Well, it seemed pretty queer to think I was about to become a husband, but there was nothin' for it—the little girl, you see, couldn't be done out of her necklace just because of that.'

'I see,' said I, trying to.

'On Christmas Day too—day of rejoicin' and that, eh?'

'Quite so,' said I.

'So I said I was his man.'

'And did he understand?'

'No. He kept on sayin' "What?" and evidently cursin' the English language in German. Then I suggested that Vicki should be called in to interpret. He understood that, for I waved my arms about till he did; but he said her mother interpreted better, and he would call her instead. I understood that, and said "Get out." He didn't understand that, and while he was tryin' to I went and told his wife that he'd sent for Vicki. Vicki came, and we got on first rate.

First thing I did was to pull out the necklace and put it round her neck. "Pretty as paint, ain't she?" I said to the old man. He didn't understand that either; but Vicki did, and laughed. "You give her to me and I give the necklace to her, see?" I said, shoutin', for I felt if I shouted loud enough he wouldn't be able to help understandin', however naturally German he was. "Tell him how simple it is," I said to Vicki. Vicki was very red but awfully cheerful, and laughed all the time. She explained, I suppose, for he went out to call his wife. Vicki and I stayed behind, and——'

'Well?'

'Oh well, we waited.'

'And what did Frau von Lindeberg say?'

'Oh, she was all right. Asked me a lot about the governor. Said Vicki's ancestors had fought with the snake in the Garden of Eden, or somebody far back like that—ancient lineage, you know—son-in-law must be impressed. I told her I didn't think my old man would make any serious objection to that. "To what?" she called out, looking quite scared—they seem frightfully anxious to please the governor. "He don't like ancestors," said I. "Ain't got any himself and don't hold with 'em." She pretended she was smilin', and said she supposed my father was an original. "Well," said I, goin' strong for once in the wit line, "anyhow, he's not an *ab*-original like Vicki's lot seem to have been." Pretty good that, eh? Seemed to stun 'em. Then the son came in and shook both my hands for about half an hour and talked a terrific lot of German, and was more pleased about it than any one else, as far as I could see. And then— well, that's about all. So I pulled off my little game rather neatly, what?'

'Yes, if it was your little game,' said I, with a faint stress on the your.

'Whose else should it be?' he asked, looking at me open-mouthed.

'Vicki is a little darling,' was my prudent reply, 'and I congratulate you with all my heart. Really, I am more delighted about this than I can remember ever being about anything—more purely delighted, without the least shadow on my honest pleasure.'

And all Joey vouchsafed as a reward for my ebullition of real feeling was the information that he considered me quite a decent sort.

So, you see, we are very happy up on the Galgenberg just now; the lovers like a pair of beaming babies, Frau von Lindeberg, sobered by the shock of her good fortune into the gentle kindliness that so often follows in the wake of a sudden great happiness, Papa Lindeberg warmed out of his tortoise-in-the-sun condition into much busy letter-writing, and Vicki's brother so uproariously pleased that I can only conclude him to be the possessor of many debts which he proposes to cause Joey to pay. Life is very thrilling when Love beats his wings so near. There has been a great writing to Joey's father, and Papa too has written, at my dictation, a letter rosy with the glow of Vicki's praises. Joey thinks his father will shortly appear to inspect the Lindebergs. He seems to have no fears of parental objections. 'He's all right, my old man is,' he says confidently when I probe him on the point; adding just now to this invariable reply, 'And look here, Miss Schmidt, Vicki's all right too, you see, so what's the funk about?'

'I don't know,' said I; and I didn't even after I had secretly looked in the dictionary, for it was empty of any explanation of the word 'funk.'

Yours, deeply interested in life and lovers,
ROSE-MARIE SCHMIDT.

LXV

Galgenberg, Dec. 31.

DEAR MR ANSTRUTHER,—My heartiest good wishes for the New Year. May it be fruitful to you in every pleasant way; bring you interesting work, agreeable companions, bright days; and may it, above all things, confirm and strengthen our friendship. There now; was ever young man more thoroughly fitted out with invoked blessings? And each one wished from the inmost sincerity of my heart.

But we can't come to Berlin, as you suggest we should, and allow ourselves to be shown round by you. Must I say thank you? No, I don't think I will. I will not pretend conventionally with you, and I do not thank you, for I don't like to have to believe that you really thought I would come. And then your threat, though it amused me, vexed me too. You say if I don't come you will be forced to suppose that I'm afraid of meeting you. Kindly suppose anything you like. After that, of course, I will not come. What a boy you are! And what an odd, spoilt boy! Why should I be afraid of meeting you? Is it, you think, because once—see, I am at least not afraid of speaking of it—you passed across my life convulsively? I don't know that any man could stir me up now to even the semblance of an earthquake. My quaking days are done; and after that one thunderous upheaval I am fascinated by the charm of quiet weather, and of a placid basking in a sunshine I have made with my very own hands. It is useless for you to tell me, as I know you will, that it is only an imitation of the real thing and has no heat in it. I don't want to be any hotter. In this tempestuous world where everybody is so eager, here is at least one woman who likes to be cool and slow. How strange it is the way you try to alter me, to make me quite different! There seems to be a perpetual battering going on at the bulwarks of my character. You want to pull them down and erect new fabrics in their place, fabrics so frothy and unreal that they are hardly more than fancies, and would have to be built up afresh every day. Yet I know you like me, and want to be my friend. You make me think of those quite numerous husbands who fall in love with their wives because they are just what they are, and after marriage expend their energies training them into something absolutely different. There was one in Jena while we were there who fell desperately in love with a little girl of eighteen, when he was about your age, and he adored her utterly because she was so divinely silly, ignorant, soft, and babyish. She knew nothing undesirable, and he adored her for that. She knew nothing desirable either, and he adored her for that too. He adored her to such an extent that all Jena, not given overmuch to merriment, was distorted with mirth at the spectacle. He was a clever man, a very promising professor, yet he found nothing more profitable than to spend every moment he could spare adoring. And his manner of adoring was to sit earnestly discovering, by means of repeated experiment, which of his fingers fitted best into her dimples when she laughed, and twisting the tendrils of her hair round his thumbs in an endless enjoyment of the way, when he suddenly let them go, they beautifully curled. He did this quite openly, before us all, seeing, I suppose, no reason why he should dissemble his interest in his future wife's dimples and curls. But alas for the dimples and curls once she was married! *Oh weh*, how quickly he grew blind to them. And as for the divine silliness, ignorance, softness, and babyishness that had so deeply fascinated him, just those were what got most on to his nerves. He tried to do away with them, to replace them by wit and learning combined with brilliant achievements among saucepans and shirts, and the result was disastrous. His little wife was scared. Her dimples disappeared from want of practice. Her pretty colours seemed suddenly wiped out, as though some one had passed over them roughly with a damp cloth. Her very hair left off curling, and was as limp and depressed as the rest of her. Let this, Mr Anstruther, be an awful warning to you, not only when you marry, but now at once in regard to your friends. Do not attempt to alter those long-suffering persons. It is true, you would have some difficulty in altering a person like myself, long ago petrified into her present horrid condition, but even the petrified can and do get tired of hearing the unceasing knocking of the reforming mallet on their skulls. Leave me alone, dear young man. Like me for anything you find that can be liked, express proper indignation at the rest of me, and go your way praising God who made us all. Really it would be a refreshment if you left off for a space imploring me to change into something else. There is a ring about your imploring as if you thought it was mere wilfulness holding me back from being and doing all you wish. Believe me, I am not wilful; I am only petrified. I can't change. I have settled down, very comfortably I must say, to the preliminary petrifaction of middle age, and middle age, I begin to perceive, is a blessed period in which we walk along mellowly, down pleasant slopes, with nothing gusty and fierce able to pierce our incrustation, no inward volcanoes able to upset the surrounding rockiness, nothing to distract our attention from the mild serenity of the landscape, the little flowers by the way, the beauty of the reddening leaves, the calm and sunlit sky. You will say it is absurd at twenty-six to talk of middle age, but I feel it in my bones, Mr Anstruther, I feel it in my bones. It is, after all, simply a question of bones. Yours are twenty years younger than mine; and did I not always tell you I was old?

I am so busy that you must be extra pleased, please, to get a letter today. The translation of Papa's book has ended by interesting me to such an extent that I can't leave off working at it. I do it officially in his presence for an hour daily, he, as full of mistrust of my English as ever, trying to check it with a dictionary, and using picturesque language to convey his disgust to me that he should be so imperfectly acquainted with a tongue so useful. He has forgotten the little he learned from my mother in the long years since her death, and he has the natural conviction of authors in the presence of their translators that the translator is a grossly uncultured person who will leave out all the *nuances*. For an hour I plod along obediently, then I pretend I must go and cook. What I really do is to run up to my bedroom, lock myself in, and work away feverishly for the rest of the morning at my version of the book. It is, I suppose, what would be called a free translation, but I protest I never met anything quite so free. Papa's book is charming, and the charm can only be reproduced by going repeatedly wholly off the lines. Accordingly I go, and find the process exhilarating and amusing. The thing amuses and interests me; I wonder if it would amuse and interest other people? I fear it would not, for when I try to imagine it being read by my various acquaintances my heart sinks with the weight of the certainty that it couldn't possibly. I imagine it in the hands of Joey, of Frau von Lindeberg, of different people in Jena, and the expression my inner eye sees on their faces makes me unable for a long while to go on with it. Then

286

I get over that and begin working again at my salad. It really is a salad, with Papa as the groundwork of lettuce, very crisp and fresh, and myself as the dressing and bits of garnishing beetroot and hard-boiled egg. I work at it half the night sometimes, so eager am I to get it done and sent off. Yes, my young friend, I have inherited Papa's boldness in the matter of sending off, and the most impressive of London publishers is shortly to hold it in his sacred hands. And if his sacred hands forget themselves so far as to hurl it rudely back at me they yet can never take away the fun I have had writing it.

Yours sincerely,

Rose-Marie Schmidt.

Joey's father is expected tomorrow, and the whole Galgenberg is foggy with the fumes of cooking. Once his consent is given the engagement will be put in the papers and life will grow busy and brilliant for Frau von Lindeberg. She talks of removing immediately to Berlin, there to give a series of crushingly well-done parties to those of her friends who are supposed to have laughed when Vicki was thrown over by her first lover. I don't believe they did laugh; I refuse to believe in such barbarians; but Frau von Lindeberg, grown frank about that disastrous story now that it has been so handsomely wiped off Vicki's little slate, assures me that they did. She doesn't seem angry any longer about it, being much too happy to have room in her heart for wrath, but she is bent on this one form of revenge. Well, it is a form that will gratify everybody, revenger and revengee equally, I should think.

LXVI

Galgenberg, Jan. 7.

DEAR MR ANSTRUTHER,—I couldn't write before, I've been too busy. The manuscript went this morning after real hard work day and night, and now I feel like a squeezed lemon that yet is cheerful, if you can conceive such a thing. Joey's father has been and gone. He arrived late one night, inspected the Lindebergs, gave his consent, and was off twenty-four hours later. The Lindebergs were much disconcerted by these quick methods, they who like to move slowly, think slowly, and sit hours over each meal; and they had not said half they wanted to say, and he had not eaten half he was intended to eat before he was gone. Also, he disconcerted them—indeed, it was more than that, he upset them utterly, by not looking like what they had made up their minds he would look like. The Galgenberg expected to see some one who should be blatantly rich, and blatant riches, it dimly felt, would be expressed by much flesh and a thick watch chain. Instead, the man had a head like Julius Caesar, lean, thoughtful, shrewd, and a spare body that made Papa Lindeberg's seem strangely pulpy and as if it were held together only by the buttons of his clothes. We were staggered. Frau von Lindeberg couldn't understand why a man so rich should also be so thin—'He is in a position to have the costliest cooking,' she said several times, looking at me with amazed eyebrows; nor could she understand why a man without ancestors should yet make her husband, whose past bristles with them, be the one to look as if he hadn't got any. She mused much, and aloud. While Vicki was being run breathlessly over the mountains by her nimble future father-in-law, with Joey, devoured by pride in them both, in attendance, I went down to ask if I could help in the cooking, and found her going about her kitchen like one in a dream. She let me tuck up my sleeves and help her, and while I did it she gave vent to many musings about England and its curious children. 'Strange, strange people,' she kept on saying helplessly.

But she is the happiest woman in Germany at this moment, happier far than Vicki, for she sees with her older eyes the immense advantages that are to be Vicki's, who sees at present nothing at all but Joey. And then the deliciousness of being able to write to all those relations grown of late so supercilious, to Cousin Mienchen who came and played the rich, and tell them the glorious news. Vicki basks in the sunshine of a mother's love again, and never hears a cross word. Good things are showered down on her, presents, pettings, admiration, all those charming things that every girl should enjoy once before her pretty girlhood has gone. It is the most delightful experience to see a family in the very act of receiving a stroke of luck. Strokes of luck, especially of these dimensions, are so very rare. It is like being present at a pantomime that doesn't leave off, and watching the good fairy touching one grey dull unhappy thing after another into radiance and smiles. But I lose my friends, for they go to Berlin almost immediately, and from there to Manchester on a visit to Mr Collins, a visit during which the business part of the marriage is to be settled. Also, and naturally, we lose Joey. This is rather a blow, just as we had begun so pleasantly to roll in his money; but where Vicki goes he goes too, and so Papa and I will soon be left again alone on our mountain, face to face with vegetarian economies.

Well, it has been a pleasant interlude, and I who first saw Vicki steeped in despair, red-eyed, piteous, slighted, talked about, shall see her at last departing down the hill arrayed in glory as with a garment. Then I shall turn back, when the last whisk of her shining skirts has gleamed round the bend of the road, to my own business, to the sober trudging along the row of days allotted me, to the making of economies, the reading of good books, the practice of abstract excellences, the pruning of my soul. My soul, I must say, has had some vigorous prunings. It ought by now to be of an admirable sturdiness. You yourself once lopped off a most luxuriant growth that was, I agree, best away, and now these buds of friendship, of easier circumstances, are going to be nipped off too, and when they are gone what will be left, I wonder, but the uncompromising and the rugged? Is it possible I am so base as to be envious? In spite of my real pleasure I can't shut out a certain wistfulness, a certain little pang, and exactly what kind of wistfulness it is and exactly what kind of pang I don't well know, unless it is envy. Vicki's lot is the last one I would choose, yet it makes me wistful. It includes Joey, yet I feel a little pang. This is very odd; for Joey as a husband, a person from whom you cannot get away, would be rather more than I could suffer with any show of gladness. How, then, can I be envious? Of course, if Joey knew what I am writing he would thrust an incredulous tongue in his cheek, wink a sceptical eye, and mutter some eternal truth about grapes; but I, on the other hand, would watch him doing it with the perfect calm of him who sticks unshakably to his point. What would his cheek, his tongue, and his winking eye be to me? They would leave me wholly unmoved, not a hair's breadth moved from my original point, which is that Joey is not a person you can marry. But certainly it is a good and delightful thing that Vicki thinks he is and thinks it with such conviction. I tell you the top of our mountain is in a perpetual rosy glow nowadays, as though the sun never left it; and the entire phenomenon is due solely to these two joyful young persons.

Yours sincerely,
ROSE-MARIE SCHMIDT.

LXVII

Galgenberg, Jan. 12.

DEAR MR ANSTRUTHER,—I did a silly thing today: I went and mourned in an empty house. I don't think I'm generally morbid, but today I indulged in a perfect orgy of morbidness. Write and scold me. It is your turn to scold, and by doing it thoroughly you will bring me back to my ordinary cheerful state. The Lindebergs are gone, and I am feeling it absurdly. I didn't realize how much I loved that little dear Vicki, nor in the least the interest Frau von Lindeberg's presence and doings gave life. The last three weeks have been so thrilling, there was so much warmth and brightness going about, that it reached even onlookers like myself, and warmed and lighted them; and now in the twinkling of an eye it is gone—gone, wiped out, snuffed out, and Papa and I are alone again, and there is a northeast wind. These are the times when philosophy is so useful; but do explain why it is that one is only a philosopher so long as one is happy. When I am contented, and everything is just as I like it, I can philosophize beautifully, and do it with a hearty sincerity that convinces both myself and the person listening to me; but when the bad days come, the empty days, the disappointing, chilly days, behold Philosophy, that serene and dignified companion so long as the weather was fine, clutching her academic skirts hastily together and indulging in the form of rapid retreat known to the vulgar and the graphic as skedaddling. 'Do not all charms fly,' your Keats inquires, 'at the mere touch of cold Philosophy?' But I have found that nothing flies quite so fast as cold Philosophy herself; she would win in any race when the race is who shall run away quickest; she is of no use whatever—it is my deliberate conclusion—except to sit with in the sun on the south side of a sheltering wall on those calm afternoons of life when you've only got to open your mouth and ripe peaches drop into it. I used to think if I could love her enough she would, in her gratitude, chloroform me safely over all the less pleasant portions of life, see to it that I was unconscious during the passage, never let me be aware of anything but the beautiful and the good; but either she has no gratitude or I have little love, and the years have brought me the one conviction that she is an artist at leaving you in the lurch. The world is strewn with persons she has left in it, and out of the three inhabitants of a mountain to leave one there is surely an enormous percentage. Now, what is your opinion of a woman with a healthy body, a warm room, and a sufficient dinner, who feels as though the soul within her were an echoing cavern, empty, cold, and dark? It is what I feel at this moment, and it is shameful. Isn't it shameful that the sight of leaden clouds—but they really are dreadful clouds, inky, ragged, harassed—scudding across the sky, and of furious brown beech-leaves on the little trees in front of the Lindebergs' deserted house being lashed and maddened by the wind, should make me suddenly catch my breath for pain? It is pain, quite sharp, unmistakable pain, and it is because I am alone, and my friends gone, and the dusk is falling. This afternoon I leaned against their gate and really suffered. Regret for the past, fear for the future—vague, rather terrifying fears, not wholly unconnected with you— hurt so much that they positively succeeded in wringing a tear out of me. It was a very reluctant tear, and only came out after a world of wringing, and I had stood there a most morbid long time before it appeared; but it did appear, and the vicious wind screamed round the Lindebergs' blank house, rattled its staring naked windows, banged in wild gusts about the road where the puddles of half-melted snow reflected the blackness of the sky, tore at my hair and dress, stung my cheeks, shook the gate I held on to, thundered over the hills. Dear young man, I don't want to afflict you with these tales of woe and weakness, but I must tell you what I did next. I went up and got the key from Johanna, in whose keeping Frau von Lindeberg had left it, and came down again, and unlocked the door of the house lately so full of light and life, and crept fearfully about the echoing rooms and up the dismal stairs, and let myself go, as I tell you, to a very orgy of morbidness. It was like a nightmare. Memories took the form of ghosts, and clutched at me through the balusters and from behind doors with thin cold fingers; and the happiest memories were those that clutched the coldest. I fled at last in a sudden panic, flying out of reach of them, slamming the door to, running for my life up the road and in at our gate. Johanna did not let me in at once, and I banged with my fists in a frenzy to get away from the black sky and the threatening thunder of the storm-stricken pines. '*Herr Gott*,' said Johanna, when she saw me; so that I must have looked rather wild.

Well, I am weak, you see, just as weak and silly as the very weakest and silliest in spite of my big words and brave face. I am writing now as near the stove as possible in Papa's room, glad to be with him, glad to be warm, grateful to sit with somebody alive after that hour with the ghosts; and the result of deep considering has been to force me to face the fact that there is much meanness in my nature. There is. Don't bother to contradict; there is. All my forlornness since yesterday is simply the outcome of a mixture of envy and self-pity. I do miss dear Vicki, whom I greatly loved, I do miss the cheery Joey, I miss Papa Lindeberg who likened me to Hebe, I miss his wife who kept me in my proper place—it is quite true that I miss these people, but that would never of itself be a feeling strong enough to sweep me off my feet into black pools of misery as I was swept this afternoon, and never, never would make me, who have so fine a contempt for easy tears, cry. No, Mr Anstruther, bitter truths once seen have to be stared at squarely, and I am simply comparing my lot with Vicki's and being sorry for myself. It is amazing that it should be so, for have I not everything a reasonable being needs, and am I not, then, a reasonable being? And the meanness of it; for it does imply a grudging, an uneasiness in the presence of somebody else's happiness. Well, I'm thoroughly ashamed, and that at least is a good thing; and now that you know how badly I too need lecturing, and how I am torn by particularly ungenerous emotions, perhaps you'll see what a worthless person I am, and will take me down from the absurd high pinnacle on which you persist in keeping me, and on which I have felt so desperately uncomfortable for months past. It is infinitely humiliating, I do assure you, to be—shall we say venerated? for excellences one would like to possess but is most keenly aware one does not. Persons with any tendency to be honest about themselves and with even the smallest grain of a sense of humour should never be chosen as idols and set up aloft in giddy places. They make shockingly bad idols. They are divided by a desire to laugh and an immense pity for the venerator.

I add these observations, dear friend, to the description of my real nature that has gone before because your letters are turning more and more into the sort of letters that ends a placid friendship. I want to be placid. I love being placid.

I insist on being placid. And the thought of your letters, with so little of placidness about them, was with me this afternoon in that terrible house, and it added to the fear of the future that seized me by the throat and would not let me go. Is it, then, so impossible to be friends, just friends with a man, in the same dear frank way one is with another woman, or a man is with a man? I hoped you and I were going to prove the possibility triumphantly. I even, so keenly do I desire it, prayed that we were. But perhaps there is little use in such praying.

Yours sincerely,

ROSE-MARIE SCHMIDT.

You may scold me as much as you like, but you are not to comfort me. Do not make the mistake, I earnestly beg you, of supposing that I want to be comforted.

LXVIII

Galgenberg, Jan. 13.

DEAR MR ANSTRUTHER,—Just a line to tell you that I have recovered, and you are not to take my letter yesterday too seriously. I woke up this morning perfectly normal, and able to look out on the day before me with the usual interest. Then something very nice happened: my translation of Papa's book didn't come back, but instead arrived an urbane letter expressing a kind of reluctant willingness, if you can imagine the mixture, to publish it. What do you think of that? The letter, it is true, goes on to suggest, still with urbanity, that no doubt no one will ever buy it, but promises if ever any one does to send us a certain just portion of what was paid for it. 'Observe, Rose-Marie,' said Papa, when his first delight had calmed, 'the unerring instinct with which the English, very properly called a nation of shopkeepers, instantly recognize the value of a good thing when they see it. Consider the long years during which I have vainly beaten at the doors of the German public, and compare its deafness with the quick response of our alert and admirable cousins across the Channel. Well do I know which was the part that specially appealed to this man's business instinct——'

And he mentioned, while my guilty ears burned crimson, a chapter of statistics, the whole of which I had left out.

Yours sincerely,
ROSE-MARIE SCHMIDT.

LXIX

DEAR MR ANSTRUTHER,—I see no use whatever in a friend if one cannot tell him about one's times of gloom without his immediately proposing to do the very thing one doesn't want him to do, which is to pay one a call. Your telegram has upset me, you see, into a reckless use of the word 'one,' a word I spend hours sometimes endeavouring to circumvent, and which I do circumvent if I am in good bodily and spiritual health, but the moment my vitality is lowered, as it is now by your telegram, I cease to be either strong enough or artful enough to dodge it. There are four of it in that sentence: I fling them to you in a handful, only remarking that they are your fault, not mine.

Now, listen to me—I will drop this playfulness, which I don't in the least feel, and be serious:—why do you want to come and, as you telegraph, talk things over? I don't want to talk things over; it is a fatal thing to do. May I not tell you frankly of my moods, of my downs as well as of my ups, without at once setting you off in the direction of too much kindness? After I had written that letter I was afraid; and I opened it again to tell you it was not your comfortings and pityings that I wanted, but the sterner remedy of a good scolding; yet your answer is a telegram to ask if you may come. Of course I telegraphed back that I should not be here. It is quite true: I should not if you came. I will not see you. Nothing can be gained by it, and everything might be lost—oh, everything, everything might be lost. I would see to it that you did not find me. The forests are big, and I can walk, if needs be, for hours. You will think me quite savagely unkind, but I can't help that. Perhaps if your letters lately had been different I would not so obstinately refuse to see you, but I have a wretched feeling that my poor soul is going to be pruned again, pruned of its last, most pleasant growth, and you are on the road to saying and doing things we shall both be for ever sorry for. I have tried my best to stop you, to pull you up, and I hope with all my heart that I may not be going to get a letter that will spoil things irreparably. Have not my hints been big enough? Let me beg you not to write foolishnesses that cannot, once sent, be got back again and burned. But at least when you sit down to write you can consider your words, and those that have come out too impulsively can go into the fire; while if you came here what would you do with your tongue, I wonder? There is no means of stopping that once it is well started, and the smallest thing sets it off in terrible directions. Am I not your friend? Will you not spare me? Must I be forced to speak with a plainness that will, by comparison, make all my previous plainness seem the very essence of polite artificialness? Of all the wise counsel any one could offer you at this moment there is none half so wise, none that, taken, would be half so precious to us both, as the counsel to leave well alone. I offer it you earnestly; oh, more than earnestly—with a passionate anxiety lest you should refuse it.

Your sincere friend,

ROSE-MARIE SCHMIDT.

I suppose it is true what I have often suspected, that I am a person doomed to lose, one by one, the things that have been most dear to me.

LXX

WELL, there is no help, then. You will do it. You will put an end to it. You have written me a love-letter, the thing I have been trying so hard for so long to stop your doing, and there is nothing to be done but to drop into silence.

LXXI

BUT what is there possible except silence? I will not marry you. I cannot after this keep you my friend.

LXXII

Jan. 19.

OH, I have tried, I have hoped to keep you. It has been so sweet to me. It has made everything so different. For the second time you have wiped the brightness out of my life.

LXXIII

Jan. 21.

LEAVE me alone. Don't torment me with wild letters. I do not love you. I will not marry you. I cared for you sincerely as a friend, but what a gulf there is between that and the abandonment of worship last year in Jena. Only just that, just that breathless passion, would make me marry, and I would never feel it for a man I am forced to pity. Is not worship a looking up? a rapture of faith? I cannot look up to you. I have no faith in you. Leave me alone.

LXXIV

LET us consider the thing calmly. Let us try to say good-bye without too great a clamour. What is the use, after all, of being so vocal? We have each given the other many hours of pleasure, and shall we not be grateful rather than tragic? Here we are, got at last to the point where we face the inevitable, and we may as well do it decently. See, here is a woman who does not love you: would you have her marry you when she had rather not? And you mustn't be angry with me because I don't love you, for how can I help it? So far am I from the least approach to it that it makes me tired just to think of a thing so strenuous, of the bother of it, of the perpetual screwed-up condition of mind and body to a pitch above the normal. The normal is what I want. My heart is set upon it. I don't want ecstasies. I don't want excitement. I don't want alternations of bliss and terror. I want to be that peaceful individual a maiden lady,—a maiden lady looking after her aged father, tending her flowers, fondling her bees—no, I don't think she could fondle bees,—fondling a cat, then, which I haven't yet got. Oh, I know I have moods of a more tempestuous nature, such as the one I was foolish enough to write to you about the other day, stirring you up to a still more violent tempestuousness yourself, but they roll away again when they have growled themselves out, and the mood that succeeds them is like clear shining after rain. I intend this clear shining as I grow older to be more and more my surrounding atmosphere. I make the bravest resolutions; will you not make some too? Dear late friend and sometime lover, do not want me to give you what I have not got. We are both suffering just now; but what about Time, that kindest soother, softener, healer, that final tidier up of ragged edges, and sweeper away of the broken fragments of the past?

LXXV

Jan. 23.

I TELL you you have taken away what I held precious for the second time, and there shall be no third. You showed me once that you could not be a faithful lover, you have shown me now you cannot be a faithful friend. I am not an easy woman, who can be made much of and dropped in an unending see-saw. Even if I loved you we would be most wretched married, you with the feeling that I did not fit into your set, I with the knowledge that you felt so, besides the deadly fear of you, of your changes and fits of hot and cold. But I do not love you. This is what you seem unable to realize. Yet it is true, and it settles everything for ever.

LXXVI

MUST there be so much explaining? It was because I thought I was making amends that way for having, though unconsciously, led you to fancy you cared for me last year. I wanted to be of some use to you, and I saw how much you liked to get them. By gradual degrees, as we both grew wiser, I meant my letters to be a help to you who have no sister, no mother, and a father you don't speak to. I was going to be the person to whom you could tell everything, on whose devotion and sincerity you could always count. It was to have been a thing so honest, so frank, so clear, so affectionate. And I've not even had time really to begin, for at first there was my own struggling to get out of the deep waters where I was drowning, and afterwards it seemed to be nothing but a staving off, a writing about other things, a determined telling of little anecdotes, of talk about our neighbours, about people you don't know, about anything rather than your soul and my soul. Each time I talked of those, in moments of greater stress when the longing for a real friend to whom I could write openly was stronger than I could resist, there came a letter back that made my heart stand still. I had lost my lover, and it seemed as if I must lose my friend. At first I believed that you would settle down. I thought it could only be a question of patience. But you could not wait, you could not believe you were not going to be given what you wanted in exactly the way you wanted it, and you have killed the poor goose after all, the goose I have watched so anxiously, who was going to lay us such beautiful golden eggs. I am very sorry for you. I know the horrors of loving somebody who doesn't love you. And it is terrible for us both that you should not understand me to the point, as you say, of not being able to believe me. I have not always understood myself, but here everything seems so plain. Love is not a thing you can pick up and throw into the gutter and pick up again as the fancy takes you. I am a person, very unfortunately for you, with a quite peculiar dread of thrusting myself or my affections on any one, of in any way outstaying my welcome. The man I would love would be the man I could trust to love me for ever. I do not trust you. I did outstay my welcome once. I did get thrown into the gutter, and came near drowning in that sordid place. Oh, call me hard, wickedly revengeful, unbelievably cruel if it makes you feel less miserable—but will you listen to a last prophecy? You will get over this as surely as you have got over your other similar vexations, and you will live to say, 'Thank God that German girl—what was her name? wasn't it Schmidt? good heavens, yes—thank God she was so foolish as not to take advantage of an unaccountable but strictly temporary madness.'

And if I am bitter, forgive me.

LXXVII

It would be useless.

Jan. 27.

LXXVIII

I would not see you.

Jan. 29.

LXXIX

I do not love you.

Jan. 31.

LXXX

Feb. 2.

I will never marry you.

LXXXI

Feb. 4.

I shall not write again.

THE END

THE HISTORY OF VINTAGE

The famous American publisher Alfred A. Knopf (1892–1984) founded Vintage Books in the United States in 1954 as a paperback home for the authors published by his company. Vintage was launched in the United Kingdom in 1990 and works independently from the American imprint although both are part of the international publishing group, Random House.

Vintage in the United Kingdom was initially created to publish paperback editions of books bought by the prestigious literary hardback imprints in the Random House Group such as Jonathan Cape, Chatto & Windus, Hutchinson and later William Heinemann, Secker & Warburg and The Harvill Press. There are many Booker and Nobel Prize-winning authors on the Vintage list and the imprint publishes a huge variety of fiction and non-fiction. Over the years Vintage has expanded and the list now includes both great authors of the past – who are published under the Vintage Classics imprint – as well as many of the most influential authors of the present.

penguin.co.uk/vintage-classics